TRUE S

Fiona Kidman, born in 1940, is a full-time writer who lives in Wellington. Author of thirteen books, including novels, a play, poetry, non-fiction and two collections of short stories. Her novel *The Book of Secrets* won the 1988 New Zealand Book Award. She has held the Writer's Fellowship at Victoria University and has received a number of awards, including the Queen Elizabeth II Literary Fund's annual Award for Achievement.

OTHER BOOKS BY THE SAME AUTHORS

Search for Sister Blue (play)
Honey and Bitters (poems)
On the Tightrope (poems)
A Breed of Women (novel)
Mandarin Summer (novel)
Mrs Dixon & Friend (short stories)
Paddy's Puzzle (novel)
Gone North (non-fiction)
Going to the Chathams (poems)
The Book of Secrets (novel)
Unsuitable Friends (short stories)
Wakeful Nights (poems)

Fiona Kidman

TRUE STARS

V
VINTAGE

Although there are references to living politicians in this book, Kit Kendall, Rex Gamble and Alan Smart are fictitious characters. Any resemblances are coincidental. As a work of fiction, it does not represent a chronological account of the events of 1988. All the other characters are fictitious too.

Acknowledgements

Much of this book was written while the author was Writer's Fellow at Victoria University in 1988. Thanks are expressed to the QE II Arts Council/NZ Literary Fund, the University, and particularly staff in the English Department. Thanks are also due to Owen Dance for his help with research and interested support.

The author and publisher are grateful to the following companies for the use of their material:

'Angel of the Morning' by C. Taylor, lyrics reprinted by kind permission of SBK Songs Australia Pty Ltd;

'Knock Three Times' by L. Brown and I. Levine, lyrics reprinted by kind permission of SBK Songs Australia Pty Ltd and Festival Music Publishing Group;

'River Road' by Sylvia Tyson, lyrics reprinted by kind permission of Salt Music (Lcosong);

'Lara's Theme' by Maurice Jarre, lyrics reprinted by kind permission of J. Albert & Son Pty Ltd;

'Daybreak' excerpt from *Mortal Act. Mortal Words* by Galway Kinnell. Copyright © 1980 by Galway Kinnell. Reprinted by kind permission of Houghton Mifflin Company.

Vintage New Zealand
Random Century New Zealand Ltd
(An imprint of the Random Century Group)

18 Poland Road
Glenfield
Auckland 10
NEW ZEALAND

Associated companies, branches and
representatives throughout the world.

First published 1990
This edition first published 1992

ISBN 1 86941 156 0
Printed in Hong Kong

For Flora, my mother,
and the indestructible memory of Warwick Flaus

. . . . dozens of starfishes
were creeping . . . . . .

. . . . they sank down
into the mud; they faded down
into it and lay still; and by the time
pink of sunset broke across them
they were as invisible
as the true stars at daybreak.

(from 'Daybreak', a poem by Galway Kinnell)

Part I

★

1

Imagine: picture this. Kit Kendall weeping, with his head down, in his parliamentary office.

Kit, who had listened to the Beatles, marched in protest against the Vietnam War, fallen in love once by moonlight, cried when Kennedy was shot, written poems in treetops and saved forests from destruction. Today he could hear only the roar of the crowd, and it was not for him.

It might be called a mid-life crisis of sorts. Kit Kendall was forty-five years old, had been married for the past twenty-two of them, had two children, a son and a daughter, commonly known as a pigeon pair, to whom he was devoted, and lately he had acquired a mistress. He had been chosen by the constituents of Weyville, a small town close to the centre of the North Island, to be their elected representative, and sworn an oath of allegiance in the House of Representatives not once, but twice, to serve them and his country.

In return for this honour he occupied a very small office which could be found by his visitors when they had walked down several long varnished corridors in Parliament Buildings, only a small remove from the area known as Siberia. He had done little to warrant such an undistinguished corridor but, quite simply, that was the trouble; he had done very little. The office floor was covered with green carpet squares and the walls painted institutional cream. On his desk stood a studio portrait of his family. In his desk lay, face down, a snapshot of the woman who had his unlisted telephone number. Kit drew a salary of $49,000 (due to rise soon) with fringe benefits—he franked his personal and electorate mail for free and ate cheap meals at Bellamy's. Today, for lunch, he had eaten spiced pork spareribs, apple pie with cream, and cheese and biscuits, accompanied by a bottle of rather young local wine, in the company of two backbench colleagues who had already taken drink for breakfast and a trade unionist who considered putting his knife and fork together on the plate to be the province of the bourgeoisie. This meal, subsidised by the taxpayer, had cost him $9 per head. He sat on two Select Committees and the trade unionist had briefed him and his colleagues on a late submission to one of them. The trade unionist and the three politicians all knew that it would not be considered. They all knew, too, that evidence of its presentation would salve several consciences, and the fact that it was late would permit them to salve their own.

His first meeting of the afternoon had been with a Weyville citizen who wished him to lend support for a dispensation to build a factory amongst houses in his electorate. In times of hardship, anything should be possible, the constituent argued. The prospect of a position on the board of directors if the proposal went through had been implicit. The citizen, whom Kit suspected of having once been his wife's lover, though he didn't have any real evidence to support the idea (and indeed, he was prepared to pander to every suspicion he could entertain about his wife, by way of alleviating his own guilt), was a key player in the proposal because he was arranging finance for it. He did not hold shares in the open market himself; they were held in his own wife's maiden name. Kit, who was shorter of money than he ought to be these days, found the idea attractive though he said only that he would think about it. It was a temptation he intended to refuse for the moment but the offer held hope for an uncertain future.

He listened to the crowds outside; he could identify voices speaking through loudhailers. There was a large police presence in the building. The people outside were shouting in a monotonous chant *We want jobs we want jobs what do we want? Jobs jobs jobs.* Kit could visualise them, the scruffy jeans, the headbands, the street theatre, the tired faces animated by the momentary excitement, the way they would all wilt away into the afternoon when the speeches had been made and they couldn't think what to do next.

He could go outside if he chose. But he didn't have to. He was not a Cabinet Minister, nor, he had realised, ever likely to be one. His seat was far from safe. An air of inalienable permanence was not on his side. He had no responsibility to the mob outside. He saw himself when he was young, thin, bearded, long-haired, his arms raised and his mouth wide open, shouting into the face of authority. He remembered being dragged away by the police; it still stunned him that his parents were proud. You could say he came from a good family, according to your definition.

He could not bear to go outside and lift the megaphone to his mouth and stand while being shouted at on the other side of protest. It was not what he had come here to do. But then neither were most of the things he did.

Imagine. He could not have.

The bells summoning him to the debating chamber began to ring, shrill electronic blasts which went on and on.

Still he sat crying. He had learned, minutes before, that another march of the unemployed was to take place, only this one would originate from Weyville, from his own back door, as it were. *Keep your cat in your own backyard* the kids at his school used to taunt each other when fights spilled over from one family to the next. Not that he was part of the scraps. But he was now.

Soon he would have a mob all of his own to face.

He was as unlikely to have help then as his one or two unhappy colleagues had right now.

He stood, wiped his eyes with a handkerchief which he refolded and put in his breast pocket, checked that there were no specks of dust on his twinkling black shoes, and set off to debate the affairs of the nation.

2

When the phone rang for the second time Rose approached it like a cat circling, then backed away.

'Oh goddam you,' she said softly. 'You'll speak to me one day.'

It was 1.30 in an afternoon in late March. For over a year someone had been ringing Rose Kendall when she was alone at home, and replacing the receiver without speaking to her when she answered. She said she had no idea who it was when she talked to people about it, which lately had been less and less, although the problem had got worse. In fact, she had many ideas, but they varied from day to day.

The police had told her that they would do what they could to help but it was a hard crime, which they described as an offence, to crack. The people at the phone company were convinced that it was a domestic problem which she was covering up, or even inventing, although in the circumstances this was what they implied, rather than stated. It was considered untactful to tell the wife of a Government politician that she was a dingbat. They could not understand why the caller never rang when her husband was home. If the motivation was political they hinted, surely it was him that the caller would ring.

She retreated the length of the room. When she felt she was far enough away she stood holding herself together with her hands pressing her elbows into her sides. On the fourteenth ring the phone stopped, as if it had exhausted itself. If it was an overseas call they would have lost their money more than twice she thought with satisfaction. She was remembering a hotel she and Kit stayed in off Fifth Avenue, the best they could afford then at two hundred a night. If you are making an overseas call, the notice in the room had read, allow the number to ring for a minute, which is ten rings, or you will be charged for the call as if it had been connected.

Only she did not believe this was an overseas call. She believed that the person who was ringing was someone in Weyville, the town where she had lived all her life: someone who knew her.

She referred to the caller in her head as they, for the person could not be identified by their sex, and besides she had begun to see them as having several dimensions, maybe heads. At first she had thought of the caller as him, but now she was not sure.

They will think I am not here, she told herself now. Soon they will stop calling me.

'They must, mustn't they?' She addressed the dog at her feet, pushing him with her toe. A small black and tan spaniel crossed perhaps with dachshund. He had stirred restlessly when the phone rang, aware of her agitation. Now he stretched and settled again. Her children had named him Roach when they brought him home. They assured her it was short for cockroach, but she was not sure. They were in high school at the time.

These days, Rose addressed many questions to the dog.

The afternoon sun lay across the ordinary furniture. Rose could see dust against the grain of the oak. We should get new furniture, Kit said, at the weekends when he was home from Wellington. His eyes would appraise their old furniture in the new house. Their new old house.

It was a large house set well away from all the other houses in the street. It had a wide entrance way, and stained glass with knots of roses repeated in the same patterns but different colours throughout the house. A cathedral window dominated the stairwell. The house had been built by an early settler, on farmland that was now a suburb. It was the kind of dwelling that is few and far between in towns like Weyville, a town set on broad plains against the open sky, where an old house usually means a weatherboard box built in the 'thirties. But this was different, the kind of house, at least in the sum of its parts, that Kit and Rose often talked of owning, when the children were small. When they got rich; when they struck it lucky — then they would spend hours lovingly renovating it together.

Only this house was sleekly functional when they bought it. 'We won't have time to fiddle around,' Kit said, then. It had to work now; they needed the space. He meant, to entertain.

So as well as roses and tall windows there was a kitchen that looked like the inside of a space re-entry vehicle, and an added-on patio, a barbecue area outside, and a swimming pool. Everything worked. Sometimes at the weekend when Kit was home they did entertain. They entertained people whom they wished to encourage to vote for Kit again at the next election. During the week the house was often empty except for Rose and Roach.

Kit appeared to be pleased, though he didn't have time to sit around dreaming these days. She used to wonder where he would be without her to think about the practical things in life. He had been an industrial chemist at the mill before he entered Parliament. It was trees that really interested him. When he was a student and she had first known him, he had spent his vacations fire-watching trees from a mountain top. She was used to managing.

It was late autumn but the heat lay over the town as if it were summer. A thick encrustation of grapes hung around the windows. The leaves had a filtering effect on the sharp bright sunlight outside.

Who, on a still summery afternoon, could be bothered to make pointless telephone calls that required no answer except the sound of her voice, Rose wondered.

She was a short woman with wider hips than she liked but not so wide that she would not wear jeans. She wore blue stonewashed pants this afternoon and a white muslin blouse with yellow thread embroidery across the chest. She had bought it at Narnia the last time she was in Wellington. Kit would like it, she imagined, but when she showed it to him he hadn't said one way or the other. Her scrubbed features, bare of make-up, were neat and unremarkable except for wide cheekbones that made her face look broad when she slept, and heavier eyebrows than one expected in a woman. At times she looked brooding, but when she was happy her face became mobile and the sleek brows dramatic. This did not happen often, of late. Her frizzy reddish-brown hair was pulled back with a purple scarf. For women's suffrage, she had told herself when she put it on this morning, and for an instant, smiled at herself. She suffered moments of panic about her worthiness, and whether she served causes well enough.

Recently, she had been interviewed by one of the new glossy magazines as part of a survey of changing attitudes in provincial electorates. Should she do it, she asked Kit, who, after speaking to his advisers in Wellington, had said that it was a good idea, as long as she was careful. The article read as follows:

> Weyville's population is 22,000, which includes 1,500 unemployed. It is a neat town with the usual quota of new shopping malls and glass facades, although a number of shops are currently standing empty. Four high rises dot the centre of town; suburbs spread away, mostly in the direction of the local timber mill, which has been going through a period of restructuring and what its management describes as retrenchment. The eastern suburbs reflect the former rural and farming nature of the district. Rose Kendall was in the process of moving house when I caught up with her. Her

new residence is an old homestead property surrounded by one of the area's more upmarket housing developments.

A friendly, apparently forthright woman, Rose Kendall has been associated with causes, in particular the feminist and peace movements, since the late 1960s, although she wryly admits to having developed her political consciousness when the Vietnam War was already in its closing stages.

'That's what came of living in the provinces, I suppose,' she says with a reflective smile. 'And of course, the children were tiny then.'

Pictures of her children, Olivia and Richard, adorn the family home. Olivia, the older, attends university in Dunedin, while her son is currently living in America where he was an American Field Scholar last year, and is now doing a computer studies course.

There is little sign of early hardship which Kendall, 43, claims she was surrounded by as she grew up. Born and bred in Weyville, a once traditionally blue ribbon seat which changed hands six years ago, ex-schoolteacher Kendall is the daughter of a trucking family which held contracts to service a local quarry and various milling operations. Her father, the late Tom Diamond, may have been rough and ready but he had a nose for business. Her brother, Jim, now runs the family firm.

Pressed to comment on the region's problems, and the growing discontent of her husband's constituents, Kendall says she has faith in the Government's policies. 'Economic miracles don't happen over night,' she says, 'This is a caring Government.'

Asked to explain how she relates present record levels of unemployment with her own history of civil liberty campaigning, she flushes angrily: 'You only have to look at my record to know that I've been consistent,' she says.

Kendall doesn't wear a wedding ring these days, but she twists a large topaz ring, which she says was a legacy from her grandmother, as she speaks.

The article didn't say that she suffered from pre-menstrual tension, came quickly when she made love, and was bossy in bed — when she had the chance — or that potato salad was her favourite food, although lately she had taken to eating cold potatoes straight out of the fridge.

It didn't mention her stepmother whom she had disliked, although she had done her best for the family, or her mother who had died when the family was young, the delicate migrant daughter from a tea-planting family that had given up on Malaysia, or Malaya, as it was, or that Tom Diamond had spent the rest of his life after her death trying to eradicate the traces of her style while at the same time grieving in secret for her. 'She's a right little corker,' he would say about his second wife when they went to the RSA together. They sang *Roll me over/in the clover/roll me over, lay me down, and do it again* on Saturday nights, drank flagon beer, brought a couple of dozen home, and some mates, stunk the house out, and on Sunday morning, Elsie, that was her name, Elsie, would go at the house like a maniac, polishing the ornaments, and dusting the knick-knacks, getting everything ready for them to work hard until the next weekend. On Sunday night Tom did the accounts, his black eyebrows clenched in concentration. He said he didn't know who his family was, it wasn't worth talking about. One night, after a flagon, he elaborated, just the once. Afterwards Rose would think that she dreamed it, that his grandfather who had brought him up in Australia was really called Diamantis; but whatever drop of diluted Greek blood lurked in his veins now, Tom would tell you *I'm a Kiwi joker, don't get me wrong mate, if you didn't fight for New Zealand, you're a nobody.*

Rose met Kit, or maybe it was the other way round, one night by the lakefront when she was dancing on the flatdeck of one of Tom Diamond's trucks, drinking beer and naked to the waist. Kit had come down to town for the weekend from the mountain.

'Tell me about your family,' Kit's mother said, the first time they met.

'My mother's dead,' Rose had said quickly.

'Oh dear, I am so sorry,' Mrs Kendall said then.

'You weren't to know,' said Rose. 'Look, here she is, here's a picture of my mother.' The photograph showed her mother when she was very young, perhaps about the time when she left Malaya. She was sitting on a verandah surrounded by bougainvillaea. She wore a wide-brimmed hat, and a tremulous smile hovered about her mouth. Even in the black and white photograph her skin looked translucent.

It wasn't as if Kit's parents were very wealthy, or superior. They were a pleasant family who lived in a modest house on the outskirts of Auckland. But they took holidays, read books, and believed in education in principle, although they didn't make demands on their family to be educated. They were proud that Kit had done so well, that was all.

But after she met them, Rose began coaxing her fizzy cloud of hair into a neat French roll, and stopped wearing red fingernail polish. She was teaching Standard Three at Weyville Primary, and her school inspection visits started going very well after she met Kit and began visiting his family. It was as if she had come home.

She and Kit didn't mean to stay in Weyville. But they had good jobs and they could get five per cent mortgages. It made sense to buy a section and build, which meant they also had to get married. People didn't live together in Weyville, not then, anyway, and Rose had to get away from Elsie somehow. Tom Diamond gave Rose a flash wedding even though it was not what she wanted. In the local paper it was written up as the Weyville Wedding of the Year:

> The bride wore a shimmering gown of French lace, made in a princess line with piping at the seams. Roule roses scattered the train...
>
> The bridesmaids wore pearl-white picture hats and pale pink accessories. Their crinoline gowns were supported by hoops...
>
> The bridegroom's mother wore a powder-blue suit with black accessories...
>
> The bride's stepmother, Mrs Elsie Diamond, wife of well-known road haulage contractor, Mr Tom Diamond, wore a cheerful cherry red outfit and a large black and white hat with an appropriate diamond pattern...

They did, definitely, mean to leave Weyville.

But the article didn't mention that either.

Kit hadn't been pleased about the article. 'I didn't say a word out of place,' she said when he had looked at it, frowning.

But she knew that it had revealed a chink.

'Apparently forthright,' he had said, and walked out of the room.

She had sat and stared at the topaz ring. Later she put it away in a drawer for awhile.

Like the dog, Rose began to relax. Clearly the phantom caller thought she was out.

She opened the pull-down lid of the desk which Olivia used to have in her bedroom. Rose had taken it for her electorate work now that her daughter no longer needed it. There were piles of paper stacked inside it in methodical rows. On the left-hand side there was a pile of invitations to be answered: two to attend school functions, one to open a kindergarten, one to judge a flower show, one to present prizes at the rodeo when it came to town—with a follow-up for her and Kit to attend the country and western dance in the evening, and for the same evening was an invitation to have dinner with the president of the local businessmen's association—and three to have afternoon tea with old-age pensioners.

Appeal forms for campaign funds which she had prepared ready for handing out to fund-raising volunteers were stacked on the right-hand side of the desk. In the centre stood more letters, all from local party members, divided into two piles. The complaints were on one side, the good wishes on the other. In its fourth year the Lange Government was going through another crisis and the sheaf of good wishes was slim. Amongst the complaints there was an anonymous letter written in red ink which, of course, she could not identify as having come from a party member but it slotted into the category of things that had to be dealt with, and so she put them all together. The letter made certain suggestions about Rose's sexuality, throwing in the possibility that she slept with seamen off foreign fishing boats when she visited Wellington. She had no answer for this, and if she did she would not have known where to send it, although the postmark was local.

She sat at the desk, pulling an end of her hair, pondering whether to show the letter to the police or not. By itself, the letter was a routine fact of political life, but for the moment everything must be regarded as suspect. If there was someone out there, the police had warned (she had noted the use of the word 'if'), who had a hang-up about her (no pun intended, they said, with melancholy humour), he might move on from phone calls to some more aggravating form of harassment. It was this decision, whether or not to visit the police again, which had been hanging over her all day. As much as the phone calls it was making her day unbearable.

She did not want to see the police again. *Life's a bitch — and then you die, see Stevie Smith, passim* her daughter, Olivia, had written on the lid of the desk, and underneath that *SHAKESPEARE WAS A SEXIST BASTARD*. Rose wondered sometimes if it was either of the children's friends that rang her night and day. Or even the children themselves.

But Olivia and Richard had gone. And anyway she trusted them. She loved them. She might not know them any more, but there was that, her love for them, a passion as clear as sunlight. She raised her head as if to smell them, but they were not part of this house.

Rose replaced the lid. Kit was right. They should get new furniture. They should get rid of the rubbish. She, in particular, had to stop living in the past. She thought that it was immediately apparent to most people that she did this; she appeared to be an efficient woman with little time for reflection and less for regrets. Some said, when Kid entered Parliament, that she would have done the job better.

It was since the phone calls began that she had been pushed back into the past, to re-examine every thread of her life. 'It's driving me crazy,' she said to Kit one night when he was home, willing him to understand. She did not express a desire, even to herself, that he believe what she was telling him.

He had glanced at her reflectively. 'It's over to you, isn't it?' he had said. When she turned to ask him what he meant they were interrupted by a caller with electorate business, and the matter hadn't been raised again.

She leaned and straightened a table resting on an angle because one of its legs with barley sugar twists was broken. When she had done that she opened the desk again with new resolve. She would write a list of all the things she needed to do, starting with the piles of paper in front of her. She wrote: *answer letters*; her eye strayed, which ones first? She crossed out *answer letters* and wrote *answer invitations (decide which ones to accept)*, *complaints from members*, *good wishes from members*, *ring Kit tonight*, crossed out *ring Kit*, she had rung him the night before, and doodled. She put down *get a conservatory*, *new dining room table*, *establish conversation nooks*, *get new covers on the sofas (probably dullish-coloured with shiny surface)*, *look out new fillings for sandwiches for fund-raising mornings* (because they had become the party of broad appeal now and scones were not enough), *check out style book about food presentation* (lately she had eaten a great deal of food that looked better than that which she cooked and tasted worse), *do something about clothes*, *get a haircut*; she crossed out *haircut* and wrote *body wave*. There were more ways than one to serve a cause. She wrote *I am an emblem* and was going to write *for every woman* but this didn't feel right, maybe a bit unrealistic; even though she was the only person who would see it, she didn't put that down.

She looked back over the list. Shades of Elsie, she thought. God help us. Fortunately Elsie was dead. Finally.

In the silence the phone clicked, signalling that it was about to ring.

She stiffened but nothing happened. A man had once sent signals to her in this fashion, dialling to let her know when she was working in the kitchen of her old house that he was thinking of her even though she would not be able to pick up the phone and talk to him. The silliness of it. Her face burned. Surely it was not him. She hoped it was not. Still, it was not the first time she had thought of him, for she had racked her brains for months thinking of anyone and everyone she had ever known. This was a possibility she had always dismissed.

But it could be anybody.

Nobody could be discounted any more.

While she was thinking of this, the phone began to ring again, properly this time, a steady persistent buzz. Rose lurched towards it knocking over the table with barley sugar twist legs; it fell, scraping her shin, and the thing she had been holding back, because she had to be calm, had to remember at all times that this might be a genuine call, maybe one of Kit's constituents, or a call from Wellington, even the Prime Minister himself, it was not beyond the bounds of possibility, leapt out and was said as she picked up the phone: 'Go away you bastard, you fuckwit,' she screamed. As she caught her breath there was a sharp indrawn one at the other end. 'You horseshit. You. I'll kill you, I'll do it myself,' she added, still shouting.

She slammed the receiver down, and leaned against the wall, wondering what irretrievable thing she had done.

In a second the ringing began again. She picked it up. 'Rose Kendall,' she said dully.

'That was better out than two teeth I guess,' her sister said at the other end.

'So how long's this jerk been ringing you?'

'A year. On and off.'

'For Chrissake. Why didn't you tell me? Or did you think it was me?'

Katrina did not look much like Rose. Her hair was dyed black, and in repose her face was tired. It was a handsome face with a large nose which she had talked about having bobbed for years, if only she could afford it. She was dressed in an ultra-short puffy black skirt and a sheer orange lace jacket over her bra. She wore laced black boots and heavy silver rings. One of her ears was bleeding slightly from having a new stud put in.

Her square acid-blue Housing Corporation house sat in a straight row of houses that ran exactly parallel to another row, and another beyond that. The corner of the intersection nearest her house had a McDonald's filled with a queue up to the counter; on the far side stood a dairy painted scarlet to advertise Coca Cola. Three doors up the burnt-out hulk of a car, and the charred remains of a cross as tall as a man, stood on a lawn. The people who had lived in this house, a Samoan and his white wife and their children, had moved away.

'It's the Klan,' said Katrina with apparent indifference when Rose commented.

'I know, of course, what happened,' Rose said. 'But I didn't realise it was so close to you.'

'Down among the boongs. You ought to come here more often. There's some brides of Christ up the street, they're out to get the Jews but the pickings are a bit lean. The Jews all live in your street.'

'This is New Zealand, not the Bible belt of Middle America,' Rose snapped.

'Tell me about it. This is the Blake Block.'

Katrina's unfenced lawn straggled to the edge of the road, littered with paper and tins from the food barns. Her house smelled of ashtrays overflowing with Winfields. Her ancient car was like that too, Rose recalled. The only time she'd been in it she had to put her head out the window while Katrina drove. This afternoon there was a stack of dishes in the sink beside them. They sat on chrome-legged chairs at a green formica table with tea stains on it. Rose resisted the urge to get a cloth. Katrina would love that, the excuse to throw her out.

'I know it's not you that's doing it, Sis,' said Rose. 'I could tell from the way you reacted. Well you wouldn't have rung back and spoken to me, would you?'

'But you thought it might have been me? Jesus, why would you think that?'

Rose nearly said: *because you've caused us a hell of a lot of trouble on and off over the years*. But it didn't seem like the moment for all-or-nothing honesty. Instead, she said: 'I'm ready to think it's anybody.'

'One of your political buddies that's gone sour on you? There must be plenty of those.'

'I expect so.'

'But you're not sure?'

'I don't know, Katrina. I feel like it's me they're out to get.'

'You're meant to. You'd make a lovely victim. You'd end up just like me.' Katrina blew a smoke ring. Our father taught her to do that, Rose thought. She's reminding me whose favourite she was.

'I know it wasn't you, Sis.'

'So why did you come?'

'You rang.'

'And you came running. What's happened? Have you run out of shoulders to cry on?'

'I don't... do that.' Rose made as if to collect her bag. 'So why did you ring me?'

'I don't see you that much. You're too busy with good works.' Katrina drew on her cigarette, eyeing her speculatively. 'Or does that bore you now? What do you do when you've got everything you want?'

Rose checked a quick response. She knew now that there was a course to be run, that she wouldn't find out easily what it was that Katrina wanted. Her sister had caught her off balance for a moment and now she would have to wait until Katrina was ready.

'Or haven't you got what you want after all? Christ, you marched for this, and marched for that, and sat in for the workers here, there and everywhere, do they thank you now that Kit's in Parliament? I mean, wasn't that what it was all about?'

Rose was silent.

'You look done in,' said Katrina, getting up. 'Here, the sun's over the yard-arm, drink this.' She poured some Seagers into a couple of tumblers and slopped them under the tap. 'I haven't got anything to go with it.' She put one down in front of Rose. Water trickled down the side of the glass, making a pool beside it. A match floated.

'Tell me,' said Katrina, producing a packet of opened Cheezels and flapping them in a cloud of their yellow dust onto a plate, 'did either of you ever think what you were taking on? Or was it just part of the fun, standing for Parliament?' She shook her head. Her voice was soft. 'Kit never meant to get in, did he? It was the last thing either of you expected.'

When Rose still didn't reply, she said, 'Not everyone liked him. Not everyone's pleased about the Government.'

'I know that,' said Rose. 'I've thought about that a hundred times. I don't know where to begin looking. Which one of them it could be. But I don't believe it's that.' She paused. 'It does feel personal.'

'What does Kit say? He must get it too.'

'They don't ring when he's home.'

'Yeah? Well, I see.'

'How's Larissa?' Rose asked, holding her breath and swigging the gin. It was best to swallow quickly, though she had to be careful or Katrina would fill it again.

'That bitch. I hope I don't see her for about a hundred years.'

'She's your daughter.'

'Oh God. Here we go.' She tipped the bottle sideways with a deft little motion towards her own glass. Rose covered hers with her hand, even though she could see how much this irritated Katrina.

'Is she still with Gary?'

Katrina shrugged.

Rose supposed, whenever she thought about it, that it was easier now for Katrina to pretend that Larissa hadn't existed. Like Paul, Larissa's father. Maybe Katrina never thought anymore of Paul, the first of her children's fathers. When she married him she wore her black hair in a lacquered bouffant and taught dancing. She tripped everywhere with a bright, studiedly alert expression and taught little girls to stand on their toes and spin, and adults to ballroom dance in the evenings. For these sessions she wore sequined dresses which she sewed at the weekends, and when there was time she made extra ones for her pupils who were dancing in the competitions. She and Paul were dancing partners. He had slicked-back hair and sold cars on a second-hand lot. Rose used to think he was like a character out of a comic strip, he was so true to type. When he went off with a driving school instructor who used to be a marching girl she and Kit laughed, at least to themselves. It was later they learned how truly Katrina had grieved.

Or perhaps they never really did. 'You don't understand,' Katrina had said, in some excess of sorrow late at their house one night, and it was true. They still looked sideways at Paul when they saw him in town. He lived in a huge hacienda-style house in north Weyville and went to fundamental revivalist meetings with his wife and their three well-washed children. Richard said, last time he was home, that Paul grew cannabis in the greenhouse, but Rose didn't know about that, nor did she ask Richard how he knew.

In an adjacent room a baby cried.

'Shall I pick her up?' asked Rose.

A flicker of apprehension darted across Katrina's face. She caught her top lip between her teeth. They were big strong teeth. 'I'll do it,' she said, getting up. Straight away Rose guessed what condition the baby was in.

As she sat thinking how she would kill her sister if the baby was sick, the back door was pushed open and a face appeared. It was Minna, Katrina's friend, whom Rose had met a couple of times at the hospital last time Katrina was in, having the baby.

'Oh, it's you,' said Minna. 'I wouldn't have come in if I'd known. I thought you were the bailiffs.'

'Getting ready to give a hand were you?' Rose didn't trust Minna. She was English, with a tiny doll-like face full of apparent naïvety. Her blonde hair fell straight to the curve of her rump. Her top and jeans were exquisitely laundered and ironed; through her T-shirt her nipples poked out fashionably from her skinny breasts. She was a vegetarian and practised organic gardening; at the hospital she had turned up with brown rice and bean shoot dishes, and thrown out

Katrina's dinners when they brought them round. Minna had left a child behind in England with a former husband and was proud that she had the courage to walk out on what she termed 'a bad situation'. Rose placed her age at around thirty, though she could pass for eighteen.

Katrina emerged from the bedroom with her youngest child in her arms. Sharna was a pinched little girl, nearly nine months old. Katrina said the baby's father was named George and he had been staying on the Block for awhile, but she didn't know where he was now.

Rose hadn't seen the baby for months but straight away she put her arms out with a desparate urgency as if anyone would do rather than her mother. Katrina handed her over; Rose could see that she wasn't keen, but there was not much else she could do.

Sharna clung to her, nuzzling into her neck. If she had been dirty in her cot, she was changed now. Her jumpsuit, though matted from the wash, was clean and dry, and her hair damp as if it had had a flannel passed over it. One of her eyes was huge and blue, the other walled. Rose looked at the hand bunching her blouse up into a fist.

'She's lovely,' she said, and meant it. She rubbed her face against the child's. There was a sourness on her skin, but apart from that she smelled all right.

Katrina shrugged and said abruptly, 'I'll feed her.' She reached out and took Sharna back, at the same time releasing her bra under the orange lace.

'You're still feeding. That's good.' Rose disliked the hearty note in her own voice.

'It's easiest. And cheaper than SMA.'

Because Minna was there, Rose couldn't ask Katrina if it was money she wanted. As she sat watching the baby greedily feed she started planning things she could buy for Sharna. If Katrina would let her. It was one thing for Katrina to ask for something, but it was often another matter to tell her what she needed.

Minna got up to help herself to the gin and the phone rang; because she was beside it and Katrina didn't seem bothered, she picked it up and answered.

She said *Hullo, hullo, are you there, speak to me gorgeous*, and replaced it. 'Must be a wrong number.'

'You get them all the time,' said Katrina, pushing her breast back inside her clothes. 'Kids playing with phones.' She glanced at Rose.

The back door opened again, or rather burst open this time, and a boy wearing a military-style *Bundeswehr* sweatshirt raced at them, as if to pass between them, pushing everything in his way aside.

Katrina grabbed him. 'It's your aunt,' she hissed. 'Speak to her.'

Basil, his six-year-old face that might be a hundred, squinted at her.

'How's school?' said Rose. They looked at each other, measuring up each other's weak spots. When he was smaller Rose used to come and collect Basil for an afternoon, but it always turned into a disaster. If Sharna was pinched from an overt neglect, Basil had the appearance of a child whom nobody could improve. He had always been underweight and scrawny, his head almost too large to sit comfortably on his neck, his freckles brilliant on his luminous skin, his hair permanently spiky. She could swear he had the beginnings of crow's feet around his eyes. He had never slept properly when he stayed with her, crying fretfully for his mother from the time of his arrival until he was taken home.

He looked at Katrina, ignoring Rose's question and wrinkling his nose as if sniffing for something. 'You old bitch,' he said, 'you're just a bloody old milk tanker.' He punched Katrina's chest, hurting her. 'I'll smash that baby in.' He pushed Sharna hard; Minna snatched her from Katrina's lap.

Rose thought she could use some more gin after all.

'It's like coming to a horror movie here, isn't it?' said Minna companionably. Katrina had Basil in a wrestling hold, then flipped him quickly over into her lap. He fought for a moment, all teeth and fists, then subsided against her, his head tucked under her chin. She took some Cheezels from the plate and delicately inserted them between his lips.

Rose opened her mouth to tell Katrina what she thought: *You shouldn't let Basil do this*, she wanted to say, *he's too big to behave like this*, then she saw her sister's face. For a moment, it was at peace. Her eyes were closed; perhaps she was thinking of Wolf, Basil's father.

Rose had met Wolf only once, seven years before.

They were at open-air tearooms by the lake, the afternoon was dull and cloudy, the water looked yellowish-brown. It was a shallow lake, man-made, unvaried by turbulence, lacking depth or mystery. But the peacocks walked around them, spreading their tails and prancing, and Katrina's face shone. Her dark hair had fallen round her shoulders, her eyes never left the face of her lover. She explained about New Zealand to him, that Maoris did not live in huts as at the model pa they had just visited. She reminded Larissa patiently that she must thank the young German for the drink and that she must not frighten the birds. Larissa was eleven, and bored. She didn't want to be with them, though Rose was not sure whether it was because she disliked the German or because she was playing him off against Paul, her father, with whom she was supposed to have spent the afternoon. Wolf stroked Katrina's leg. She stroked his. They were surrounded by an aura.

'You look a leetle tired,' he said.

'Do I?'

'Perhapz only becoz I feel it.'

'I wonder what time we got to sleep.'

She began to tell him some other story, about a flood that had been in the district. It was without point but she sounded articulate and reasonable as if these were things he ought to know. She either didn't see Rose there, or didn't remember that she had asked her to come. It was as if Rose was not there at all. After awhile Rose and Larissa wandered away and threw crusts of their afternoon tea to the peacocks, and then into the sludgy bulrushes at the edge of the water where ducks shoved one another. Larissa began to laugh, for the first time that afternoon. Her hair slapped against her back, a plait as thick as the rigging on a tall ship. Then she took Rose's hand, as if she were much younger; they walked away from Katrina and Wolf. The sun came out and the water glittered and when they had walked far enough they turned to go back to the tearooms. Katrina was animated and greeted Rose as if it was the first time she had seen her that day, though she didn't introduce her to Wolf again.

She ran away to Europe with the beautiful German youth. She said he was her new beginning. Larissa stayed behind. It was not the first time she had lived with the Kendalls. When Wolf abandoned Katrina, Rose and Kit scraped together her fare and sent it to her so she could come home. After her return Paul stopped her maintenance. He didn't have to pay her any more, he wasn't looking after someone else's kid, he said, and when she took him to court he won.

She got to keep Larissa.

It was true though, Basil was her special child. He was always in trouble at school. Katrina was supposed to take him regularly to a child psychiatrist, but she had taken him only once. Shrinks didn't know anything, she said, there was nothing wrong with Basil. She loved this dumb kid whom Rose had never been able to take to.

He stood up, wiping crumbs from his mouth, then coughed as if something had caught in the back of his throat. He heaved, close to wretching.

'Shut up,' Katrina said. He gasped, choked. She stroked his head idly as he subsided. 'He's always doing that,' she remarked to nobody in particular.

'Shouldn't you take him to the doctor?' Rose asked.

'That's the answer to everything,' Minna said. 'See the doctor. Bugger up his central nervous system with drugs.'

Rose felt Minna's dislike of her as a tangible force in the room.

Minna said, 'How do you think she can pay for the doctor anyway, with what your lot's done to the health system?'

'What would you do?' Rose asked, stung, her tongue loosened by the gin. She must be crazy, drinking gin at a constituent's house. But this was her sister Katrina, not just a constituent, and Minna was her guest. Rose would have liked to hold Sharna again but it was too late. She had a meeting to attend.

Rather more than you're doing,' Minna answered, suddenly sounding prim and English. 'Look at this place.' She waved towards the window, and the line of houses that stood outside.

'Did you see *EastEnders*?' Katrina asked hurriedly, as if spurred to change Minna's line of conversation and stop Rose from walking out, as clearly she would at any moment.

'Oh yes,' Minna conceded. 'But I'm sick of it. I don't like the blacks that are in it ri-aght now. That's another thing,' she said, turning to Rose. 'This place down here's getting taken over by the blacks.'

'So Katrina says. If that's what you'd call it. You have to try and fit in when you come to another country, Minna. Otherwise they'll say *you're* taking over.'

'Uh huh. Pommie bashing. I suppose that's what got you lot into power. I don't see you sitting in the roadway with the blacks now.'

'We don't call them blacks here.' She couldn't understand why Minna didn't leave. She lived next door to Katrina, saw her every day, had time on her hands to come some other time. Rose was waiting to find out what it was that Katrina wanted, and to find out more about Larissa if she could.

'Yes you do,' Minna persisted. '*They* say it. You're supposed to say *black*.'

'It depends on who's saying it.'

'Selective morality. Anyway, what's it matter, blacks, Polys, they're overrunning this place.'

'I have to go,' said Rose. Katrina jumped up to follow her out, tucking the baby on her hip. Minna reached for the gin at the same time as the phone began again. Her hand left the bottle for the receiver, but the line was dead. Katrina glanced towards Rose, suddenly uneasy; her sister fumbled with the door handle, frantic to get outside in the open air.

'Coincidence,' Rose said, when she reached the car.

'It is weird,' Katrina admitted, although Rose hadn't wanted that, nor to talk about it now.

'Nobody knows I'm here,' she said firmly. 'You can see how easy it is to get jumpy about nothing.'

Katrina leaned against the car door. 'It's like somebody must have followed you.'

'Nonsense.' Rose looked around her. At least on the surface it was a quiet street. She strained to remember cars that had passed, but they were a blur, she didn't watch things like that. Not so far. 'That's crazy. Forget I mentioned this whole thing, all right?'

'Suit yourself.' Katrina dropped her cigarette on the ground, grinding it with her heel. 'Rose?'

'Yes?' *Now for it.*

'Could you look in on Larissa?'

'What's the matter with her?'

'Nothing.'

'Why don't you?'

'She doesn't want me to, eh?' Starting to play the role of a downtrodden Blake Block inhabitant, whining slightly.

'Katrina, tell me.'

'I don't know,' said Katrina, as if Rose was persecuting her. 'Look, I heard something, all right? Her and Gary, they're into something heavy, I dunno what it is.'

'Dope?'

'So how should I know? Half of Weyville is.'

'Are they?'

'Pardon me? I forgot you were mates with the cops these days.'

'That's not true. They think I'm nuts.'

There was a silence.

'I don't know what's with Larissa,' Katrina said. 'That's God's truth, Sis. I heard that Gary's been beating up on her, and that he's got a bit of money.'

'What do you want me to do?'

'Oh I dunno.'

'Yes, all right, I'll go and see her. They're still at the caravan park?'

'I hear so.'

'Is it urgent?'

'I thought you wouldn't be able to wait.'

'She's not that keen on seeing me either,' Rose said. 'You know that.'

'No. Well. It's over to you. She deserves her lot.'

'I mean, I can't go right away, this minute. But in the morning, is that okay?'

'Whenever.'

As she drove away Rose fancied that Minna was watching her from behind the cracked venetian blinds in Katrina's house. She had become used to people behaving angrily towards her since Kit got into Parliament, but she did not understand Minna's antagonism; it was as if she disliked her being near Katrina. For a second she thought crazily that it could be Minna making the phone calls, then remembered that Minna had been in the room when the phone had just rung.

If it was the caller. She looked in the rear-vision mirror; someone might be following her now. The road was clear. She shook her head. Nobody could have known where she was.

It might have been a coincidence at Katrina's, in which case it could still be Minna.

Or anyone, she argued with herself.

Skinny blue shadows were lengthening across the road. She avoided a dead-looking trike with a slewed wheel that had run out on the roadway, and drove over the railway tracks, past the remnants of the railway station. Outlines of gardens could still be seen, ragged trees and broken lines of fences where once there were railway cottages; the land was zoned industrial, but since the stockmarket crash plans for building on it had lapsed. Rose pulled into the dairy on the edge of the shopping mall which served the Blake Block.

As she picked her way across the parking lot an old woman dressed in a long brown raincoat nearly to her ankles, with thin blunt-cut hair covered by a shocking pink hairnet, rushed at a group of street kids who had been sniffing. She carried a broken spade handle. One of the kids pushed his paper bag of glue into her face and she tottered, almost falling; the kids saw Rose, retreated, and the woman recovered herself. Rose ran towards her, calling out, *Are you all right?* The woman glanced at her and backed into a shop verandah, as if nothing had happened.

Inside the dairy Rose smiled at the proprietor, a young Indian named Gandhi with a moustache. She knew him of old, from when she and Kit used to collect donations for the Party. He had been a generous giver. He turned away, staring at the wall as she picked out milk from the refrigerator. She saw that the shelves were half-empty, with the goods pulled up to the front leaving dead space behind.

'Thank you,' he said when she gave him the money. He still did not look at her.

She sat in the car for a moment before starting the engine. Perhaps Katrina and Minna were right. She didn't know how she would cope in the Blake Block. Across the road a telephone dangled in a doorless phone box. Public telephones here were almost all out of order. Above her stood a row of hoardings. Sweet Harmony were playing a gig at the local theatre at the weekend, and the Topp Twins the following week. An advertisement for insurance had been defaced. Somebody had painted, in big red letters that had run, BLACKS AND LESBIANS RULE, OKAY?

She thought about it on the way home, as she turned her navy-blue Metro into the tree-lined street that branched away to her right. A few lights had come on in Cedarwood Grove, shining behind silver trophies or careful floral arrangements standing in the windows, or down on to acres of carpet beyond picture windows; falling across large empty lawns. Otherwise there was nobody around, no kids playing in the street, no one out talking over the fences. The eerie hush of each house's isolation from its neighbour was suffocating.

She directed the car up the driveway towards the automatic doors of the new garage, recently built under the old house. The door between the garage and the kitchen was standing open. Inside, the phone rang, a persistent unrelenting drone.

As she sat in her car, waiting for the sound to cease, she turned out the contents of her bag. At the bottom there was a pile of credit card slips including four Visa dockets for petrol and two American Express for alcohol, a card for a dental appointment she needed but had forgotten to keep, three hard jubes, and five tablets of Valium.

3

'If that's Rose, tell her I'm in the shower,' Toni Warner called.
'It sounds urgent.'
'I don't care.'
Toni owned an eight-place Hutschenreuther dinnerset, which she used often, cultivated an all-white garden in the style of Vita Sackville-West, and was the mother of two children who were perfectly integrated into the State school system and had begun to learn Maori. She was Rose Kendall's best, if younger, friend.
Lyle walked into the kitchen trailing the phone by its cord. His hand covered the mouthpiece. 'I told her you were free.'
'Shit.'
She reached for the phone.
'I'm flat sticks, can I talk to you later, lovey?'
'Yes, sure.'
'You're all right?'
'Yes, of course.'
'What is it?' Toni was contrite.
'Nothing. You got the radio on?'
'Umm . . . it's on . . . I wasn't listening . . . it's Anne Murray isn't it?'
The singer was performing an old Cole Porter number with a surprising bitter-sweet accuracy . . . *Are you still in love with me-ee*? Toni sensed Rose's tearfulness down the phone.
'*Are* you all right?'
'Do you know if she's still getting that guy round her house? The one they're always arresting and sending to jail because he keeps turning up and saying he's in love with her?'
'Rose!'
'I was just thinking. How could she sing that? It might make him worse.'
Toni's tone was sharp. 'For God's sake, Rose. Anne Murray lives on an island off the coast of Canada.'
'I know.'
'I've been listening to Tracey Chapman lately,' said Toni. 'You need educating.'

She put the phone down and looked at Lyle, standing in the doorway.

'Did you tell her?' he asked. She often felt that her husband listened to her phone calls.

'She didn't ask.'

'You'd better shift it if you're going, hadn't you?'

★

The meetings of the Weyville branch of the Labour Party were held in the Presbyterian church hall. A trestle table was set out at the front. The electorate committee sat along the table facing the members. Of late, there had been more committee than audience.

But this evening, when Rose Kendall arrived, there were at least twenty cars outside, and inside the hall fifty or so people had gathered. She was on the point of being late and tried to walk slowly as if it didn't matter. She had put on make-up and changed into an off-the-rack emerald green silk shirt with an Eloise label, and a grey linen skirt with boxer pleats. She smiled at everybody and nobody in particular.

Harry Ryan, the secretary, was already seated behind the table while the chairman, Matt Decker, walked up and down alongside it, doing a head count among the rows.

Rose pushed her way through a crowd round the kitchen door to deposit her plate of supper sandwiches. Toni was amongst the knot of women setting out cups and food, applying herself to the wrapping of bread around tinned asparagus spears. When Rose caught sight of her small pointed face bent over her task, she thought, absurdly it seemed at that moment, how pretty she was. Her eyes, turned away from Rose now, were blue-ish green and wide-spaced, her dark hair cropped short. Her throat rose out of a crisp cotton blouse; she seemed to work intensely. Rose longed for Toni to look up and speak first. The women were laughing about something.

After a moment, she said, 'You didn't tell me you were coming tonight.'

'I only decided at the last moment.' Toni sounded defensive.

'What's the joke?'

'How many men does it take to wallpaper a room?' asked Toni quickly, lightening up.

'How many?'

'Six if you slice them thinly.' The women laughed, as if for the first time, small hooting noises.

Matt had come up behind them. 'That's all right. How many women does it take to paint a ceiling?'

Toni groaned. 'Go on.'

'Three. One to hold the ladder and two to form a support group.'

While they pretended uneasily that they had stopped laughing, Rose moved away towards Matt, looking for a quiet word. As a rule he appreciated this. She knew it made him feel privy to the news from Wellington, even more because he was deputy editor of the local paper. She and Matt had had many serious and important discussions about nothing in these interludes while the party faithful were gathering. He was a tall bulky man, fleshy and handsome in his way, with thick curly grey hair. He had had his disappointments, which included a continual failure to become the paper's editor. His critics suggested that this was hardly surprising given his political stance. They accused him of naïvety; this was the country, boy. While he wore his second ranking like a martyr's badge of honour, others more unkindly promoted the notion that it was his wife's family ties with the newspaper's proprietor that kept him in a job at all. A play he once wrote for television had been accepted, only to have the producer change his mind at the last moment; more recently he had been passed over for selection as candidate for the Weyville seat in favour of Kit. It had soured him for a time, especially when Kit surprised everyone and got into Parliament. Now, it seemed, he was easygoing and affable and cooked couscous for dinner parties when his wife let him. Kit told Rose that she should watch him, because sooner or later he would take his feelings out on the world. Yet he exuded decency and discretion, even a slight jaunty courage. She could not believe that he would hurt her or Kit.

'Looking for somebody?' Matt asked.

'You,' she said, irritated.

'Oh, well, we're about to get started.' He nodded towards the seats.

Dismissed, she took a place in the front row. Something felt wrong. She looked over towards Harry, who was avoiding her eye. The last time she had seen him he had been standing outside welfare, his rumpled hair still showing the remains of a smart cut. He had blinked uncertainly, as if he couldn't believe it was him standing there; and she hadn't been able to either. She had started towards him in the street, and then, looking at his face with its expression of misery, thought better of it. Besides, she didn't know what to say. She could see it wasn't her place to say how sorry she was that he was unemployed. Now he sat turning his thick gold wedding band over and over.

She wished that she hadn't come. But Kit had told her to go to the meetings whenever she could make them. It was a way of pressing the flesh, a visible reminder that all of them in the Party movement had got this Government together between them, that they had united once with common purpose.

A group of them made the decision that they would have a new Government as they sat in a roadway in 1981.

A cold day gleaming with a distant rim of sunlight behind dense grey cumulus. Twenty-two of them, men and women, sat across the roadway north into Weyville, blocking the highway before a football game was due to start. There had been orders out not to bring children. The Springboks were due to start playing football against the local team in half an hour. Spectators headed towards the grounds; so far they had been deflected away from the group of protesters. There were two routes in. The group had decided to block only one entrance in order to make a show of strength together, there being no hope at all, with their numbers, of covering both roads. They were wearing motorcycle crash helmets. They had all heard about Molesworth Street in Wellington, when the police waded into the crowd with batons, breaking open the skulls of women in the front row of the demonstration.

'At least there were a lot of them,' someone in the group said nervously. Somebody else pointed out the disadvantage of this, the way they were pressed back into the crowd behind, so they couldn't escape — there was nowhere to run.

Rose and Kit sat side by side. For a moment Rose wanted to giggle, they looked so silly dressed up like this, as if this were a game in itself. The group caught one another's eyes, grinned; she was not the only person thinking that. But her stomach rumbled and she remembered what Kit had said, don't have too much breakfast, just in case you end up hurt, needing an anaesthetic or something. Someone passed a flask of hot coffee. Maybe nothing would happen. She reached for Kit's hand, his fingers closed around hers. His scarf was wrapped around his beard. At the same time that he held her hand with his free one he rubbed Nick Newbone's back as if he were a kid; she felt sorry for Nick, he looked so scared. They were all scared in different ways, but Nick was terrified, and although she didn't like him much it seemed to her that he was much braver because he had come anyway, anticipating the fear before it happened. Hortense, his thin energetic wife, sat beside him but she didn't seem to notice how scared he was.

Alongside them, Toni pulled her coat around her and shivered. 'Will Lyle be very angry?' Rose asked her. It would be a long time before Lyle seemed to accept Toni's political activity. Today he had asked her not to come. He was going to the game.

Toni shrugged and gazed up the road, as if seeking him out. Matt turned and smiled at her, brushed her face. Rose sometimes wondered about them. Matt, and Harry and his new girlfriend Belinda, and Morris Applebloom, had been carrying a banner between them at the front. It read GO HOME BOKS. *At the moment it drooped as they waited for action.*

Henare Muru and his mother Wiki handed out sweets. The boiled lollies dissolved down the backs of their throats as they sucked. Rose didn't know Wiki before the tour began, now she saw her as a friend. She had been to several of their meetings. Her presence formed a bridge with four gang members who had turned up.

'What about a song?' someone called. 'Give us a chant.'

'Amandla-a-a,' cried Toni, as if driven.

'Amandl-a-a, Ngawhetu, Amandla Amandla,' they responded, full throat.

In the distance a car approached travelling fast. It was a big dark car and it did not look as if it was going to stop.

'Hold fast,' screamed Toni. Her face was contorted, her eyes shining, her mouth pulled back against her teeth.

Still no police.

The car ground to a halt just in front of them, brakes squealing. A man sat at the wheel, dressed up in a suit. A large woman wearing an enormous pink and grey hat leapt out on the passenger's side.

'We're going to a wedding, not the bloody game. What do you think you're doing?'

'One, two, three, four. We don't want your racist tour.'

'We're not going to the bloody game, didn't you hear us?'

'You would if you bloody could. If you didn't have a bloody wedding to go to.' Toni was beside herself.

'Toni, you don't know that,' Matt said. He was the only person who could say it to her. Mind you, they all knew she was right.

The man in the car got out.

'Keep back, this mob'll do you, Kev,' screamed the woman. 'Just see if they dare lay hands on a woman.'

Rose called out, 'Mrs Hawker, we're not going to hurt you.'

The woman's eyes singled her out. 'You. A teacher. You ought to be ashamed of yourself.'

'Who's wedding is it?' Rose asked.

'Mind your own bloody business.' Mrs Hawker was close to tears, her heavy powdered cheeks quivering.

'Is it Yvonne? Is it your brother's girl?'

The hat trembled as she heaved herself across the road towards them, hands up like a boxer's.

'It's okay, Mrs Hawker, you can go through,' Kit called.

The group parted and Mrs Hawker hesitated, then stumped back to the car. It started up and the car drove through, Mrs Hawker restored to the side of her husband, both of them looking straight ahead, thanking no one.

'Why did you do that?' Matt asked. 'You didn't ask us.'

'Are you here to stop a wedding or a tour?' Kit responded.

And the next moment the rugby supporters had broken ranks up ahead of them near the ground and were streaming back towards them, seeing the interference with the Hawkers as a blow against them, uncertain of what had happened. 'We want the tour, we want the tour.' Their chants lifted skywards.

There were more than a hundred in the approaching group; as they closed in bottles began to fly. One of the supporters held a softball bat like a weapon, menacing them.

'Kill, kill, kill the motherfuckers.' He lifted the bat above his head. A full can of beer sailed past Rose's head and landed with a dull thunk beside her.

'Where the fuck's the police?' muttered Morris. A banker, he had not lived here for long. He was not the kind of person they had expected to turn out with them; they held him in special awe and respect, the courage of it, laying his job on the line like this. He was married to Sarah who had stayed home today because of the children (not just hers and Morris's — several of the group had left their children with her today); she made the banners for them too. Morris's face shone with one of his usual close shaves, but there was a film of sweat and fear on his skin now.

Then the police emerged from behind the garden fence where they had been hidden all the time, almost too late to stop the onslaught, but not quite.

The supporters were turned back, marched away up the road under police escort. 'Are they going to arrest the bloke with the bat?' someone asked.

'Don't be silly,' Kit said and he was right, there were no arrests, only talk between the police and a knot of supporters.

Still nothing happened. Nearly time for the game to begin. 'I think we're a fizzer,' Harry said. 'What's the point, we should have tried to get on to the field.'

'There's not enough of us.'

'Some people should have come up from the city.'

In a way that was what they were all thinking, though they understood the need for orchestrated chaos in the cities. And the barbed wire was so thick around the game nobody in their right mind would have believed they could get through today unless there were hundreds of them. Later in the tour there would be crowds of protesters from throughout the country at all the games, but it was still too early for the danger to have sunk in. It was like a dream unfolding.

A great cheer erupted in the grounds.

'They've begun,' somebody said glumly, 'Nobody even noticed we were here.'

'We're a bunch of wets,' Toni announced. She was strung right out, tension and frustration bringing her close to despair. 'They'll say we didn't care.'

'That's not the point,' said Morris sharply. 'We do, and we're here, that's the point.'

At that moment a squad of police dressed in riot gear moved down the road towards them, shields up, batons at the ready, cantering along in a half-run with rhythmical, even tread. There was an almost light-hearted note in that steady beat. That was something they would remember.

'Oh Jesus,' said Kit. On either side of her, Rose felt him and Morris leaning towards her, protecting her, but at the same time afraid, holding their hands up to protect themselves too. Kit stood up and was knocked down by the first policeman. She jumped to her feet, throwing herself forward to protect him, taking the full force of the baton on her side.

Afterwards, lying dazed by the roadside, holding each other, trying to stem the flow of blood from wounds that sprouted above their eyes and over their ears, several of the men holding themselves in the groin where they had been kicked, somebody, it might have been her, or Toni, or Wiki Muru coming round from being knocked out, or maybe just all of them, said it wouldn't happen again, that they were going to do something, change the Government for a start, if it took them the rest of their lives. They weren't going to sit down and wait for any more to happen to them, not just like that.

But you got hit either way.

Tonight the meeting was business-like, Nick Newbone's apology was registered which Rose thought ominous. Nick was always there. Nick had served on the committee for years. Of course Hortense was present, but Hortense never missed anything.

The minutes and financial statement were dealt with in ten minutes, even though the branch's bank account was overdrawn. The only dissident was Larry Verschoelt, the big Dutchman who had been true blue for as long as anyone could remember but who had crossed over to join them a couple of years back when things were booming. He grew orchids up until last year, when the bottom had dropped out of the market. He had sold his Range Rover and drove a pick-up with a curling bumper sticker that read *I love Naomi's pink cardies*. Rose saw that he was drunk. When the figures were read out, demonstrating what everybody already knew, that nobody was giving money to the Party any more, he went up to the table and bent his head down holding his nostril as if he was snorting a line of cocaine.

Voices called out *Sit down Larry, for Chrissake, you'll get your turn.*

You'll get your turn. That was when Rose knew that it was all on, for sure. Whatever it was.

A few minutes later, a motion was put. The mover was a small woman named Denise. She wore open-and-sniff perfume samples and jumpers with glittery thread. 'Great high-tack, isn't it?' Toni said, whenever they discussed Denise. She was compiling a list on her. Denise had bought into Rada before the crash and lost a fortune. Toni had added owning Rada shares and losing them in the crash to her high-tack list, which meant her corresponding list of okay people had become suddenly quite small.

But for the moment Denise appeared to be fulfilling a role.

'I move that this branch works to amalgamate a march of the unemployed and the rural sectors, presently convened as separate events for next week, into one major march to demonstrate against the policies of the present Government, thereby making a single massive protest by the Weyville electorate.'

Rose looked to see whether Matt was laughing. But his head was inclined towards Denise and he was calling for a seconder. There were so many that Harry did not know whose name to write down.

Rose was surrounded by cheering as the motion was carried. *You can't do that*, she thought, *you can't come to meetings of the Party and plan an action against it.* That was not the way it worked. You had to go to a different meeting if you wanted to plan a march against the Party. There were unwritten rules in political life and she thought she understood them. Kit had always said, just sit there and be nice, don't get involved, that's not your job. Your job is to let them know that we're still in it together. And this was a rule she understood too. So she sat in silence, although she could feel herself going numb, as if she was protecting herself from some giant pain whose threshold seemed very close.

She looked for Toni. Toni was grinning hugely. It was that old smile that said, *We're doing something. We're not just sitting down and taking it.*

Rose knew then that there was no Party any more, not here anyway. She had known it for months. Beside her, an old couple, both with their scalps shining pinkly through their white hair, smiled at each other.

A young woman with spiky hair, wearing metal-framed glasses, who usually organised the pro-abortion petitions, looked elated. 'We should take the march all the way to Wellington,' she cried. The cheering in the room nearly drowned out the end of what she was saying.

For awhile Rose did not hear what was going on in the room, she sat thinking: *Is this what it was all for*? And then, *Where's Kit?;* and later, *What shall I tell him*?

Nobody appeared to be looking at her, though she knew they were all aware of her presence. If she sat very still perhaps they would forget that she was there, or perhaps she would be able to slip away without them noticing. Only she didn't really believe that.

Denise was on her feet again, fired up with all the attention.

'I further move that we pass a motion to censure our local Member of Parliament, Kit Kendall.'

They quietened then, as if a wave of nerves had caught them, almost like children who have been caught smoking behind the bikesheds and respond with that aggressive hysteria that reduces them to giggling.

'We might as well,' Denise shouted, still excited, the flag-bearer, it seemed, in a pink tracksuit tonight with fluffy moccasins.

'What good'll that do?' called Larry Verschoelt, thickly. 'It won't make a blind bit of difference to what he does down there in Wellington. We just dump him at the next election.'

'It's like we don't exist to that man any more,' the old man next to Rose told her, as if, in fact, she did not exist either.

Toni stood up then. 'Mr Chairman,' she called, attracting Matt's attention over a new volume of noise. He signalled to her to speak. 'Matt, there's not much we can censure Kit Kendall for at present. He still represents us. It's just that nobody listens to him down there. It's what he stands for that we're attacking, not the man. Isn't it?'

Rose could hear Katrina's voice in her head: *He never meant to get in, did he*? It was something she and Kit had never faced, never voiced out loud: what the consequences would be for them both if there was a landslide in the Party's favour at the polls, if in this most unlikely provincial town there was a swing to the left. When it happened it had been too late even to talk about it. It was true, they had meant to change the Government, but had they ever meant to go this far? Had they intended, by changing it, that they would also become it? The past is the present we live in, that is our territory, she thought, what is happening now is simply a rehearsal for the future. The journalist who had interviewed her had not asked her, either, what she thought of herself. If he had, she might have said, not especially good or evil, or even clever; nothing special—only I believe in what's right. Only then, she realised, she might also have been asked to define what was right, and was grateful that these questions had gone unasked.

Toni was still on her feet, and Morris stood too. Rose looked for Sarah, whom she had liked, but for reasons she would now prefer to forget, had never known as well as the others did. She was nowhere to be seen.

'One at a time,' said Matt, and there was another fluttery laugh in the room which Rose did not understand.

Morris said, 'The Government's standing firm on nukes. Kit Kendall's always been against nuclear ships and the Government's still supporting that view. Kit's quite influential in that respect.'

The old man beside Rose muttered to her, as if he really did not recognise her any more. 'That doesn't give my boy a job,' he said.

Toni had taken the floor again. 'Kit put himself on the line against the tour. That's where I'm coming from in respect of Kit. I'm not ready to censure him yet, not personally. We know he's capable of tough options. We need him still, to listen to what we believe in now.'

'We can put up another bloody good candidate at the next election if he doesn't,' shouted Larry.

'Shut up.' Matt stood, shouting back. 'Order.'

We meant to do good, Rose thought, *and that is still what we want, but the reality is different*. She would have liked to be back on the edge of the road with them all, faced by the drama and the challenge of what was to come.

When the meeting was over, she slipped out without waiting for supper. As she stood fumbling in her handbag for her car keys, Toni came up behind her and touched her arm. Rose fought the urge to throw it off.

'Am I supposed to thank you for saving Kit's skin?'

'Not unless you want to.'

'What's happening, Toni? What's really happening?'

Toni didn't answer.

Abruptly, Rose changed the subject. 'I feel like I'm spooked, Toni. Do you think there's spooks out there?'

Toni laughed uneasily. 'Shall I walk to the car with you?'

'No. Thank you. Look,' she said, turning, 'I don't mean ghosts.

I'm not a child. I mean, spooks.'

'The SIS? Being followed, that what you mean?'

'It's just a thought.'

'But why? You're not a security risk.'

'I don't know. Why not? They have to follow someone.' She checked the impulse to say that it might be Kit who was the risk, though she supposed that must be clear to Toni.

'The Prime Minister's falling apart,' Toni said at last, 'don't let it happen to you, Rose.'

'Thanks for the advice.' She pulled away, wanting to leave.

'Are you sure you're all right?'

'Don't keep asking me that.'

The car was sitting under a street light and when she reached it she saw that its paint had slid all down its sides and it didn't look like her car at all. She was about to touch it until she realised that it had had paint stripper thrown all over it.

It was nearly 2 a.m. before she was able to track Kit down in Wellington. He sounded tired, or a bit drunk, she was not sure which. 'I tried to let you know about the meeting, I tried to warn you not to go,' he said, 'but you weren't answering the bloody phone.'

'Who told you?'

He hesitated. 'It doesn't matter.'

'It does,' she shouted, 'everything matters.'

'Harry,' he said finally. 'Harry told me.'

That figured. Trust Harry to go soft at the last minute when it came to Kit. 'He might have told *me*,' she said. A picture of Harry turning his wedding ring over floated in front of her.

'Maybe he tried,' said Kit. 'Perhaps you didn't answer when he rang either.'

'You don't know what it's like.'

'No. So you keep telling me.' His voice faded with weariness.

'It rings twenty times some days and ten times there won't be anybody there.'

'It's too bad.' When she said nothing, he sighed and said, 'I'll speak to Telecom again.'

'Kit, it's not just the phone any more. After tonight, I don't know what they'll do next. Kit, will you come home?'

'Rose, the car can be fixed.'

'I know.'

'The House is in session. You know I can't come home.'

★

'Another parcel from your mother?' Sergeant Jeffrey Campbell placed a large square object in front of the constable at the desk. 'Animal, mineral or vegetable?'

'It'll blow you away,' said Teddy O'Meara.

Campbell winced.

'Bad-taste joke,' said Teddy, 'you shouldn't laugh at my mum's cakes.'

'Do I get to eat it?'

'Say pretty please.'

'You're getting too big for your boots, lad,' said Campbell. He meant it too, although he felt affection for the tall young man. At night he sometimes lay awake and thought about Teddy. He often lay awake at nights; years of night shifts in earlier days, before he had moved into the relative safety and permanence of the uniformed inquiry branch, had destroyed his sleeping patterns. His thoughts about Teddy were not specific to him, he dwelt on all the young staff. He called them the kids. Sometimes an edge of bitterness, quickly suppressed, crept into his reflections. Where had his familiarity with them got him? Nowhere much. He had been in the job for thirty-two years, and Weyville for fourteen; he should have left by now. But his wife didn't want to leave. And maybe he didn't either, perhaps she was an excuse for lethargy. The kids liked him and the way he was always there. His wife had a son (she had been a widow when he met her), but he had no children of his own. He supposed that what he felt towards the youngsters was paternal. They all seemed so lonely when they arrived in this town.

Not that Teddy gave the impression of needing friends, not these days. He was self-confident in a way that Campbell himself was once, and now the older man envied him. Weyville had been Teddy's first posting, but he had gone away after that, spent years in Wellington and then come back. Almost as if he liked the place. If anything, since his return it was Teddy O'Meara to whom the new recruits turned. The boy was made of tough metal, thought Campbell with admiration. No wonder he blushed when his mother sent him fruit cake from the King Country.

'Here's a knife,' he said encouragingly while Teddy pulled the wrappings off.

The cake was a lustrous brown object with clumps of cherries sticking out all over it. Teddy cut a hunk and put it on a plate beside Campbell's coffee cup.

'Have you looked at last night's work sheets?' he asked the older man.

'Not yet. What were you doing on night shift?'
'I did one for Reg. He's crook.'
'So you did.' He could see, now that he looked, that the constable was a trifle grey. 'And you're doing a swing shift today? Bloody hell, they muck you around, don't they?'
'Yep, sure do.'
'Anything special last night?'
'Couple of domestics on the Blake Block. A burglary. We picked him up. One alleged rape, probably false. And that Kendall woman was in here ranting and raving again.'
'That's all we need. Telecom's supposed to be handling her complaints now.'
'Yeah, well, maybe. But she's got a new problem. Somebody chucked paint stripper on her car.'
'Christ. How much damage?'
'It'll need a new paint job. Her insurance'll fix it.'
'It's not good enough. Where was the car?'
'Outside the Presbyterian hall.'
'What was she doing there?'
'She wasn't saying her prayers.' Teddy looked at Campbell. 'Sorry. She was at a meeting. It's just,' he hesitated, 'well, if you don't mind me saying so, she seems a bit out to lunch, that lady.'
'Was anyone else's car done over?' asked Campbell, ignoring this opinion for the moment.
'No.'
'There was a whole row of cars, and hers was the only one that got done?'
'That's right.'
'What did she do?'
'Walked all the way down here bawling her lights out . . .'
'Walked? Why didn't she go back inside and phone? They've got a phone in that building.'
'Seems she didn't want to go back inside. Said she didn't want to show her face. Has she got a boyfriend, sir?'
'Not that I know of. Doesn't mean she hasn't. Why?'
'Dunno. Just a thought.'
Campbell scratched his head. He liked old-time dancing and he did it with his wife. Sex, too. He liked the music on the National Programme. He could see why people thought he was soft. He was also unsurprised by almost anything and that was a facet of himself that he cultivated. He liked Rose Kendall. He couldn't agree with her politics but he had been taught not to discuss politics in polite

company from the time he was a child and so he didn't. It had been pleasant calling on her, even if she was upset whenever he had had occasion to talk to her over the last year or so. There was a homely quality about her, he considered. Once he had mentioned something along those lines to his wife, called her a nice lady. His wife, who worked in a dress shop—she called it a frock shop, or sometimes, lately, garment retailing—had told him tartly that his girlfriend's (that was how she put it) bras, which she had seen, were, if not grubby, at least rundown. He remembered Rose's children doing traffic patrol when they were at intermediate; he could still see first Olivia and a year or two later Richard holding out the lollipops to let the other kids go over the zebra crossing. Bright kids. Their mother missed them since they went away. He supposed she got lonely. It was possible she could have a lover.

He thought about the bra. Possible, but unlikely. 'I'll check the idea out,' he said. 'Have you any thoughts?'

Teddy fingered his moustache. 'Could be any of half a dozen.'

'But all your contenders were inside the hall last night?'

'As I said . . . it was a thought.'

I asked him to help, Campbell thought, I should listen to him. But it was so easy, such a young man's response. Teddy had been present when Rose Kendall laid her first complaint. It was a coincidence: Teddy was on patrol section, there was no need to involve him. But he hadn't laughed. Most cops did just that when people came in to complain about things like obscene phone calls, or at least as soon as the complainant was out of sight. So what, they said. Or, I expect it's her old man's girlfriend (or the other way round). Always assume it's a domestic, Campbell had been told once, and though for Rose Kendall's sake he had tried to forget that advice, it was there at the back of his mind. He was known as a thorough cop—don't discount any possibilities.

But: 'She could have quite a lot of enemies,' Teddy had said thoughtfully at the time. 'It can't be easy for her.'

So Campbell had kept on referring the matter to him, talking it over when it troubled him. There had to be something to it, surely. He hoped Teddy might come up with some fresh perspective when others he spoke to laughed.

Seemingly Teddy had had enough, and in a way he couldn't blame him. There was enough real crime burgeoning in Weyville to keep double the staff in this station busy. Still, something had happened to Rose Kendall last night, something more than voices in the air.

'What happened next?'

'Jack and I went back to the car with her and found she'd run off leaving the keys in the lock where anybody could lay their hands on them. Lucky the car was still there. I told her that too. We asked her to come back to the station and talk it over.'

'That was when you got the old megila?'

Teddy glanced sideways at him.

'The ear-bashing.'

'I know what it is. How we weren't doing our job and nobody cared, all that stuff. The same crock of shit they all trot out.'

'O'Meara!' Still, he could see why he was so wound up. He probably would have been himself. She had received more consideration than she realised.

Teddy looked at him, taking his time. 'It was a long night.'

'All right then.' Campbell knew it was true, they were short-staffed and the pressure had been on; he didn't have any answer for it. You had to let the kids run their course in here where they couldn't do damage. The boy looked strained; it was time he had a break. Campbell thought he had a girlfriend in Wellington. 'I'll check where Telecom's at with Mrs Kendall's complaints,' he said.

'I did that, first thing.'

Campbell looked surprised, but nodded approvingly. 'Well done. And?'

'Two leads, same as before. Phone boxes on the opposite ends of town.'

'This turkey knows what he's about.'

'Why do you say that?'

'The calls are damn near impossible to trace in phone boxes.'

'I expect that's right, sir.'

'Well of course it's right. Those calls were made late at night, weren't they?'

'I believe so. It's awhile back since they were intercepted. The last few weeks she's been getting them in the daytime. She says.'

'Is there still surveillance?'

'Alternate weeks. Telecom says it costs money to keep a line open on her—means they have to tie up a staff member doing nothing else but check her calls. They're getting fed up.'

'Why do we have to spend time on stuff like this?' Campbell sounded weary and it was true, the pettiness of this case suddenly disgusted him. He cut himself another piece of cake without consulting Teddy O'Meara.

'Because she's a politician's wife,' said Teddy idly. 'Or wasn't I supposed to answer that?'

'She's entitled to peace and quiet like everyone else.'

'I knew I shouldn't have answered.'

'Bugger, I've chipped my filling. Could you tell your mother not to put nuts in her cakes?'

'Yessir. A big chip?'

'It's all right, it happens all the time. So how d'you know what megila is, O'Meara? That's New York.'

'I know, sir. I stayed with my uncle on the way back, last time I went to Ireland.'

'Might have known. Your uncle's a New York cop?'

'Bronx. How d'you know, sir?' Teddy was relaxing, back in charge of himself.

'Eh? Oh, the same. There're plenty of Irish Campbells.'

'And here's me thinking you were a Scot.'

'O'Meara, you offend me.'

Teddy smiled.

'I stayed with my cousin twice removed when I was on my way back. It's twenty years now. You going back again to the old sod?'

'I hope so. It feels like home.'

Campbell looked troubled. 'I reckon it's good for a look; once is enough. Even my father didn't want to go back. They treat us like foreigners.'

'Not me, sir,' said Teddy.

Again, Campbell was aware of his confidence. At the same time, he realised that it was not correct to think of O'Meara as a boy. He had been in the department for eight years now. Nor was he certain how well he knew him, or how accurately he gauged him.

'Myself, I can't even understand them when they talk,' he said, sounding short, wishing he hadn't let this conversation go on for so long. 'You're a New Zealander anyway.'

'Sure,' said Teddy easily, 'when it comes to rugby, that's what I am all right.'

The phone rang then.

'I think there's going to be some trouble at the Blake Block,' said Teddy when he had replaced the receiver. It was five to three in the afternoon.

4

The kid stood on the corner of Hyde Street and Blake Pass. The look was nonchalant, leather jacket drawn up round the chin, dark glasses, cigarette trailing from the hand at the side. Opposite to where the watcher stood was a Christian video shop with a big pile of tapes labelled 'CHRISTIANS AND COMMUNISM — What the Russians are Hiding' in the window. It was a temptation not to throw a rock through it, given what the kid thought of fundies. Neither it nor the fish and chip shop on the far side of the service station were open. Wind whipped up a scatter of rubbish and rolled it along the gutter.

A row of cars was pulling out of the service station. The last one had just finished gassing up, and the attendant had gone inside with the motorist's credit card. There were no other cars in sight.

A Studebaker, 1951, reconditioned engine, painted metallic grey, bonnet like a bullet, appeared from round the corner, cruising for the third time. The kid had time to feel a thrill of happiness, a certainty that she was not alone. Then she tensed up; now, now. The conditions were just right. She turned her cigarette palm out, holding it in front of her mouth, and at this signal the Studebaker slowed, passed, and drew into the kerb a hundred or so metres down the road, engine idling under its cylindrical sheath.

Larissa walked into the service station, not hurrying unduly, flicking her scarf up round her mouth. Her blue hair stood in a row of spikes along the top of her head, like a dog that is afraid. Only she wasn't scared.

The last car left as the attendant checked the till. He was a good-looking young man, clean-shaven and broad-shouldered, a bit on the short side. It had been a busy afternoon; he had only finished his cut lunch ten minutes before, eating on the run. He was thinking about taking a Moro bar off the stand when Larissa entered. She picked up a packet of gum and fumbled change from out of her pocket. The till was still open when Gary and Jason walked in behind her, in their greatcoats, slipping balaclavas over their heads.

Gary dropped down on the attendant's wrist before he had time to look up properly, or perhaps his eyes were still on Larissa's legs which went all the way up to her backside, just out of sight beneath her mini-skirt.

'Don't fuckin' move,' Gary said.

The attendant jerked his arm up in a reflex which might have thrown him sideways but for the fact that Jason had come up behind him and jabbed a sawn-off shot-gun into his ribs. His head was caught round the neck in Jason's grip.

'Quickly,' said Gary; he held out a thin blue plastic bag bearing a supermarket label. 'I want the lot.'

'Is it a gun?'

'Is it a gun, Je-siss. Look, I don't want to touch this stuff, will you just pick it up. Nothing funny, no buzzers, no little tricks, because we're watching, okay?'

The attendant's eyes were bulging and he seemed incapable of movement. Jason prodded him from the rear.

'We're helping you,' he said, 'we want you to survive. We're kind.'

'Thick as pigshit, if you ask me,' said Gary. The light was gleaming on his shaven skull. He picked up one of the attendant's limp wrists and held it over the till. The hand dropped and Gary chopped down on the wrist so that it gave a messy crunch on the edge. The man screamed, but the pain had jolted him into action. He brought up the uninjured hand and dipped it in the till, beginning to scoop out the money.

'That's better,' said Jason, 'Faster.' A frantic edge was developing in his voice.

Outside, a car purred in the distance. Larissa's eyes flashed around, lit on the CLOSED sign standing behind the door. She picked it up and banged it down outside, shutting the door fast. The car carried on.

'Ah, clever,' said Jason approvingly, as she stood, back to the roadway, hands spread against the wall, and starting to look wide-eyed.

Five, maybe six hundred, had gone into the bag.

'Where's the rest?' snapped Gary.

The attendant whimpered in the back of his throat; Jason jabbed.

'There isn't any more.'

'Is that all?' It was the first time since this operation began that Larissa had spoken.

'They do it with credit cards,' whispered the attendant.

'I ain't got no credit cards and I buy petrol,' Gary said.

'It's enough,' said Jason. 'C'mon, we've got to move.'

Larissa noticed the attendant's lunchbox. It was the same as a kid's school lunchbox, may even have been one, for it had a Mickey Mouse transfer stuck on its lid. She picked it up, threw it at its present owner's face. 'It's not enough.'

Sticking her hands in her pockets, she turned away as if she had no further interest in the proceedings.

'What's the matter, baby?' Gary was rapidly knotting the top of the bag together by its punched-out shopping bag handles. 'He offend you?'

'He makes me puke. Lunchboxes. Little kids. Shit.'

'I'll fix it. In a minute.' The bag was tied up, a harmless-looking little bundle. Gary reached for the phone, started dialling.

'Don't muck around, Gary.' Jason was scared shitless now.

But Gary poked the phone towards the attendant, wiping it down at the same time with a grease rag. 'Tell the cops there's some people hanging around the service station who bother you. Tell them, there could be trouble if they don't get over fast. Speak nicely to the policeman.' He nodded to Jason.

Jason pushed the weapon into the man's back. 'Do as he says,' he said softly. 'I can't help you if you don't.'

The man did as he was told, his voice as much glazed as calm, the pain hovering behind his words. It was five to three in the afternoon.

'Okay?' Jason asked.

Gary nodded and Jason stuffed the gun under his khaki greatcoat.

'Right, move, nice and easy but fast,' Gary said to the others. He turned to the attendant and sliced his face with the side of his hand, and then the top of his head with a tyre lever, and they all walked out the door together, leaving the man slumped across the counter.

'That was for you,' Gary said to Larissa as they piled into the car.

'Why did you get him to make that call, bro?' Jason asked, as they turned off the road. In the distance they heard sirens.

'Why not? Say, man, look at it this way, it's his voice, the guy at the service station's, and according to him the robbery hasn't even started. Finesse, that's what it is. Doubt and confusion in the mind of the enemy.'

'Hmm. I suppose he smacked his own head in?'

'Maybe, maybe he did. Or one of his partners in crime. You never *know* do you?' He stroked Larissa's thigh with the tips of his fingers: they jutted out of black fingerless mittens. She was sitting very close to him, almost in his lap. Her face was feverish with excitement; he knew she couldn't wait to get at him. As he switched off the engine, he said, 'Besides, it was a joke on O'Meara. A real joke, he'd have thought he was going to make an arrest. I like to play jokes on O'Meara. We should have fun when we go out, doncha all think?'

In the ablution block at the camping ground Larissa let the water run through her hair for a long time, sluicing out the blue rinse that she had put in it that morning. She was sorry the colour was only temporary; she liked having blue hair. She wondered what colour she might turn next. Maybe pink. Or how about an ordinary blonde? She had enjoyed having all the colour bleached out of her hair at one stage, a snowy cap moving swiftly and lightly through the streets of Weyville, earrings hanging nearly down to her shoulders. That was when she got kicked out of Weyville High. Thank God. She'd have killed someone if she'd stayed there any longer. She could still hear her aunt up-herself Rose preaching, po-faced, about what a good mind she had and what a waste it all was.

Here her head switched off-course for a moment. Her aunt, she supposed, was an improvement on her mother. One thing was for sure, she'd never have black hair, not as long as she lived. Which, more or less, she hoped would not be for too long. The idea of anyone having fun after they were about twenty-two at the outside was over the top. Really off the wall.

She leaned her head against the small rectangular mirror glued to the concrete wall. She felt tired and rather small. It occurred to her that Jason, hers and Gary's best and neatest friend, who took chances with them whether he liked it or not, was maybe twenty-four. But look at him, stumping along on a wooden leg. It didn't make sense. If she was Jason she thought she would probably rather be dead. She towelled some bruises on her shoulders and left thigh. They still hurt.

The trick was not to cry out when Gary did this to her. Living in a caravan park everybody got to know your business unless you were real careful. If she made any trouble Gary would kick her out. And then where would she go? And to whom? Without Gary there wouldn't be anything. Nothing in the world that she could imagine, just a great void like the sky at nights when they slept outside the caravan in summer without even the benefit of stars. Sometimes Gary pulled the awning over when it got cold and then it was simply dark and still and she got lonely, even though he was there. That was what it would be like if he sent her away.

Sometimes she dreamed that she would go up to her father's house and it would be all right, that he would open the door and say *Oh hi, it's you Larissa, come along in*, and he would cook up some crumpets and stuff, and make her some Milo, and maybe show her to a bedroom with a primrose-coloured duvet for her to sleep under on the bed; when she woke up it seemed like a good joke. The last time she had been near Paul's house she had broken three windows and the cops had come down and interviewed her about it. Or one cop, anyway.

O'Meara, that was the guy's name, O'Meara. Gary said the guy was a bit of a card, made you laugh, that joker. *Cunning as a bunch of shithouse rats you lot* O'Meara said, last time he came round; *shithouse rats*.

Afterwards, they all laughed. 'Shithouse rats, that's what we are.' They called themselves that, though sometimes, thinking about it at night, Larissa began to shiver violently at the idea, and when she had to get up for a pee she picked her way really carefully out to the Portaloo dunny.

Jason said O'Meara was a guy you couldn't trust, which they all agreed was so from the very fact that he wore a uniform; you couldn't trust any of the fuzz.

But you could sort of get along with him.

Larissa gave her hair a final rub and examined it carefully in the mirror; there was hardly a trace of blue left in it. She pulled on her jeans and a clean T-shirt; she reckoned she could pass for just about any ordinary teenager in Weyville. What a laugh.

Flicking a comb through her hair and pinching her cheeks a bit, she decided she was ready for whatever interviews were in the offing. Come to think of it, she felt pretty good. Gary had been really nice to her after they got back, kind of affectionate. He'd sent Jason packing real fast and told him to get some beer out for them, they'd be over in ten minutes. 'And tell your old lady to go take a walk or something, we don't want the old bitch hanging around,' he called after Jason's departing back.

Then, later, she said hadn't she better be doing something about changing her appearance, the way they'd agreed, weren't they wasting time, and he had said, *Don't worry, time's never wasted with you kid*, as if she was still special to him and more important than doing time, if they did get caught. Only he seemed relaxed and not too worried about it, as if he knew it was going to be all right. She'd done a real good job, he told her, making sure that there were no cars around, her timing was just perfect, and that was important for them with the Stude which he loved but was a dead giveaway.

Still, if the mutt in the service station had come round yet he might have said something about her hair, so in the end she'd come over and taken a shower. She stepped out into the afternoon light and looked down the length of the caravan park.

At the head of the park just behind the gates stood Herbert's lodge and the office and camp store. Herbert decided who could enter the reserve and who stayed out. There was a cattle stop at the gate so that he always heard the clank of approaching vehicles even if he didn't see them, which was not often. He was talking about having surveillance cameras installed so that he could watch people coming and going wherever he was in the house. Grilles had been put up in front of the window where people came up to make enquiries. It seemed a bit of a laugh to Larissa that there were so many security precautions in force for people like them who wanted to live a free life out in the open air, but Herbert was a bit of a fanatic. The other night there had been a bunch of bikies through and he had chased them with a hammer. The fool, they all said afterwards, he could have got himself killed, rushing in like that. They all whooped and hollered around him, so that he thought they were helping, but what the idiot didn't realise was that none of them was actually doing anything, just making a noise. The cops had been cruising and it was settled pretty smartly. O'Meara again.

Just as well he was around.

The caravans were parked in two rows facing each other. Some had been there longer than others. The ones on either side of theirs had gardens around them. Jason and his mother, Poppy, lived in one of them, and alongside them were a couple of housetrucks. Jason had gone to school from the caravan. He said the kids at school called him a gypsy. When he tried to tell them that his home never moved, just stayed in the same place all the time, the same as theirs, the kids laughed. He was glad to get out of school, he said. She could understand that. It was one of the reasons she got on that well with him, even though he was older.

'Isn't there anything you liked at school?' her aunt had asked her when she was having the big soul-searching rave to her.

'Yeah. *Brighton Rock*.'

'Brighton Rock?'

She was like a parrot, repeating you all the time. Poppy hung brightly coloured felt parrots outside the caravan on fine days, just like it was an aviary. She brushed them regularly instead of feeding them. Aunt Rose would look good hanging outside on a hook.

'I liked Pinkie.'

'Pinkie?'

Jesus, you'd think she was doing indecent exposure, maybe that's the sort of pinkie she thought she was on about.

'The bloke. He's like my boyfriend Gary.'

'Gary.'

'Jesus.' There she'd said it that time. 'Yeah, like Gary. Cool.'

'But. Pinkie was a, yes. Well, Gary's your first boyfriend. You'll have lots of boyfriends.'

Larissa thought then how dumb her Aunt Rose was. She didn't seem to understand that she was telling her something about life, about her *taste*, about, like, the way she was. She took Gary round to see her aunt once, but it was useless. Aunt Rose had taken her aside and offered her some Clearasil for Gary's spots. Larissa said to her, at the time, that she liked his spots.

Which was true. She liked picking them, it made her feel close to him, getting stuff out of his body, like monkeys playing with each other. She got to hurt him a bit when she did it, in a way that he didn't seem to mind.

Poppy put stones round her garden and painted them white; she grew flowers and vegetables. Her trailer wasn't nearly as big as hers and Gary's, being old, but as Jason said, it was almost like a real house. She had knick-knacks all over it, a black Sambo to stick pencils and knitting needles in, and a yellow felt donkey with a sequinned bridle that she kept in the china cabinet along with her vases, nine of them, coloured yellow, violet, green, pink, and the rest were crystal. She shook her mats every morning with cracks like whips. You had to keep mats in their place, she said, because they always moved towards the rising sun. She looked about seventy though Larissa figured she couldn't be that old and still be Jason's mother. Maybe she was really his grandmother. Larissa didn't care much about things like that, who was related to who. Families, as such, were a bore.

Their caravan was bigger. It was just about the biggest in the park. It was a thirty-foot Gulf trailer. She couldn't remember what it was in metres and anyway nobody in the camp understood metrics — 'I've got a thirty-footer,' (or a twenty-eight footer) they said when they were bragging. Never anything fancy; the caravan made its own statement. She kept it tidy though. People thought they lived like pigs in the caravan park, but it was a lie. They'd get kicked out if they didn't keep things tidy. Herbert had standards and that was that, even if he was a hammer-wielding idiot. And the thing was, though Jason and his mother had lived there for yonks, and never moved, it was always there, the possibility that you could. Just get up and go one morning. That's the way the people in the bright chimneyed housetrucks did it. Just came and went. And maybe one day they would. Just hook up to the Stude and go somewhere. Her and Gary, and maybe Jason could come for a bit, though it wouldn't be too good if he stayed for long. Just came and went a bit.

That's what she'd like, though, she said to Gary when they lay out under the awning in summer nights. She couldn't understand why he didn't jump at the idea, why he kept sticking round in Weyville, but he worked things through in his own time, Gary did, and sooner or later, she guessed, he'd wake up one day and it would be like it was his idea.

In the meantime, he said he still had a bit of work to do on the Stude, and it was no good taking the old girl on the road until he was sure she was shipshape, and sending all that work down the drain.

She walked down between the rows of caravans, heading for Poppy and Jason's trailer. She expected to see Jason and Gary sitting outside with some tinnies on the table. That was the best possible scenario. But Poppy was sitting outside with a shawl wrapped round her shoulders, and even though the sun had gone in, a broad-brimmed shiny basket-weave hat on her head, and a pale pink chiffon scarf wrapped right around its crown and under her whiskery chin. She was talking to the parrots as they swayed in the breeze.

Larissa experienced a stab of fear, more like a thrill. Her eyes travelled up the lane, expecting to see the fuzz parked outside hers and Gary's caravan.

Instead, she saw a once dark-blue Metro that had had its paint rubbed down. Her aunt leaned against it, smiling and nodding to Gary as she spoke to him, even though he sat on the caravan step, staring dead pan at her, right through her in fact. Then he saw Larissa coming down the lane towards them; she could see from this distance that he was turning talkative.

Jason walked past her, as if in a dream. Who knew what went on in that guy's head. It would be easier to stop and talk to him, have a rap about their adventure of the afternoon. But his face was closed off, and knowing Jason he might never speak of it again. Besides, there was her relative, her aunt, waiting for her, talking to her lover while she waited.

★

Rose had put off her promise to visit her niece all day. It was not that she did not want to see Larissa. But she was afraid of what she might find. And of what she and Larissa might have to say to each other. Or worse, simply what they would not say.

Gary leaned against the door frame of the caravan, his knees drawn up under his chin. He had hardly said a word to her. Suddenly he turned his head in the direction of her car and smiled. His teeth looked yellow when he spoke.

'Pity about the car. Been in an accident?'

'Not exactly.'

'Tsst. Bit of careless driving, eh?'

'No.'

'Sorry. Nosy parker, eh? That what you're thinking?'

'No.'

'Well what were you thinking?'

That was when she tossed her head and smiled. 'What fun it must be to live in a park like this. Friendly.'

'What fun.' He mimicked her. 'Want to trade? Want to live here?'

'No. Thank you.' She raised her eyes and saw Larissa as she walked towards them. She stood very still. Going back, further again, no stopping once you'd begun. She saw Larissa across the edges of her life. She saw her always. She did not tell her children that she saw Larissa, that she was special. They would never have understood why the child occupied her heart. They would have felt themselves betrayed, as if Larissa, their unkempt and wayward cousin, had staked out an area that was specially reserved for them.

'You can keep her,' Katrina said. Paul had gone and Katrina was alone.

'We've got two children already,' said Rose. Indeed, Richard was newborn. 'How long do you want us to keep her?'

'For good.'

'Katrina, we'll help you. You'll get over this.'

'I am. That's why I'm giving her to you.'

'What about Paul?'

'He doesn't want her either.'

In the gaunt suburb where Rose cared for her, Larissa learned slowly to play like other children. She ate, seemingly all the time, even dirt. Especially dirt. She shitted black earth. She ate with her hands; she grew fat.

Rose feared that the child was mute, maybe retarded. Sometimes she didn't seem to recognise her, turned her attention to total strangers in shops and reached out her arms to them. Rose was always tired and Richard kept her awake at night. One day she hit Larissa and shook her until her nose began to bleed. At the sight of the blood she stopped, appalled, and fell to her knees in the garden with the child. 'Forgive me,' she said. 'Forgive me Larissa, be all right, please. Give me another chance.'

Olivia, who was four, stood watching with wide, strained eyes. She walked away from her mother as if she could not bear what she had seen.

Days, or maybe it was weeks, later, Rose could not remember, for time passed in a blur, the child put her arms up to her and spoke: 'Mummy.'

And later, the same day: 'Kiss. Gizz a kiss.' After that she had new words every day.

Katrina came to visit one day, taking time off from her new job in a chemist's shop. She was pale but she looked all right, just ordinary. She acted as if she was Larissa's distant aunt, as if she was really one of Rose's children. Larissa ignored her mother, chanting songs to herself and playing with Richard who had begun to crawl.

An appointment was made the next day for Rose to see welfare. Kit came with her. He had been trying to get her to see the doctor or anyone who might help, because she was so quiet and thin that he was frightened for her.

'I'm afraid her mother might come and take her away,' Rose said to the welfare worker.

'She's not yours to keep,' the welfare woman said. She was kind, patient, but didn't appear to understand what Rose was saying. 'You're not trying to abduct the child, are you?'

'Abduct? She was given to me.'

Months passed. One day, Katrina came and took Larissa away. She felt better about having her now, she said, and Paul had said he would see her at the weekends. The minute she picked her up, actually touching her, Larissa turned her back on Rose, ignoring her as totally as if she had never seen her.

For awhile her children grieved, mystified that their sister had gone, then gradually seemed relieved as their mother had more time for them. Rose picked up again with some of her more interesting friends whom she hadn't had time for lately, and went to coffee mornings. She got elected to some committees, and started to speak forthrightly on a number of topics.

Then for a year or so Katrina and Larissa stayed away, although Katrina and Rose phoned each other from time to time. When they began to visit again Larissa had resumed her position as a cousin. She was a helpful quiet child, compliant when she was with Rose, usually guarded, although sometimes when they were alone, like the day at the lake, she seemed very pleased that Rose was there.

It was when Katrina went away with Wolf, and Larissa came to live with them the second time, that the violence began. 'You let her take me, if you loved me you would never have given me back to her,' Larissa screamed once when she and Rose were fighting. The interminable shrieking arguments of early adolescence wore Rose down.

'She was your mother. She is. She had a right.'

'She was a drug addict.'

'Don't be stupid.'

'She'd got sacked from her job for pinching pills.'

'Bullshit.'

'Bullshit, bullshit, is that all you can say? Who's la-di-da now? I know. My friend's father is the chemist that sacked her. Everyone knew. Except you.'

There was the moment of suddenly knowing it was true, what she'd never thought of. And of Kit nodding when she told him. He'd always known.

'Your mother's okay now,' Rose had said, the next time the subject came up.

'Yeah, run away with the big bad Wolf,' Larissa sneered. 'I suppose if she turned up tomorrow you'd hand me back again.'

'I expect I would.'

'The caravan looks nice,' said Rose.

'Want it?' said Larissa, stopping in front of her. She tapped a cigarette out of its pack.

'I've already offered it to her,' Gary said. 'The lady's choosy about her accomodation.'

'Fits. What the fuck do you want?'

'I brought you some tomato preserve. I thought it might come in useful.'

'Christ, what do you think this is? The church fair?'

'You used to like it.' Rose held out a jar in each hand.

Larissa stood, not moving to take it, blowing smoke towards Rose. Gary leaned forward and plucked a jar out of Rose's hand.

'Lady Bountiful, eh?' He contemplated the jar, smiled, turned it over, rocking the contents under the lid.

Feeling foolish now, she wanted to retrieve it or apologise.

'Pretty weird stuff,' Gary said, rotating the bottle. 'Pretty weird fucking juice.'

Rose stepped forward, holding out her hand. She couldn't take her eyes off the jar.

With a quick stabbing movement he smashed it against the metal frame of the caravan door. Glass flew through the air. The red tomato preserve bled down the wall, carrying more glass with it.

'Here.' He shoved the jagged dripping edge towards her and bared his teeth.

Stepping backwards, she put up her hands as if to ward him off.

'You'll have to clean that up,' he said to Larissa, tossing the jar on the ground.

'Yeah.' Larissa contemplated the mess, looked sideways at Rose. 'Tell that bloody whoring mother of mine to keep her dogs off me.'

Clumsily Rose turned to open the car door.

'If the cap fits wear it,' Larissa said, softly, but not so much that Rose would miss it above the noise of the motor.

Back at home Roach had had his throat cut. His body was laid neatly across the driveway in front of the garage door. It was natural to think of someone like Gary. Only Roach's body was still very warm, as if he had died only minutes before.

Wiki Muru, whom Rose Kendall had once thought of as her friend when they sat demonstrating on the road leading into Weyville, had become disenchanted with her alliance with the liberal Pakehas in the town. It was a gradual process at first, but then it accelerated faster than anyone, herself included, could have seen.

After the tour she had started supervising one of the work schemes that the Labour Department ran. She got several gang members who had been unemployed for a long time into work, and a lot of young people who had gone away to the cities started coming home because they'd heard there might be temporary work there which was better than none. You couldn't say things were great, because Muldoon had left such a bad taste in everyone's mouth and the town, like most of the country, and especially the smaller towns and cities where people most liked rugby, was still split in two over what had happened about the tour. There were those who said the protesters were shit-stirrers and communists who had tried to interfere with people's freedom and that Maoris should be kept in reserves like the blacks in Africa; and those who had been on the tour and wanted to change things. The people who wanted Maoris put in reserves, and said as much, claimed that do-gooders like Wiki were turning Weyville into one of the reserves, which was not exactly what they had in mind; they meant reserves away from them. Maybe in the cities, where the wanky liberals were anyway.

But the work schemes kept the lid on things. Wiki slaved her butt off night and day. She lost weight, stopped smoking, and wore her bone carving with new pride.

After the Government changed, just the way they had all hoped, the work schemes got closed down and the kids were still in the town and had nothing to do. Neither she nor the elders could stop the gangs starting up trouble again. Two of her sons, including Henare, had moved into the Mob. Henare had recently imported a pit bull terrier illegally through the wharves at Napier and he never took his black sunglasses off day or, as far as anyone could tell, night. The Muru boys' chapter was importing junked down Japanese cars that were so short on parts you could class them as disposables. Street fighting broke out most nights round pub closing time and there had been seven rapes in the town in four months. People began staying inside after dark. Wiki went to see Kit Kendall twice to find out if there was any way the gangs could get back into work; he said he was sorry, but in a free market economy work schemes were just not on. He'd told her that the youth of this country, Maoris included, had never had a greater incentive to get off their backsides and do something for themselves.

'Do you mean that?' Wiki had asked him.

The story went that Kit Kendall had simply stared into middle distance, though he had not discussed the matter with Rose.

It was some time since Wiki had spoken to the Kendalls, Toni Warner, the Ryans, the Deckers, the Appleblooms or anyone else who had been on the tour marches, but when she heard about the unemployment march she had got a group together and they'd all gone along. In justifying it to the kaumatua she said they had to do something; maybe something good would come out of it and she was still ready for a fight, she'd just been waiting for one to come along. You couldn't give up hope.

When the march was over and the television cameras stopped rolling, everyone was flushed with triumph. Wiki's group were part of the crowd, shouting and cheering, and jeering as well, every time the Government was mentioned. They would march all the way to Wellington, they said.

Then Larry Verschoelt got up and said that was all very well, but what sort of work did these people want? There wasn't enough work for white people these days, and he didn't see why niggers should be doing white men's jobs. When Matt went over and tried to explain to Wiki about Larry, she said they'd all decided to march, but if any of the local branch members came along she wouldn't guarantee their safety because some of her people were talking about killing a few whites and she might just help them do it. Matt and Harry and Toni had a meeting and drafted a statement saying that they thought it would be culturally insensitive of them to join the march, and how really pleasing it was that Wiki's group had taken this initiative. So far they hadn't issued the statement.

★

In the high early morning sun, Rose worked steadily. She cleared dead broom and gorse away from a corner of the garden. Rotted leaves had formed a rich dark layer across the earth where camellias and a holly bush fought for survival. She tied the holly bush back, being careful not to scratch her hands and bare arms. A hydrangea stood revealed for the first time and the two flowerheads that had struggled towards the light were such deep purplish-blue that she paused to consider them with regret. She could imagine cultivating colour like that.

A kingfisher flashed across the expanse of sky between the overgrown ngaios rearing above the spot where she was digging, and away down the bank. The ngaios' leaves undulated like the green Indian Ocean in which she had once paddled; the boughs were sharks among the waves. Tucked behind the trees stood a small glasshouse with several broken panes, indiscernible from the house.

On the rainbow in the white face of her watch she noted that it was 10.15. She made the decision there and then to leave Weyville.

She went inside and got bread and laid it on the ground. Starlings and some sparrows congregated, scuffing the long grasses with their feet and beaks. She watched them squabble and squawk, and smiled. She could have put nesting boxes in the trees.

Somebody else would have to do it now.

She took her spade and turned the soil where she had cleared a space. It was a new spade, purchased the day before. The blade sliced cleanly through the damp earth, disturbing slaters. When she had been working for five minutes or so, she stood back and surveyed the hole she had dug, glanced at the cardboard carton in which she had brought home her last lot of groceries. It would almost fit.

'Can I help?'

Toni's voice startled her so much she almost put the spade through her shoe.

'What are you doing here?'

'Passing by.'

'Come to gloat?'

Toni looked at her, *as if she was strange*, she thought. Toni had no right to look at her like that.

'I hear your march gets underway again today. Why aren't you on it?'

'It leaves at midday. It's not my march.'

'But you'll be going?.'

'I'm not marching to Wellington.'

'Who is? Or is that top secret?'

'I don't know. Not many.' Her face reddened.

'You had a great time yesterday, I thought you'd all have gone.'

Toni couldn't help exulting. 'There were two thousand.'

'You got on telly. Congratulations.'

'Oh Rose.'

'Oh Rose, what? I could have been there too?'

'Don't be silly.' She hesitated. 'Wiki's leading the Wellington march.'

'Brilliant. It should be a good show. Just what you all need. Maori land march all over again.'

'It's a march of the unemployed.'

'C'mon Toni, where's your spirit? You should be getting your tent together. Your billy. New pair of Reeboks.'

'It's not like that.'

'Isn't it? What's it like Toni, tell me.'

'I didn't come round to talk about that.'

'But I'm asking you.'

'Wiki just wants a small group from Weyville, a really representative group of the unemployed...she says we got things started but now it's over to them. She's probably right, if all the middle-class hangers-on want to get on the bandwagon it'll look like something else.' She blushed.

'Wiki's not talking to Pakehas any more? Even Martin Luther King used to ask the whites along.'

'Some of the union people are going.'

'So what happens, does she hold interviews along the way? What about all the rural poor you were spouting about the other night? I mean, hell, you want a big march don't you?'

'You sound as if you want it to happen.'

'I just want to know what went on between your moments of high drama in the main street of Weyville and this morning's attack of the bleeding hearts.'

Only of course Rose did know, because Harry the wet had already told Kit.

'Rose, you don't know what's going on around you.' Toni squatted on the ground beside her friend.

'No? You mean people don't tell me things to my face any more?'

'You're not engaged with reality.'

'Thank you. That's very profound and meaningful, Toni.'

'People *like* you.'

'Thanks, I've noticed.' Rose turned another lump of earth, uncovering beer bottles and a rusted can. She picked up the can and studied it. 'I'm worried about chlorofluorocarbons,' she said. 'And the hole in the ozone layer. And slam dancing. And mercury levels in the sea. And the greenhouse effect. I'm scared especially shitless about the greenhouse effect, it's just as well I don't live by the sea. And about glue sniffing, though not by the people who sniff, though I wish I knew how to get them to stop. And about my kids dying in some random and senseless way and, almost worse, about them wanting and planning to die. And designer drugs, and the moral majority, and buildings falling down when I'm inside them.'

'And the state of race relations in this country and the closure of the post offices, and why they're cutting back on the DPB?'

'I love Kit.'

'Oh sure. That's a good idea. Love Kit and don't worry about any single goddamn thing that you can actually do something about. That all makes sense, everything you've said.'

'What d'you want me to say? That I don't support Kit? Anyway, I can do something about the things that worry me. I don't buy things in spray cans any more.' She dropkicked the rusty can, lifting it skywards, caught it in her hand.

'The rest of us don't need to love Kit. It's got to be too much of a hassle.'

'You'd better bugger off, Toni. I've got work to do.'

'I can see. Jesus, this stinks.' She curled her nose up in the direction of the box. Rose pushed it further away with her foot.

'So where did you go last night?' Toni asked.

Rose started to cry, and then after awhile she stopped.

'Who told you?' she asked presently.

'The Wrights.'

'They bought the house?'

'You ought to know. It was your house they bought.'

'I didn't ask the land agent.'

'You see, you don't know what's going on under your nose.'

'I didn't want to know.'

'Never mind Kit, I do love you Rose.'

'I know. Hey, I wish I'd been in films, Toni. If I couldn't make director at least I'd like to have worked the boom. Do you think it's too late for me?'

Toni's silence stilled her. 'So what did you hear?'

'They said you were walking around in their garden at midnight carrying a box in your arms. You crouched down by the beans like you were going to take a pee, then you crawled along on your hands and knees parting the dahlias and peering into them in the moonlight.'

'I bought all those dahlias. They should have been lifted last season. They weren't up to much this year.'

'And then you had a wander round under the nectarine tree and shook a couple of branches, and they still weren't sure it was you but Tassie Wright who's actually okay stopped Dan from ringing the cops because she could see it was a woman and she had a hunch who it was and thought maybe it was best not to call them, for which Allah be praised. Then Dan had had enough and said he wasn't going to be spooked out of his own house and put the light on.'

'And I took off. Yes. I wanted to bury Roach at the old house. He never liked it much here. And I thought the kids would have wanted to put him there. Stupid really.'

'Is this Roach in here?' Toni tapped the carton. 'What happened to him?'

'Hold your nose.' Rose ripped the wide band of tape holding the carton together with one sweeping motion. Toni peered in, her face registering disgust; she drew a sharp retching breath. Rose picked up a stick and lifted the body under the muzzle so that she could see it better.

'Still think people like me?'

She flung the box into the hole she had dug and the body spilled out of the box. She shovelled dirt over Roach in quick angry bursts.

'So the Wrights've got a good story. Who else have they told it to? The whole town? Will it be in the paper tonight?'

'They told me. They knew you were my friend. They were worried.'

'Worry, oh shit. People love gossip. Kendall's wife on hands and knees. All right, so that's what I did. I'm a retard. But look, it was bad luck they got up then, they don't usually stir at that hour of the night.'

'You've been there before? Since you moved?' Toni was shaking her head, trying to get rid of the image of the dog.

'Yes. Now and then.'

'Why?'

'I liked that house. L-shaped beastly Beazley. Ticky tacky box. I miss it. Bloody awful colour we painted it, but the paint was on special, d'you remember us buying it and all the summer we spent weekends painting it?' She hesitated. 'It's okay, I won't go back again. I've finished with it. Will you tell them that? Will it shut them up?'

'How long's that dog been dead, Rose?'

Rose considered her friend Toni Warner whom she had known, more or less, for ten years.

She thought she knew her, but then again she was not sure.

She knew about Toni's periods and fluid retention and what she was taking to help the situation, like Vitamin B6 and when that didn't work primrose oil, and how she'd given it all away and was simply practising TM because she realised it was stupid doing work on the body without doing work on the head.

She knew, too, that Toni was sharp and clever and had a great capacity for remembering things, like quotes out of books and bits of poetry; she was very good at almost everything she undertook and careful about not going in for things she might do badly.

She cultivated a dangerous outspokenness.

Sometimes Rose almost wished Toni would make a mistake. Yet when it came down to it, where it mattered, there was nobody else like Toni.

'Three days. And no, I haven't told the cops because I didn't want to talk to them any more. I needed some space to work something out.'

'Have you?'

'Yes.'

Inside the house the phone began to ring. Rose packed the earth down flat on the ground with the back of the spade and stood up, wiping her face. To Toni, she appeared not to hear the phone. Out of habit Toni began to walk to the house, her step quickening, even though it wasn't her phone, arriving in time to pick it up before it stopped. When nobody answered, she put it down. Behind her Rose stood in the doorway.

'That is the thirty-fifth time that telephone has rung and the caller has hung up without answering in forty-eight hours,' she said.

'God. Truly?'

'Yep.'

'Is this your phantom caller? You didn't tell me that it was still happening.'

'I didn't think you believed in him.'

Toni looked uncomfortable. 'I didn't realise it was so bad.'

'It's worse than that.' She touched the side of her head, let her hand fall.

'Forty-eight hours? That's two days, what about the day before that?'

Rose's forehead wrinkled. 'There were no phone calls the first day. But it goes like that, sometimes there aren't any.'

'So there must be a pattern?'

'You'd think so. But I can't see it. Anyway, seriously, why should anyone believe me? I mean, I could have invented them all, couldn't I? Well, you can see I'm nuts, absolutely doolaley, you've got proof. Haven't you?'

'Look, I've just picked up your goddamn phone and heard them hang up.'

'That could be someone who doesn't want you to know they ring me.'

'Is that what Telecom says?'

'Something like that. I mean, that's what they would say. It's called covering every eventuality.'

'Listen, didn't you hear me? I believe you. I believe *in* you.'

'Okay. So that's good. Thanks.'

'Has Kit got a girlfriend?'

'He says not.'

'Of course he'd say that. But he's a politician.'

'Do you know something I don't?'

Toni looked sideways at her. 'Lots of people have girlfriends and boyfriends. Lovers, if you prefer.'

'So you think this scumbag that's driving me out of my skull is a woman that's after Kit? That what you mean?'

'It's been known to happen.'

'Original. Look, they all say that. Well not in so many words. Anyway, these aren't toll calls. They can trace toll calls.'

Toni nodded, agreeing. 'Okay, and he doesn't have a girlfriend in town. I buy that.'

'I'm glad I've got you to keep me informed.'

'Have you kept records of the calls?'

'Miles of them. I've showed them to Telecom. Waste of time.'

'Rose, can I look at them? Would you let me take them away and study them? Please.'

Rose hesitated. 'Yes, sure. Do what you like with them.'

She opened her desk and pulled out a well-thumbed notebook. 'Dates, times, the lot. They cover the last three months, that's when I started keeping a record.'

'I'll get it back to you in a day or two.'

'There's no hurry.'

Toni followed her quick glance to a suitcase standing by the wall.

'Are you going to Wellington?'

'Probably.'

'Kit'll be pleased.'

When Rose didn't answer, Toni put her arms around her. 'I really do love you, Ro. Fuck politics.'

In the doctor's waiting room Sharna threw up and Basil ran around in a state of frenzied activity, throwing books and toys all over the place. When he had done that he sank into lethargy but at least he was quiet while Katrina picked everything up and put it back in its place. The receptionist just watched her and Katrina thought, *Stuff it, why should I do this*? but she did anyway. She couldn't bear sitting there with the woman just looking at the mess and wondering what was going to happen next. Then Basil came to life and did exactly the same thing all over again. This time Katrina didn't put anything away.

She had been waiting for an hour. A well-dressed couple in their late thirties had gone in ahead of her, not looking at each other. She thought, *I bet they're having problems about screwing, I'll bet he's impotent, I'll bet the doctor spends hours counselling them.* Sharna began to cry and Katrina fed her surreptitiously, afraid that Basil would start performing, but he looked half asleep again. It was, in all, an hour and a half after her appointment that she actually got to see the doctor.

She had planned it all so carefully, but instead of everything she meant to say, she came out with, 'If you can spare me five minutes, *if* it's not too much trouble.'

He grimaced, looking her over. Katrina reckoned Mungo Lord couldn't be more than thirty. He was new to the practice; he did paediatric work at the local hospital as well. There was no option but belief: Basil was in good hands. She thrust him in the doctor's direction.

After the examination, she asked, 'Is there much wrong then?'

'Nothing much. Here's a nutrition chart, you might like to have a look through that. And be firm about his bedtime routines.'

Katrina knew she ought to be reassured but she still felt uneasy. She thought of ringing Rose to get her opinion, but then she remembered her problem with the phone. It was kind of discouraging, and besides, phoning Rose wasn't her regular style, even if she had made rather a habit of it lately. Perhaps she would just tell

Minna. But in the end she did dial Rose's number. There was no answer.

She let the phone ring for a long time, willing Rose to answer, trying to let her know who it was, or at least, if she was in the house, to sense a friendly presence so that she would be encouraged to answer. It had begun to feel absolutely necessary that she talk to her sister.

After awhile she replaced the receiver, lit a cigarette, and leaned against the bench. The house smelled of fried onions. Minna came in, as Katrina had expected she would anyway. Katrina said, more waspishly than she meant, 'If you're going to hang around here make yourself useful.' She attacked the pile of dishes that had accumulated again and Minna picked up a teatowel. When they had done that chore they vacuumed and dusted together.

Nobody could say that Basil lived in a dirty house.

The night before, Jason and Poppy had watched *Starship Intercourse* and the first half of *Terms of Endearment* (Poppy had seen it eight times). First thing in the morning they watched *Bodacious Tatas*, then the second half of *Terms of Endearment* and finally half an hour of *Neon Maniacs — 12 Good Reasons to be Afraid of the Dark*, before Jason decided that it wasn't to his taste and went off to return them all to the video shop.

When he got back Poppy was sitting on the steps of the caravan wearing her hat. She sat up defiantly. Beside her, Larissa tried to entice her back inside but she wouldn't budge.

'What is it?'

Larissa turned a stricken face to him.

Inside, the place had been turned over. The diarama that had been the first thing he built in hospital, in the awful months when he was coming to grips with the fact that he would never ride the Harley Davidson again, lay on its side. He had made and painted each of the figures in the charge of the Scots Greys at Waterloo piece by painful piece. Sergeant Ewart, captured by Jason in lead and colour, seizing the colours of the 45th French Infantry, lay headless on his side. Scattered off the shelves was a whole detachment of cuirassiers and a half-finished charge of cavalry officers.

'Cops. Did they take anything?' He turned things over himself as he spoke, checking his stash. It was undisturbed.

Larissa shook her head. 'They were having fun.'

'Why didn't you stop them?' he shouted at Poppy. She sat up, more rigid than before, on the step. 'Ah, forget it. What about your place?' he asked, turning to Larissa.

'Yeah. They didn't break anything of ours. Gary was there.'

'Where is he now?'

She shrugged.

'Buggered off. I might have known. D'you reckon they're onto something?'

'I dunno.' She picked up a soldier. 'I'm sorry.'

'Yeah, I know.'

'You're weird,' she said. 'I don't understand these. How you've got the patience.'

'Anybody could make them.'

'I couldn't. I never had much patience for learning anything.'

'You could of. I know you could.' Then, because he did not want her to see how he felt about certain things, and because he had loved the soldiers too, he swept up a handful of them and deposited them in the kitchen tidy in the corner of the caravan.

'You could fix those.'

'Kid stuff.' He shovelled more of them up and soon there were none left. 'Why does your aunt hang around here?' he asked her when he was finished.

He asked Rose that, too, standing in the gateway while she loaded her car.

'Have you been potting Larissa to the cops?'

'Who are you?'

'A friend.'

'Of whose? Oh I know, you're at the park. Jason, isn't it? What would I pot her about?'

'Nothing.'

'Then what are you worrying about?'

'Somebody's hassling us.'

She straightened from filling the car boot. 'Somebody's hassling me too.'

'You! Don't make me laugh.'

'It's true. And I suspect everybody. So you'd better watch out.'

He saw that she meant it. Turning to go, he said on impulse, 'I look out for Larissa.'

'You do?' Her voice was surprised, a touch incredulous.

'Somebody has to.'

When he had gone a little way down the path she called after him quietly. 'Thank you,' she said. 'I appreciate that.'

He turned back again; she stared after him, smiling, a little puzzled, but friendly. He wished he knew her, and thought what a shame it was that it probably wouldn't happen.

★

As she headed south, Rose drove past the church Paul attended, on the outskirts of the town. The church was situated at the edge of the reserve that sloped away to the lake. It was the only stand of native bush left in the district; the foliage formed a backdrop to the plain white squared-off building. Paul's second wife, Joylene, was going into the church with a group of women. She was dressed in bright colours, her pelvis thrust slightly forwards as she balanced on stiletto heels. Rose had a good chance to observe the group because a traffic officer pulled her over to the side of the road. He looked embarrassed when he saw it was her.

'Are you in a hurry, Mrs Kendall?' he asked. 'There's a demonstration heading this way, and we'd like it to get straight through and out of town. People are in a funny frame of mind.'

'It's okay, I'll wait,' she said. It went through her head *How strange, he's apologising to me. It used to be me that stopped the traffic.* Did he remember this, or had the politics escaped him?

Watching in the rear-vision mirror, she saw a group of twenty or so people led by Wiki heading towards her. Getting out of the car, she slammed the door behind her and walked quickly away from the road, up the grassy verge towards the church, keeping her back to the marchers. A choir began to sing inside, Joylene and her friends at practice. *Loving shepherd of Thy sheep/ keep Thy Lamb, in safety keep.* Rose remembered watching *Places in the Heart* twice over on a flight to London with Kit last year. It was about a woman somewhere in the middle of America who nobly made friends with a black man in spite of the disapproval of the local people; she bore widowhood bravely and sang in a church just like this. Only the trouble was that the actress had also played the Flying Nun what seemed like a hundred years ago, when television was still black and white and Olivia—her child, her baby—when she was not much more than a toddler, had gone to a second-storey window and stepped out of it, thinking that she too could fly, trusting the air to hold her up, believing that anyone really could do anything.

She hadn't been hurt but she might have been; she might have died. Rose believed that the safety net that had caught her was her own love, her own will for her daughter's survival. But nets failed and love was unreliable; it had done nothing for Larissa, and Olivia was far away. So was Richard. To be in Weyville and love them was not enough, as Toni had hinted when she spoke of Kit. Neither belief nor idealism, neither marching nor friendship could sustain them. For here she was with her back turned on her own friends, who had taken to the roads against her, against belief, or perhaps on account of it.

The marchers had reached the intersection. Suddenly behind her the choir emerged from the church and began singing louder, as if in supplication, surrounding her. There was nowhere to go but to become part of them. Joylene had her head bowed over her hands. *Suffer not my steps to stray/ from the straight and narrow way . . .*

Down the road, coming towards the marchers, another group had appeared, carrying a banner emblazoned PEASANT POWER. At the front of the march a kilted bagpiper squeezed his instrument and burst into 'Amazing Grace'. A cheer went up behind the piper. Overhead flew a top-dressing plane, trailing another banner: TOWN AND COUNTRY UNITE.

The choir sang louder, and Joylene raised her arms above her head. 'Praise the Lord,' she cried. One singer could not bear it a moment longer and broke ranks, running to the edge of the road. 'Why don't you all get back to work?' she shouted at the marchers, though it was difficult to tell which group she was addressing. 'Work shirks,' cried another, and soon they all stood shouting, except for Joylene who kept on singing. Nobody appeared to notice Rose.

Now she could see that Toni had emerged from the ranks of the second group and was walking slowly down towards Wiki's. Then both groups stopped and Wiki moved towards Toni.

'It's all right, Wiki,' said Toni. 'It's just the cockies. The Party's staying home. They asked me to come and tell you.'

Symbolism was so easy, too easy, yet Rose knew that if you lived in a town like Weyville, you couldn't get away from it. There was only a limited number of things you could learn, or people you could know, or even places to go, and after awhile nothing was coincidence, it was simply the inevitable path of things. She wanted to go as far away as she could to find some place where the accumulation of evidence suggested that Weyville was no more than a place in the imagination, or the heart for those that insisted, tucked away for good like her first house, where all the life-changing events, births, partings, love had taken place, but weren't going to happen again.

She would take a back road and detour past the marchers, heading south. In the car she slipped a tape in the deck; it was Crystal Gale. *Here I go once again/ with my suitcase in my hand/ and I'm ru-unning away down River Road*: so sentimental, admit it Rose, downright conservative; so small-town, so tough. So everything.

The march snaked away to her left as she turned into the detour. The black banners on poles were held aloft, straining against the breeze. Police cars tailed behind, like butterflies drifting in the light.

5

The first afternoon Rose was away she detoured out of town, and then drove south, taking the back route round the western edge of Lake Taupo. She did this without thinking about it, realising only later that she was intent on avoiding the march. Then she thought how unnecessary this was, given that the march would take days to cover the ground that was already between her and Weyville. Half-way round the lake where the cliffs drop straight to the water she stopped the car and got out, looking across the lake. She raised her head as the sharp edge of a breeze caught her cheek, tasted winter in the air.

When she had rounded the lake she was inclined to drive further west. The car was low on petrol and at the next village she pulled into a service station. Half a dozen houses straggled along either side of the road. At their centre stood a general store with tearooms attached, which were entered by a separate door. At first she went into the store, looking for a Moro bar and some fruit, remembering that she had not eaten all day. The apples looked as if they were half-way through the drying process, and two bunches of bananas lying in the bottom of a wooden packing case were green. As she searched out the sweet rack she realised that the store was in the process of shutting down. CLOSING DOWN SALE read a sign above the remains of a haberdashery counter: a tangle of wool, pins, dressmaker's tapes, some packets of pantyhose, and an ambitious pink nightgown with lace down either side of an intended cleavage. A litter of discarded tins lay at the back of the shop, and single rows of goods were pulled to the fronts of the shelves, just like Mr Gandhi's shop, only worse. Her foot caught a rusty five-pound flour tin, empty on the floor, and sent it skidding. Nobody came to serve, although somewhere in the distance she heard raised voices.

Empty-handed, she tried the tearooms, knocking on the counter several times until the voices in the background suddenly stopped and a thin woman, neither young nor old, but who looked as if she had been crying, appeared through the strips of blue and white plastic flyscreen. Looking around her, Rose experienced the sickening sensation that she was responsible for this woman, and for a moment half-expected to be attacked. But as the woman looked through her, Rose remembered that she had already driven well south of Kit's electorate, and that few people outside of Weyville itself knew or cared what his wife looked like.

She ordered tea. The sandwiches were curling and the fillings looked diseased. BE WISE, BUY PIES: the sign above the warmer at least looked new, and she recalled with yearning what a treat it had been when Elsie Diamond had allowed her and Katrina to buy pies for their school lunches. She ordered, knowing it would be a mistake, and looked for extra sachets of tomato sauce.

'That's all we've got,' said the woman, nodding in the direction of the formica tables. The sauce was in large red tomato-shaped squeeze containers, their nozzles encrusted with rimes of blackened sauce.

Rose took her place alongside a trestle table with a cardboard sign reading ARTS AND CRAFTS FOR SALE tacked above it. Arranged on the table were dried flowers, wooden ornaments adorned with shells, Polly Masters' pottery (three jugs, two plates and a holder for Marmite jars), frilled covers for toilet rolls, several jars of what first appeared to be bottled fruit but on closer inspection was fibre knotted into strange shapes floating in liquid, grotesquely anatomical—*pickled privates, $1.30 a jar*, and for a moment the horrid pink things did look like women's vulvas; *pickled stoned, $1.80; pickled bums, $1.30.* In spite of herself she began to laugh.

Then stopped. What hope had once enlivened this place? She could not imagine who would buy these items. Perhaps local people, as jokes to play on one another; or perhaps passers-by shocked out of their complacency would take them home, in turn to shock their friends. Yet these hopes had been in vain, or else nobody had time or money for such frivolity any more. Or maybe time had simply rolled over this place and everybody but these people already knew that these were yesterday's jokes.

'Who makes them?' Rose asked, picking up a jar of pickled bums as her tray was delivered to her.

The woman took the jar and held it, studying it as if it were the first time that she had seen it, returned it to its shelf without replying.

She picked up the tray when she had deposited the teapot and wiped at Rose's table with a sponge.

'Do you sell many?' Rose tried again.

'I don't do the stocktaking.' The woman's voice was final.

'I'll take a jar,' Rose said impulsively. She took the bums back; they were obscene, she decided, but not pornographic like the others.

The two-dollar note Rose proffered lay on the table between them, as the woman approached again.

'Do you want them wrapped?'

'No. They're fine.'

'A present?'

'Maybe. Are the tearooms closing as well as the shop?'

'Nah. We get trucks past here. We'll be better off without the shop. Just drags us down.'

'Where will people shop?'

'Buggered if I know. Turangi maybe. Up the junction. Somewhere out there. Where ever they go for their welfare these days. Know what I mean?'

'The post office's shut?'

'That's about the size of it. Piss on them, I say.' She picked up a jar of privates. 'Piss on this government from a great height I say.' She put the jar down. 'I voted for the bastards, you know.'

'I guess a lot of us did,' said Rose, and out on the plain towards the mountains she heard the wind rising and creaking.

A truck's roar interrupted the quiet afternoon and a Kenworth pulled up outside. The woman straightened, touched her hair and went back behind the counter. A man shambled to the flyscreen, his face red and contorted. Across the room, Rose could smell whisky. The woman shoved the man away, spoke sharply into the passage that loomed behind the screen, and resumed her place. As if she had been there all her life. As if there was no other place to go.

Self-conscious, Rose looked for somewhere to put the jar, perhaps back on the shelf. As if it mattered.

She sat with the evidence poised in her hand, her face turned away from the door when the driver entered the shop.

His footsteps paused behind her. 'Rose Diamond,' exclaimed a voice. 'Well gidday.'

She put the jar down carefully and said without turning round, 'Ellis Hannen.'

'Let me guess,' he said, pulling a chair out and turning it back to front so that his legs straddled the back of it. 'You've been out buying antiques, poor old ladies selling up the family silver?'

'Don't be like that.'

'Okay. Buying up the last shares in the last mill so you can flog it off cheap to the Japs?'

'Ellis, if you're going to talk like that, go away.'

He raised his finger towards the woman at the counter; anticipating his order, she was already bearing down on them with hot coffee and two pies. Ellis put down ten dollars and winked at her.

'Darlin', I'm not going nowhere. This one's my place. Yeah,' and he grabbed the woman's arm for an instant and she didn't resist, 'this here's my baby.'

He was a dark thickset man with a tanned face full of white false teeth. Rose remembered that he had bad teeth even as a child. But he had very clean whites to his eyes and now, as then, they transformed his face from ordinary to engaging.

'Just touring, then?' he said, when they were alone. It would be easy for her to leave, she thought, and wondered why she did not. Her legs felt heavy and tired.

'I'm on the run, Ellie,' she said, making a joke, only it didn't come out like that.

'Yeah?'

'No, of course not. I just needed a change.'

'Bit of space, eh. Katrina said you worked pretty hard.'

'Katrina? What's she been telling you? When did you see her?'

'Hey, take it easy. Couple of months back. I went to a garage sale down the Blake Block one Saturday morning and ran into her.'

'Oh, I see.'

'You do? Well, jeez, Rose, it's a good thing you do. But at least, counting Katrina, there's still two Diamonds that speak to me without me having to hole them up in a tearoom out the back of nowhere.'

'Well that's one more than speaks to me, Ellie.'

Ellis Hannen scratched his head. You could mark him down as a type, jocular, not a thinking man, but shrewd, the sort Tom Diamond would have approved of for a son-in-law. Only he wasn't quite like that either. At school, he'd got warts on his hands and had black pencil spotted all over them for months; he'd kept them in his pockets whenever he could and then got strapped for that. She could still hear him crying, the strap on the warts on a cold morning. Then he got ringworm and had his head shaved and painted and he'd hidden out the back of his parents' farm where they couldn't find him for two weeks and Jim Diamond, her brother, took him food all that time and never let on where he was. Ellis got tough after that.

'Yeah, well, Jim'll get over it I guess.'

'He'd better not leave it too long.' Rose surveyed the crusts of congealed pie. Ellis had eaten his second one already.

'Bleeding heart liberals,' Jim Diamond said to his sister when she rang him about Christmas. They hadn't shared Christmas dinner for years but they

always spent time together during its season, usually on Boxing Day, when they had a drink at one or other of their houses and gave gifts to each other's children. It was always Jim's or Rose's house and Katrina and Larissa came to whichever place it was. Basil and Sharna never attended one of these gatherings because by the time they were born Rose and her brother were not speaking.

'What do you think you and that poncey bloke of yours are up to?'

'I don't know what you're talking about,' she said, although she did. She knew all right.

'I went to a football match earlier this year,' said Jim. 'In fact I went to several, every one I could get to that the Boks played in the North Island, not that I can say it was so great watching them play up against all that shit. I went to a football game in Weyville, and my bloody sister tried to stop me getting into it.'

'Oh Jim,' she said, then, 'it's Christmas, can't we talk about it some other time?'

'No.'

'Okay, so what do you want to say about it?' she asked, feeling the bottom drop out of her stomach, knowing even before he said it that he didn't want to talk to her at all. He had disapproved of Katrina in the past but she could tell that this was different.

'I went to Auckland and you bombed them from a plane.'

'Jim . . . I didn't bomb them.' Though secretly she was pleased to be included.

'With flour. You bombed them with flour.'

Her fatal mistake, then, was to laugh at him. When she stopped, he had gone.

'How is my big brother?' she asked. 'Has he joined Rotary yet?'

'How did you know?' Ellis's surprise was genuine. 'Mr Big of the trucking world. He owns two to one rigs on the rest of the owners.'

'I miss him,' she said. 'Dammit, Ellis, I miss him.' Her eyes were full of tears and she looked away, hoping he wouldn't notice. 'Oh goddammit, Ellis, I miss him.'

'Tell him.'

'It's gone on too long. Seven years.'

'Yep, maybe.' He shook his head.

She wiped her face with the back of her hand. Silently he handed her a clean handkerchief. Ellis had always had clean handkerchiefs.

'Remember that night at the lakefront? That time you danced on the back of the truck?'

'The truck? Oh that. Vaguely.'

She could see he wanted to talk about the past, about what he thought might have been, but she could have told him never would, no way.

'You were an amazing dancer,' she said, gathering her car keys, and, defiantly, the pickled bums.

'What about a drink,' he said, without getting up.

Then, in the distance they heard a siren, a car travelling fast. Both their heads swivelled. A police car passed at speed, slowed down momentarily outside the tearooms, and Rose experienced a flash of recognition which was so quick that a moment later she could not identify what it was that she had seen.

'I wonder what's up?'

'Probably just practising. Cops. They speed everywhere these days. They're all over the place today. I saw that march starting out of Weyville earlier in the day.'

'Yes,' said Rose. 'So did I.'

'Keep them on their toes. I thought of going.'

'You? You've got a job.'

He looked at her curiously. 'So I have. About that drink?'

'There's a pub round here?'

'Of sorts. We can drink in the private bar, they get the odd traveller staying over.'

'I'd better leave it tonight,' she said, as if hurrying somewhere; implicit, the suggestion that she would return to Weyville.

For it was nearly dusk, and the wind that had been rising throughout the afternoon had turned bitter.

She raised her hand to Ellis who was already turning to the woman behind the counter.

He had given her an idea.

'I stood and looked at her in the doorway,' Toni was saying, 'and I thought, y'know, she's so innocent; Rose doesn't know a friggin' thing. You'd think she'd know more, wouldn't anybody think she'd *know* more?'

'Neurotic, needs a job, that's what,' said Larry Verschoelt thickly. His wife, Nonie, was deep in conversation with Denise Taite about getting ruched blinds made up cheap. Nonie hadn't had a job since she finished up on Woolworth's lolly counter twenty years ago, though she called running the women's share club work. She hadn't had much 'work' since the crash though. Larry had already been drinking home-made stout with Gabby Taite, Denise's husband, before they came and now he'd drunk four or five of Morris Applebloom's gin and tonics. Toni tried to avoid his eye, wondered who could possibly have invited the Verschoelts after what had happened with the march, or the Taites, for that matter. A map of Gabby and Denise's lives had been laid out when they built their house around a bar.

'She has a job; she works damn' hard at it,' Toni said, stirring herself in the window seat. Her day seemed to have been endless. She was recapping in her head: Rose, in crisis—it had been imperative to see her this morning before the shit hit the fan and it was all over town that she was going nuts; the march, the confrontation with Wiki—Wiki hadn't said *wanker* but she might as well, even though Toni had given ground. She was still smarting, that had hurt; now this. This party, and she knew she should have stayed home. She relapsed further into the corner and rested her face against the glass.

'Being Kit Kendall's wife.' Matt spoke, sounding sour. 'Larry's right... for once. Rose was a good teacher.' Matt's wife, good dependable Nancy, had stayed home tonight to prepare lessons; she had taught with Rose. 'Politics wastes too many people,' he was saying, something she never thought to have heard from him. 'For instance, there's some damn' good doctors in politics, they'd have been more use in their surgeries. Teachers, scientists, all done for. And look what it does to their partners. Nancy'd give Rose a job tomorrow.'

'Nancy!' Larry yelled. 'Nancy Reagan, Nancy You-Know-Who-the-Cabinet-Minister's-wife, and Nancy Decker as well. Aw mate,' he slapped his own thigh, 'with wives called Nance who needs enemies?'

Even Harry Ryan, blinking uncertainly at the end of the table by himself, looked up and laughed. Stopping as quickly as he had begun, he dropped his nose towards his beer again. The puffiness around his eyes suggested that he had been crying, or sleeping badly at nights.

Matt edged over to Toni. 'Will Morris throw him out, d'you think?' he asked quietly, meaning Larry.

'I don't know,' Toni said. 'Does it matter? I give up on that man.'

'You couldn't stay away, could you?' said Matt. His eyes had followed her gaze as she watched Sarah Applebloom, the youngest in the room, with her straight ironed-looking black hair and her face like a lily. Alongside her, Morris fixed drinks for the Newbones who had just come in with Mungo Lord. He had driven them over in his new Range Rover; he exuded a faint scent of antiseptic still and looked scrubbed, as if he had just finished operating.

Hortense chattered to six people at once, and over the top of Nick; at the moment she worked on the paper with Matt. Dressed in a mannishly tailored navy suit with a tight skirt, she punctuated every sentence with gestures. Her fingers were excessively long with very large knuckles. Nick let her talk without interruption. Nowadays, he programmed the computers Lyle Warner sold; he wore dark-rimmed glasses and a red tie with his sports jacket and white shoes. Often he flicked his shoulder-pads, conscious of his dandruff problem. He'd done the computer print-outs for the elections, listing the residents street by street. Kit Kendall said, after the last election, they would have almost certainly have lost it without Nick.

Mungo helped himself to wine, deftly extracting the neck of a fresh cask as if he was doing an internal. Morris held a glass against the light for a moment. As Toni watched him move in this house, she sensed how he loved it. It was the kind of house which was exactly like the Kendalls' was supposed to have been. A group of people sat in a conservatory which was almost entirely filled by a kauri table lit from above by leadlights, while others stood in the adjoining kitchen. There were other rooms given over to conversation nooks, and fat sofas, bookcases and handblown glass, where Morris entertained other bankers and clients, but this room was the Party's, their powerhouse during Kit Kendall's last two election campaigns. The room felt right, a place that drew them together.

Nick and Hortense with Mungo joined the circle, pushing it wider. In this fourth year of the Lange Government they talked about race relations and the crime wave, about privatisation and the Auckland drift, about what happened in Wellington (they all had different theories, particularly about the way that corruption ate at the hearts of men and women who went there), about the running down of the health service and what might be contained in the report of the Royal Commission on Social Policy and the hope it held out—a last hope, somebody said—and whether Lotto should fund the arts; whether, in fact, art was over-subsidised.

'It must be,' Denise pronounced, 'because it was so hard to get into Nureyev at the Festival.' She had been dying to slip in the fact that she had seen Nureyev in Wellington. 'I was so close to the front I could hear him breathe, and see him when he scratched the back of his leg. They mucked up the bookings, you know. Somebody ought to do something about it.'

'The Government can't fix everything,' Matt said, suddenly coming to its defence. 'You can't blame the Government for that.'

Nonie clutched Denise's arm frantically at the end of the table. 'I said to Denise, didn't I, how we should get the share club going again, didn't I love?'

Denise moved closer to Hortense, the alliance with Nonie collapsing now there was someone else to talk to. She and Gabby had managed rather better since the crash than the Verschoelts, and tying herself to Nonie's coat-tails again seemed less than a good idea. In fact, there were times when she *blamed* Nonie, however cruel that made her feel in her heart.

'I've been covering the march,' said Hortense to Matt.

'God bless them,' said Denise.

'I wanted to go on the march,' said Harry. 'I've been sold out.'

'Speaking of selling,' said Denise, her lipstick hovering in the gap between her front teeth, 'did you know Nixon's have sold out, and Gabby's bought in a share of real estate. It just went through today, didn't it, Morris?'

So that explained their presence: Morris's star clients for the day. Toni looked to catch Morris's eye, but he was testing the ripeness of a cheese and arranging it on a plate. He didn't look at her. But then why should he be accountable? Every day he must make deals for people who were worse by far than Denise and Gabby. It was his job.

In the kitchen Sarah was gliding round, bending between the oven and bench, her movements like silk falling through a ring. Toni couldn't take her eyes off the two of them, Sarah and Morris, arranging food, working like a team, giving the same amount of attention to all their guests. She did a mental shrug. If it came to it, she did the same for Lyle's clients. You didn't need style to buy computers.

If only Rose were here, if she could talk to her, she might make sense of the evening. She supposed she meant, if only things hadn't gone wrong. Toni suddenly ached, acknowledging more loss than she could comprehend right now, about so many things, about what happened to people and why things changed.

'We're thrilled, aren't we, Honey Puff?' Denise was still on about their deal. She plumped herself against a cushion.

Gabby looked suitably modest.

'It'll be like the old times,' Denise babbled into the silence. 'Affluence. I love affluence, don't you all love it?'

'But weren't you against the Government yesterday Denise?' said Matt drily.

Hortense, seeing the drift of the conversation, edged away from Denise.

'Oh yes. I am. We are.' She gathered herself, defiant. 'We'd have been affluent anyway.'

'They lay the envelopes out on the table,' Harry was saying. He was drunk, too, in a slow methodical way that still allowed him to follow his thoughts through one by one. 'But you only get one if you're still employed. How about that? A envelope. An envelope, yep, that's right, *an* envelope that says you've still got a job. And you keep looking for your envelope, and there is no envelope. That's how they tell you.'

'Where's Belinda?' Matt asked Toni tersely, looking aside when she pretended she hadn't heard him.

Belinda, Harry's wife who had kept her maiden name and wasn't called Belinda Ryan, was younger still than Sarah, but then she wasn't in the room. She was in the Applebloom's bathroom with her back pushed against the toilet cistern and her legs round Lyle Warner's waist while he fucked her. She had been putting on eyeliner when he came in and shut the door behind them. She watched him undoing his zip in the mirror and drop his trousers without turning round or speaking. When he got hard she touched the reflection in the mirror.

'Kinky, eh?'

'Jesus, it kills me seeing you with him,' Lyle said.

'Get your gear on,' she said, glancing at the door, 'they'll catch us.'

'Get yours off.'

The first time, she leaned on the towel rail with her buttocks arched towards him and her skirt hitched around her waist. She leaned against him and cried when they'd finished, not brave any more.

'When are you going to tell him?'

'When are you going to tell her?' They were whispering fiercely.

'Love, I've got kids. I need time.'

'You won't ever do it.'

'I will. If we get you fixed up somewhere first. A place, you know. I can help.'

She nodded.

'So?'

'He's lost his job.'

'Belinda. C'mon, they'll find us. Promise.'

'I can't. I don't know. Don't leave me, not just yet.' She had big white teeth and a top gum that showed when she smiled and a snub nose. He thought he must be crazy, but he wanted her as much as anything he had ever had. Or owned. To stop her crying, or to extract a promise, he didn't know which, he had put her against the toilet.

★

A huge central fan mounted in a solid brass holder whirred while Rose ate her meal in the hotel dining room. A man and a woman, dressed up as if for an anniversary, ate awkwardly at another table. They were her only company. A man in a red T-shirt, emblazoned with I'M A HUNK, TOUCH ME in black letters, walked through bearing an enormous live crayfish. He slapped it until it produced an anguished squirm. 'It's alive, it's alive,' he sang.

'Sorry about the noise — one helluva row,' he said, wandering back later, holding a jug of beer this time. He pirouetted a full circle by Rose's table and stole a bread roll from the side of her plate.

Guitars stirred and strummed in the bar below her when she went upstairs to her room. The room contained a single bed covered by an orange candlewick spread, a narrow bare cupboard with chipped brown paint which served as a wardrobe, a bedside table without a lamp, and brown curtains with tasselled drawstrings. Outside, horses were tied up at the entrance to the public bar, pawing and snorting softly by the light of the single street lamp.

She went downstairs to find the private bar of which Ellis had spoken, but it was closed. The crowd, mostly Maori, through which she threaded her way to the public bar, was dense, and so was the smoke. They were singing: *Knock three ti-imes on the ceiling/ when you want me* and someone in the crowd laughed when she went up to the bar which also doubled as a bottle store with an iron grille over a shelf of spirits.

She smiled, but nobody smiled back. A Pakeha woman, one of only two in the room, stepped up to her and blew smoke in her face.

In the silence Rose heard herself say, 'A half of brandy, please.'

Back in the room, their laughter seeped through the floorboards. She tipped a measure of brandy into the tumbler on the bedside table and turned the covers back on the bed. She swallowed the brandy. Not tonight would she lie awake waiting for the phone to ring, her eyes parched, until, unable to bear it a moment longer, she downed Halcyon, only to be woken minutes or hours later, her arm lurching sluggishly through the dark space between her and the telephone beside the bed, to lie shivering afterwards with Roach at her side until the pills, or fatigue, or simply disbelief, released her into sleep again. She undressed and slid into the sheets. It was cold and clean inside.

She may have dozed; it was much later that there was a knock on the door. The man in the red T-shirt was standing outside.

'The missus says there's a phone call.'

'There must be a mistake,' she said, pulling her housecoat around her.

'There'd better not be,' he said, not at all jocular now. 'It's a bloody fine time of night to get someone out of bed.'

The hotel was very quiet as she padded downstairs in bare feet.

'It can't be for me,' she repeated. She was going to say that nobody in the whole world outside of this hotel knew that she was here, but thought better of it.

She picked the phone up off the counter. 'Hullo.' She waited. 'Hullo, who is it?'

At the other end she heard it, the firm unerring click of a phone being replaced.

Hortense had started talking dirty; it was that time of night. 'You've got to believe me, I know about vaginal orgasm,' she was telling Mungo. 'You think because you're a doctor you can tell me what I feel, but you're a man. Isn't that right, Sarah?'

Sarah and Belinda were in the kitchen smoking a joint and didn't answer her, not because they were unfriendly but they were absorbed in saying very little. Morris watched his wife and Toni watched Morris. The party had loosened up since the Taites and the Verschoelts had suddenly left.

Nick had spotted Larry in the garden leaning against a tree. Thinking him ill he had gone out to rescue him and found him peeing against a pottery urn in the Applebloom's shrubbery, his arc golden in the moonlight, his face ghostly.

'The bathroom was full,' he said.

When he came inside he had acted sober and quiet. 'I think it is time we go home,' he had said firmly to Nonie and handed her her coat before she could protest. As they and the Taites had come together they all felt impelled to leave at once.

Now everyone except Belinda talked more easily.

Lyle sat alongside Toni, his arm around the back of her chair, his fingers brushing her shoulder when she talked. She sat quite still neither responding to nor rejecting him.

'I mean, what's the matter with us, if we don't talk about these things,' said Hortense. 'We're no better than the fundies up the road.'

'I am,' said Sarah, shaking her head. 'I am.'

'Oh yes,' said Belinda wistfully, 'you are too, Sarah.'

'Talking of which,' said Hortense, turning to Toni, 'did you see them out in force when you were talking to Wiki this morning? Singing?'

'I heard something,' said Toni, surprised. 'What were you doing there?'

'Covering it, of course. Newspaper, read all about it, eh Matt?'

'You didn't tell me. You didn't *interview* me. What are you saying about it?' Toni cried.

'I interviewed you for yesterday's march, big boots. Don't worry kid. It's a new angle. Matt knows all about it. Bit of police brutality, bit of beating and thumping.'

'Tell. Why didn't you tell us before?'

'Ears.' She meant the departed guests, and Larry in particular, but Matt was glancing at her, silencing her anyway.

'Rose was there,' said Hortense, getting the message. 'Just standing there in the middle of the fundies. Kind of weird, our friend Rose.'

'Why aren't we marching anyway?' cried Belinda. Her eyes were unnaturally bright.

Sarah leaned against the stove. 'Remember when being high meant you were afraid to fall out of a tree?'

'We were thirty then,' said Hortense, with reverence, joining them. 'Or thereabouts.' She had forsaken Mungo. Now her eyes followed Belinda thirstily, as if for details. At the far end of the table, in the conservatory, Matt and Nick were huddled together, the phrase 'core strategy' escaping from the edges of their discussion. They looked slightly secretive, even in this gathering. Their eyes followed Morris from time to time, with a speculative air. Nick's glance was occasionally troubled.

'We should all be out there marching,' shouted Belinda, turning on Toni.

'Don't take it out on me,' Toni said, slipping out of Lyle's range. Aside, to her old and dear friend Matt, she said, interrupting his conversation, 'I don't know where Rose is Matt. I feel I've lost her.'

Puzzled, he said, 'But you saw her this morning, she was going to Wellington.'

'I feel scared about her.' She wiped her nose with the back of her hand. 'It's all right, I'm drunk, we're all drunk.'

Harry, who hadn't spoken for nearly an hour, raised himself at the sound of his wife's clamorous voice. 'Why did you let them in here?' he said to Morris. 'Those people, they wrecked things, not us.'

'The march is on,' said Toni, recovering herself. 'Why beef about it, the people it matters to are marching.'

'It matters to me,' said Harry. 'I'm unemployed, remember.'

'Larry Verschoelt isn't doing too well himself,' said Matt uneasily.

'You didn't tell me they'd be here tonight,' Harry said to Morris.

'You could have left, old chap,' said Morris. He was screwing caps on to bottles so that nobody was encouraged to help themselves to another drink.

Harry looked at Belinda. 'No I couldn't,' he said thickly. 'What are you, Applebloom? Who can read you, eh? Name like Applebloom. Such a lovely...' he hiccupped, stopped. 'Such a romantic name,' he began though he knew, he must know, Toni thought, how they all ached for him to stop, 'sounds like orchards, cider, green grasses, perfume, haybarns. Lovely name. You're poetry, Applebloom. And all the time you're a Jew. A Jewish banker called Appelblum...' In case anybody didn't understand, he spelt: 'B–l–u–m, programme of anglicisation of the Jews...'

'Stop it, Harry,' screamed Belinda, covering her ears with her hands. 'For God's sake, stop it!'

Harry had half-risen and was leaning against the table; Matt was moving towards him to lead him out: Harry whom they had loved, Harry who worked hard for them, and they had trusted, and was now about to be dumped like yesterday's leftovers. Then the phone rang.

Morris picked it up. He listened, spoke carefully, and turned away from them.

'Yes, certainly,' he said, 'certainly, I can make that meeting. I'll make the arrangements in the morning.'

One by one the group began gathering their belongings together, awkward that they appeared to listen to their host's telephone conversation in the wake of silence that followed Harry and Belinda's outbursts.

'Yes,' Morris said again, 'it'll be quite all right. Can you give me the venue again?'

'Who was it?' said Sarah when he had hung up.

'Nobody you know,' said Morris. He put his arm around Harry. 'You're right,' he said, 'but you're wrong too.'

'I know,' said Harry. 'I know. I'm sorry...'

'No need. Come and see us again soon. All right?'

He put out his arms to hug Harry, and around them the others laughed too loudly, relief washing over them.

'Are you going away?' Sarah asked Morris.
'Yes,' Morris replied regretfully, extricating himself from Harry's embrace. 'Yes, I have to go away tomorrow evening. I may stay overnight.'
Sarah stared at him as if the others were not there, a look of incomprehension flitting across her face. Her eyes met Toni's, puzzled. Finding no answer there, she shrugged. Turning back to the others, she acknowledged their goodnights with little cloudy smiles.

★

'Have you finished charging Muru?'
'Not yet, we're still recovering stolen goods.'
'And are they worth the trouble?'
Teddy O'Meara looked at the senior officer. Campbell thought, yes, he is trying to work out what I'm asking him. It's just as well for him to wonder.
'Here's the list . . . sir,' said Teddy, offering it.
'I was only asking. Have you given a copy to CIB?'
'I have.'
Of course he knew that O'Meara would have done it. Teddy always had. It was none of his business, strictly speaking. But he couldn't help looking over the list. He might be able to locate some missing property off it anyway. Campbell saw from the list that Matau Muru, Wiki's youngest son, who had been uplifted that afternoon from the unemployment march heading south, pending a number of charges relating to breaking and entering, had been found to be in possession of the following items: one riding saddle, two bridles, one video recorder containing film of an unidentified couple of males dressing in women's clothing, the top tier of a wedding cake, three tins of Watties baby food and two of Heinz, a bottle of Tia Maria, a Batman comic, a collection of birds' eggs, a Rover badge, two car tyres and a Hillman Hunter mudguard.
'How do you know he stole all of these?'
'They were all together.'
'Couldn't he have bought the comic?'
'Not if he could have stolen it.'
'O'Meara.'
'He said he pinched it.'
'How did you extract that startling confession?'
Teddy looked straight ahead. 'He got into some kid's stuff in one of the houses he did.'
'I gathered that.'

'He just dumped all the stuff together, he said.'
'Jesus. Make sure you get it identified. Don't miss a trick.' He wasn't usually given to sarcasm.
'Sir.'
'Is that all?'
'No . . . sir.' Teddy returned the insult with a subtle emphasis but he picked his words carefully. 'There's reason to believe Muru was the hit-and-run on that kid up Orchard Close last week.'
Campbell sighed. 'Why?'
'The car being driven at speed down Orchard Close was seen to be a Hillman Hunter. The mudguard he stole.'
'Yes. Yes, I see that. All right.' He looked at O'Meara. 'I expect you're right, O'Meara. I'd hoped . . . you know the marchers are screaming police brutality already.'
'Yessir.'
'I'd hoped the march would go without incident.'
'We all did . . . sir.'
'Did we? Did we, Teddy? A pious hope. Or was it a way of getting all the troublemakers together in one place and watching who would make the first mistake? Is that what we wanted?'
'There's a few of them left in town.'
'Maybe. Where are the marchers staying tonight?'
'They're camped on the roadside, but I understand they'll be staying on a marae tomorrow night.
'I suppose that's what they'll do all the way south.'
'Right. My mate and I sussed out a few of their locations today.'
'I understand you're staying with the march to Wellington.'
'That's the general idea.'
'You'll be on the road for awhile. You should get some sleep.'
'I like cruising. Bit of country air.'
'Try and keep the media off our backs, will you?'
'It depends on whether those bastards keep in line, doesn't it? With respect, sir.'
Campbell picked up his book where he had left it after his teabreak. It had been a quiet evening for him, and come eleven o'clock he could go home. Tomorrow he would be at home all day. He started to read and put the book down again. Even Zane Grey couldn't hold his attention. He had read *Wild Horse Mesa* fourteen times. This evening, if anything, it disturbed him. He wished life were as simple as it had been then, seeing himself as a kind of sheriff, riding away into sunsets, the glow of the sky on his horse's mane, the cheering of those he left behind. He suspected that once O'Meara

might have too, except that he was probably too young to have read westerns. Or perhaps he had and liked shooting Indians. Campbell was squeamish about that.

O'Meara was looking up phone numbers.

'Take any one newspaper, and take any one Saturday night, take this station, and what do you get?' Campbell knew he sounded agitated. 'Headlines,' he answered himself.

'Rapes, muggings, stolen cars, a couple of us getting beaten up, and threats to the blokes' families.' O'Meara ran his finger down a column of names. 'Those who have them. Tell you the truth, I'm beginning to think it's a choice between celibacy and the force.'

'And you've chosen the force?'

'For the moment.'

Campbell sighed. 'They say you beat up on them.'

The younger man studied him. 'How long've you been in the job . . . sir?

'Long enough.' He rubbed his eyes. He knew what O'Meara was thinking, that he'd been around for what seemed like centuries to him; that he was in a safe job, no night shifts, small chance of violence, a useful appendage for getting boring work out of the way, someone who could be replaced at any time.

'You've forgotten how they love to hate us. The media's all the same.'

'Is it true though, O'Meara?'

'Muru had been in a fight on the march.'

'Yes. I see, of course I do. Teddy, why don't you take leave when you get to Wellington?'

'I don't reckon the march'll get that far.'

'You don't?'

'Nah.'

'You could be right. Is that what the bosses think?'

'It's what I think. Anyway, why did you ask? Want to get rid of me?'

Campbell considered his reply. His job might be safe, but even O'Meara would agree that he worked his butt off on most shifts, just like all the rest of them. This peace was unusual, and the implications of the march hadn't escaped him. He knew exactly what he had meant when he asked O'Meara if it wasn't to the advantage of them all to have the marchers together. Nor had it escaped him that though there had been a major rally of concerned citizens in the town just days before, those who had set off to Wellington were the people they referred to as troublemakers. What sort of a town was it, he had wondered more than once during the evening, that could not keep its shit together long enough to stage a real honest protest? In Orchard Close they were partying up tonight but none of them was marching. The truly poor sleep in the highways and byways. The rest commend them for their sacrifice. These were the same people who screamed brutality when the men snapped.

Yet he could not say, for certain, that they were wrong, or dispel the images that haunted him in his worst nights, of random fists and casual boots, the cavalier young men with whom he worked turned hunters. He had seen the cruising cars, the sharp blast of joy like an adrenalin surge when a youth had been dragged from an ancient vehicle, thrown against it and frisked, his possessions tossed on the road, his groin carelessly punched; he knew that the streets out there were often no more than a glorified schoolyard, the big boys and the little ones. But O'Meara was different again. Although Campbell knew he had done all of these things, and would no doubt do them all again, there was something about him that he could not place. Increasingly, he was unsure that he knew him.

The young man held him in an intent, unfurrowed stare.

'Chronic celibacy's unhealthy,' Campbell said at last.

O'Meara smiled.

The sign at the camping ground read NO PETS ALLOWED. Larissa would have liked a dog, or even a little cat. She had smuggled a kitten in once but Herbert had caught her out. Nowadays she kicked cats when she saw them. But a big dog like an Alsatian would be neat. In her imagination it liked her better than Gary. It would be cool if it bit people, even Gary sometimes, to tune him up.

She watched the clouds skudding across the dark sky, and shivered, noting the change in the weather.

'You should put something on,' Jason said beside her, so that she nearly jumped out of her skin.

'Shit, don't do that to me.'

'It's cold as a frog's tit out here. You'll catch something.'

'You're an old woman, Jason. You're getting like your old lady. What do you want me to put on, cardigan and slippers?'

'What are you doing out here?'

'Thinking. There's no law against it.'

'Penny for 'em.'

'You are weird, aren't you? Like the Middle Ages, really.'

'What would you know?'

'You're right, not much.' She traced the edge of the step with her finger. 'I was thinking it was time we were on the road. I'd like a dog.'

'Yeah? You ever had one?'

'Not really. My aunt had this silly little mongrel I used to mind sometimes when they were away. Creepy little thing.'

'Yeah, well it's dead.'

She was still. 'You're kidding.'

'Nah. I saw her bury it this morning.'

'How did you get in on the act?'

'I didn't. I watched. She didn't know I was there.'

'You're putting me on about this.'

'Straight up. It'd had its throat cut. It was high.'

'Oh.' There was a small catch of pain in Larissa's voice. 'Well, who'd have thought she'd do that to it?'

'I don't reckon she did.'

'Who did?'

'Jesus, how should I know?'

'Seems like you're the expert.'

'I'm not.' He hesitated. 'Where's Gary?'

'Out.'

'Gone out on his own, has he?'

He felt her diminishing in the dark beside him and found himself absurdly awash with tenderness. Often at this time of night she was stoned or drunk, or both, or they might be out on a job. Mostly they stayed sober when they went out at night, Larissa and Jason anyway. Jason had sat her down and told her the facts as he saw them. *You've got to be sharp or you're half-way inside already*. He knew, he'd been there. He had tried to tell Gary too, but Gary reckoned he knew everything.

Jason didn't fancy Larissa when she was high, she swaggered a lot and puked easily. He didn't care for her when she smelled of Gary either. But like this, he wanted to put his arm around her, only he knew she would think he was wet. There was nothing in the world that he could think of that would make her care for him, and so he didn't ask that she did. But when he heard that Gary was out he felt alarmed for them all, and thought how much he wanted to protect her.

'Where did he go?' he asked urgently.

'I dunno. Maybe the pub. I thought you'd know.'

'That guy's a maniac. The town's real quiet — too quiet.'

'Don't worry, Gary's staunch.'
'Larissa, your Auntie Rose went away.'
She sat down suddenly on the caravan step. 'Are you sure?'
'Yeah.'
'Did Gary know?'
'I didn't tell him.'
'Yeah, but I said, does he *know*?'
She read his silence. 'He won't get much there. Unless she's bought up fancy gear just lately. Rose's an environmentalist. Non-materialist and all that stuff.'
'Yeah? D'you want me to roll you a smoke?'
'Why not? Jason, that bitch had it coming to her anyway.'
'If you say so.'
He shrugged, took out his pouch. He supposed it was something to sit here beside her. There were things he wanted to think about, like the size of the universe which he had lately heard was expanding, amazing though that might be, and to wonder what was the life of a seed and how many times it would regenerate before it became nothing. It seemed like a good time to talk to Larissa about things like this. And because the Studebaker was gone he guessed he would have warning of Gary's return.
'We could make highballs,' she said dreamily.
'Don't bother.'
'A Steinie?'
'No, don't put on the lights.'
'Tomorrow I'm going to paint my nails yellow and black, yellow and black, black and yellow all the way across.'
'Yeah, Larissa, yeah, do that.'
'I've got like little star transfers to put on them. Neat, Jason?'
'Yeah, neat.'

★

The bed was deep and soft. Gary lay outstretched in Rose and Kit's master bedroom jacking off. He thought about some poor sod who he heard about lying down in the street in Weyville with nothing but his underpants over his head jacking till they came and took him away. He could kind of see why it had its appeal but this was more peaceful and more full of disrespect. A kind of anarchy. Though there were times when he wished he could be rescued, that somebody, maybe his mother might come and take him away. If he could just remember what she looked like.
Afterwards he took a crap on the Kendall's dining room floor,

turned over some furniture including a desk full of papers, some of which he strewed around the room and the rest he threw out a window watching them float ghost-like into the night, kicked in the glass face of the oven, and finding nothing else of interest, departed with the stereo under his arm and a little bundle of electronic gear which as yet he had not identified, in his pocket.

As he was leaving the phone began to ring. He paused, tempted, then carried on across the lawn and into the trees.

★

The morning sun clawed behind Toni's eyelids. As she pulled the covers over her head she reached from habit to the other side of the bed; it came as no surprise that Lyle was not there. He often slept in a spare bed in their son's room these days. It was no big deal, he said, he was just a hell of a sleeper as she had always known. She could hear him laughing with the kids now. They had had such good times together. Bad dreams were not reliable.

He came into the room bearing a cup of weak tea.

'Can you face this?' he said, sitting on the bed beside her. His hand ruffling the sheet was gentle.

'How did you know I felt so bad?' She sat up and sipped gingerly. 'We were both pretty awful.'

'No, I was worse than you,' he said with contrition.

'Maybe, but I feel worse. You look, hey you look beautiful.' She meant it, liking his throat beneath his fresh shirt. She put her hand on his chest.

'You took the words out of my mouth.'

'Liar.'

'*Just call me angel/ of the mo-orning*,' he crooned. He sang in the local operatic. They begged him to go back every year. He had met Belinda there.

She gripped his hand, fighting tears. The words ran on through her head, *Touch my che-eek/ before you le-eave . . .*

'Why don't you lie down and sleep a bit, I'll get the kids off this morning. They're dressed already and started breakfast.'

'Why are you being so nice to me?' She tried to keep the edge out of her voice.

'You're getting your period, aren't you?' he said.

Mrs Jane Marment's house squatted amongst her chrysanthemums. It was a utility house, the kind that people used to build on beach fronts, and add pieces on to. In hot weather the fibrolite-clad walls overheated it until it was almost unbearable. She drew the shades lower and suffered, and in cold weather she kept them drawn for warmth. It always puzzled her how people threw open their blinds and curtains, exposing themselves to the world. Her late husband had been inclined that way. She shuddered with distaste when she thought of it, it was too revealing of a side of his nature that she would rather not dwell on in retrospect. Teddy agreed with her. People ask for trouble, he said, leaving their doors and windows open, advertising their goods. If you saw what I do. She had no wish to, she believed him, though she liked him to tell her what he had seen. Lived vicariously, she could stand the burden of her boarder's life. What he told her confirmed all the baser things about human nature that she had always suspected. 'Shoot the lot of them,' she said sometimes. She knew he didn't approve of her talking like that, but it was how she felt, especially when she thought of him being in danger.

He slept now, while she sat in her front room, breathing deeply, in and out, as if breathing with him, grateful that he had returned safely again from his last shift, willing him to sleep late. The room contained solid furniture, and little ornamentation but a framed photograph of the Queen wearing her diamonds and a tiara. A slight smile hovered at the edge of the Queen's mouth, and she stared more across the room than at Mrs Marment; but that was how it should be, she felt. On the dresser stood a smaller black and white picture of the Queen and Princess Margaret when they were children, with their mother. Mrs Marment had thought about taking it out and replacing it with something without Princess Margaret, after all that had happened, but it still brought a lump to her throat when she remembered the two children saying goodnight on the radio during the war. She had heard them herself.

She breathed, in out in. Her life had been happy since Teddy came to live in one of the added-on rooms.

Standing at the bench of her Continental Streamline kitchen, Lola Campbell sliced open a grapefruit and carefully separated the flesh from the skin. She did every small household task as if it were a minor work of art, and with precise timing. As a working wife, she told her customers, she must organise her time with care or else things would get out of control.

On the gate of the wall, which surrounded the white colonial-style house with frilled net curtains at the windows, hung a sign which read No Collectors, No Canvassers, No Hawkers. Jeffrey had demurred when she ordered the sign. 'Look,' he said, 'it looks too much as if we're saying, this is mine, and we're not sharing with anybody.'

'But why should we share?' she had responded, genuinely puzzled, 'We worked hard, it's a beautiful house and it's ours. Besides,' she added, 'it makes me feel safer. If anyone can walk up to a policeman's house they'll get to know it too well.' She put it to him, what with firebombings on police houses all over the country, and her on her own at nights so often, it was hardly fair, was it, exposing her to the risk.

And Jeff, who loved his wife, and had to agree that there was danger in his work, had said, well, he supposed she must be right and actually nailed it up. She had the feeling that he still didn't like it much, and it worried her that he might be going soft in the job.

It was just past 7.30. Lola finished preparing her husband's breakfast while the last of the news was playing. With luck, he would not wake up until ten — by the time he ate she would be unpacking new stock at the shop and pinning up hemlines. She was glad hems were going up this year, so much smarter, but the manufacturers still made garments as if they were intended for Amazon-length women with wasp waists.

Lola attached a note to the fridge door with a ladybird magnet. The note read, 'No egg this morning.' Jeff was carrying more gut than she considered healthy. He would eat eggs three times a day if she didn't keep an eye on his diet. It worried her what he got into some days when she was at the shop, after he had been on night shift. Still, she only had to remind him that his fitness test was coming up for him to try harder.

When everything was done for her husband, she sat down to smoke a cigarette, drink black coffee and check that her nails had not been chipped. She kept a bottle of Flame Glow enamel in the kitchen for quick repair jobs. This was her time to gather her thoughts before she drove down and opened up at the shop. She listened carefully to the first news assessments of the day, and tucked away information that the customers might touch on later. It made her sad, the number of things that were wrong with the world. She despaired that they would ever come right. Her father had been a Mason who recited his pledges while locked in the bathroom where nobody could hear them, not even her mother. He was head of the family; it would have been unthinkable for her mother to have questioned his right to make decisions. Lola would never have gone to work if she hadn't been left a widow with a little boy to bring up; in times of hardship she was against married women going to work and taking men's jobs away. But this hardship the country was enduring was different, not her problem at all. The Government had brought it upon themselves; she still couldn't believe that, at the beginning, a woman had been put in charge of the police. A woman, the Minister of Police. Her head still spun when she thought about it. Jeff had said, once, 'Well, we got a better pay deal under her than we ever did with anyone else.' 'That was because she was soft,' Lola told him, 'and look at her, she couldn't handle it in the end, and now they've got a Maori, you can't expect things ever to get better the ways things are, except there's a change of Government, you just think about it.'

As she stubbed out her cigarette and smoothed down her skirt the phone rang. She hurried. It might be her son ringing from Australia, or wherever he was. Though she hadn't heard from him for some time. Maybe a year or more. Probably two, actually.

It was the station. 'Jeff's only had about two hours' sleep,' she said. 'He's had one of his bad nights, can't someone else attend to it?'

Reluctantly, she went into the bedroom. The thought of taking the phone off the hook when Jeff was trying to sleep often occurred to her but the idea upset him so much the first time she suggested it that she never mentioned it again. He was already out of bed.

'They didn't say what it was, oh God, it's not an armed call-out, I hope, if it is and anything happens to you I'll never forgive myself for not telling them you weren't here, Jeff...' Though she knew that he would probably be the last they would call.

He touched her arm as he passed. He had heard her go on in this vein many times before, and although she made him so angry he could hit her, afterwards he would feel sorry; she might not understand the job but he knew she was scared of being left on her own. They needed each other, it was a definition of love. It was one that did. And he liked pleasing her.

She watched him covertly as he listened to the station call. His face creased with annoyance. 'I'm tired of their games,' he said at last. 'Well, yes I am in charge of it, but patrol section's been in on it too... O'Meara was the last person to interview her and he's done two straight shifts in a row through till last night.' He rubbed his forehead. 'I'll come down and check it out later... No, not just because it's Kendall, we can't afford to take chances like that, but I reckon she'll turn up. It's all right Constable, you were correct to call me.'

Lola, sorting through her purse, slowed down the process still further, without real hope that he would tell her. For once, however, Jeffrey seemed more than ready to unburden himself.

'Kendall's wife's been reported missing,' he said. 'Well, I'd be surprised if she is, but Kendall's been ringing their house during the night and she's not there.'

'Has anybody been round to their place?'

'Yes. There's been a fairly messy break-in. No sign of her, her car's gone.'

'That's a bit creepy.'

'There was a party at Appleblooms' last night.'

'You think she stayed the night with someone?' Lola was working to keep the excitement out of her voice.

'I don't know, she might have had too much to drink, something like that. She's careful about things like drinking and driving, y'know. I'll give her that.' Not that he felt like crediting Rose with much this morning.

'I heard she drank too much. I heard she was a lush.'

'Who told you that?'

'I forget . . . somebody in the shop perhaps.'

'Lola, who?'

'Just something Teddy said last election night.'

'Teddy O'Meara?'

'It was just a chance remark. Jeff, it was at a party, that party we went to that night. It was nothing.'

'All right. All right then.' He stood tapping the phonebook with his fingernail. Then he began dialling Toni Warner's number.

Lola, out of habit (it was to protect her, the things she knew and didn't know, Jeff told her) left the room.

When she came back he was yawning, looking creased and a little drawn around the mouth. She could see he was preparing to go back to bed.

'Toni Warner's out, but her husband said Mrs Kendall left town for Wellington yesterday.'

'But she should be there by now?'

'She doesn't have to be. She didn't tell Kendall she was going so I don't expect she intended to get there yesterday.'

'Isn't anybody going to do anything?'

'CIB's checking the break-in, but they'll probably just find it's a routine one, nothing to do with her going walkabout. Nothing I'm going to lose any sleep over.'

She pecked him on the cheek as she picked up her car keys. 'That's my lad. Commonsense, eh?'

But she felt a small pang of disappointment as she drove towards town, wondering whether, as Jeffrey was not going to pursue the matter, she might be excluded from an up-to-date bulletin.

When she had gone, her husband, rumpled and awake, looked at his watch and wondered how long he could leave it before he woke O'Meara. It was ten past eight. He drank the last coffee in the pot without heating it, and dialled.

'Mr O'Meara is not to be disturbed,' said a frosty voice at the other end.

'Disturb him, Mrs Marment, Please.'

'Is it in the line of duty, Sergeant?'

'It is.'

'Oh well... when duty calls... I'll get him.'

'No, on second thoughts... what can he do? Sorry Mrs Marment, just thinking aloud.' He put down the phone.

By 8.30 he was in the office. 'Put a Query Person through the computer,' he told the constable on duty.

Only he knew that the POI index wouldn't show up anything. That stood for persons of interest and Rose Kendall might be interesting to herself and her friends, but she was not interesting enough to have got into police files.

Not yet, anyway.

6

The road had become familiar since Kit entered Parliament. When electorate business required her attendance in Wellington at short notice Rose flew, but if she could arrange it she preferred to drive. The Desert Road in the hard centre of the North Island held a fascination for her which she could not explain, even to herself.

Most people saw it as an obstacle which had to be crossed over; the long stretches edged with tussock, the hairpin bends following one after another, the mountains lurching away to the right on the southward journey, sometimes steam escaping from a volcano; the silences, if you were forced to stop, broken by the explosion of a military cannon near the army settlement and the lines of dark-green canopied trucks hurtling in convoy towards you; the rib of the earth unfurling beside the road, rainbow-striped with veins of multicoloured earth.

But in this heart of the island Rose often stopped from choice, to stand at the edge of the road, looking at the mountains or the causeway from the power scheme which ran through a slash of the earth. There was a sense of danger here, but also the clean incorruptible force of the elements.

She had travelled the road when it glittered with snow lacing its edges, brilliant with travellers from north and south, skis stacked on the roofs of their Volvos and BMWs, fluting signals to each other on their horns as they raced, outstripping one another even before their arrival at the snowfields. At the highway cafs, before they entered the desert stretch, their voices trilled, snapping as brittle and pretty as the icicles in the air, their scarves making gay banners that proclaimed their camaraderie, their exuberance, their money.

Other times she had driven through wet nights when the sides of the roads were almost indistinguishable from the sealing in the headlights, and fog had gripped the car, turning it into a solitary capsule hurtling along on its own except for the freight trucks which moved at night. Sometimes she saw her own old name flash past her, Diamond Carriers, the sign set in a bright blue form shaped like the Cullinan diamond.

Today, the glow of fires surrounded her and smoke blew across the road. A burn-off on the tussock was taking place and rows of beaters moved across the landscape. She stopped at a high point in the road. Rosehips covered a wild creeper growing on the bank. Using the car chamois to guard her fingers, she pulled off a branch. The fruit shone in her hand; she placed it on the passenger seat of the car. Billowing smoke stung her eyes.

As she watched the flames licking the distance, an army jeep pulled up beside her.

'Could you move along?' called the driver. He was a fresh-faced tanned young man, perhaps twenty, with a dirty streak across his cheek.

'I'm just taking a rest,' she said, smiling at him.

'You'll block the traffic, didn't you see the signs back there?' he shouted over his running engine. She saw his impatient dismissal.

'The car's off the road.'

'Do you need help?'

'No. Thank you.'

'Then there's a rest area half a kilometre down the road. Use that.'

He revved his engine and roared away into the smoke.

Driving through the acrid cloud, Rose's mind switched back into the black mode it had occupied for so long. She did not see herself as running before fire. Entering it, yes, prodding it, and stirring up a blaze, but not this, hunted, and chased by the flames at her back.

Yet that was what it was like, how it had been, for longer than she cared to remember.

She had come to the desert to find space. It was why she came so often, as if there were answers to be found near the mountains. Maybe she could determine from a distance, in space expunged of junk and paraphernalia, what was causing her so much trouble.

Weyville had closed in around her. For awhile she had thought she was in charge of the town and its fortunes, as well as her own and that of her friends and family. From where the Diamonds and Ellis Hannen had come, perhaps that had been tempting fate. But she could not accept that.

She had been away to training college and she had met Kit and somehow these two events had placed her in an equivocal state, between one side of town and the other.

The easy answer, on the face of it, was to do what she was doing now, leave Weyville for good. But of course it was not easy. It was the hardest answer of all. It could finish up with her leaving Kit and causing more political scandal in the process. Every marriage break-up in political life was trumpeted across the papers. She could bear that, she supposed, but it still did not answer why she had to leave him in the first place. Or whether she wanted to.

It was all tied in with the phone calls.

In personal terms, she could not think what she had done to attract such hatred. She was certain that the caller was not Katrina. It could be Jim Diamond, but she did not believe it was her brother's style. Besides, the way Ellis had spoken of Jim made her think that he wished her no harm. Then there was Larissa, who saw herself as having been injured by her aunt. Rose did not think Larissa was capable of such sustained provocation although it was a possibility she could not discount altogether, and there were the girl's friends to consider too. They struck a chord of terror in her, especially Gary.

Essentially, she believed the key must be politics, of one kind or another.

Certainly, here in the dark heart of the desert the recurring echoes in her head were not the personal but the affairs of the nation: the unfettered and now lawless market, the cheap imports made with sweated labour that were closing down businesses, the thousands dismissed from their jobs every week, the ridicule of the unions with whom she and Kit and their friends had once been aligned, the tension which stalked the streets and the ugly face of greed.

If this was what Kit believed in now, then it was time for them to admit to each other that they believed in different things after all, and to be done with each other.

But she was not ready, she decided, to bow out without finding who dogged her footsteps. This was one of the more indefinable shapes of terrorism, the fear within. She glanced behind her in the mirror to check whether she was being followed.

There had been a fight the night before. In the main street of Taupo glass lay in piles in the gutters. It had happened after the pubs shut, and weary and footsore marchers who should have been in bed hours before clashed with local gang members.

Wiki Muru left the march in the morning and was driven back to Weyville by a friend to arrange bail for her son, Matau. His arrest had taken place the previous afternoon, before the fighting broke out. By the time she arrived, her uncle had attended the court and fixed it all up. She picked up her own car and drove fast, heading back towards the marae, hoping that there would be nobody there, the mess in town cleaned up and the march underway again.

Matau sat sullen and uncommunicative beside her. He had large bruises on his chest and forearms where he had tried to protect himself from kicks.

'Did O'Meara do it?'

'I didn't see.'

'They say you ran over that kid.'

'They got no proof.'

'Did you do it?'

'Nah.'

'Don't bloody mess with me. Did you or didn't you?'

'Fucken let me outta here,' screamed her son, tearing at the door handle. She slewed, slowed the car, and braked to a halt.

She looked across at her weeping son and the welt above his eye. *That'll be a beauty*, she said to herself.

'I don't reckon you did,' she said aloud, but gently so as not to scare him away.

Matau had flung the door open and sat with one leg poised over the edge ready to take flight.

'That don't matter, does it.'

'Yes,' she said, forcing her will to communicate with him. 'It's all that matters.'

He put his head on the dash and sobbed. 'They done me over, they done me. They never fucken listened Ma.'

'They never listen full stop,' she said, and her mouth was thin.

At the marae people were milling around in front of the meeting house. Word had come through that the farmers were sloping off back to Weyville. On reflection they felt that few of them could afford the time that it would take to march all the way; besides, they wanted to dissociate themselves from the violence that had taken place and from lawless elements amongst the marchers.

Lyle Warner looked straight past Larry Verschoelt's shoulder into the jewellery shop window in the main street. A shiny black hand held a fan of gold cards. A crystal bull rotated on a stand.

'I saw the light, by God, I did,' Larry said. He leaned against his pick-up.

'Sure,' said Lyle. 'Conversion to the Labour Party's like religion.'

'By God, it is no reason for you to joke. I am a poor man, Mr Warner.'

'Money?' Lyle said incredulously. Blackmail was something that happened to other people.

Larry spat, hitting a slick of oil in the roadway, and thrust his hands into the pockets of his workshorts. 'I saw you gettin' into Harry's missus, Mr Warner.'

The bull twinkled with refracted light. 'How much?'

'Say, ten.'

'Ten grand?'

'I reckon.'

'I don't have it.'

'Aw, you don't?' Larry waved to someone across the street. 'There's a coupla other things I know, Mr Warner. Interesting things. You know what I mean?'

It was lunchtime when Basil slunk in the back door. The teacher had been in touch and Katrina had told him he was not to run off home any more. The kid never listens, she complained to Minna, who was sitting cross-legged on the floor, sewing. She had sewn up seams on Sharna's overall, patched a hole in one of Basil's school jerseys, and now was putting buttons on one of Katrina's blouses.

'You don't mean him to,' said Minna, biting a thread. Her teeth were very even, a little too small for perfection.

'If you must do that, use the scissors,' said Katrina. 'It doesn't need buttons anyway.'

'Are you going to let your tits hang out?'

'Don't be vulgar, I'll wear a singlet under it. Anyway, what do you care?'

'You're a sloppy cow. I'll make Basil some cheese sandwiches.'

The child had crawled under the sofa and was staring out at them with malevolence.

'Did you get into trouble with the teacher?'

'Yes.' He inched out from under the furniture. 'I hate her.'

'She'll hate you if you don't behave, you rotten little sod.'

'Shut up Minna.'

'Somebody should look out for him. Anyway, I'm making him sandwiches, aren't I?'

'You're a priceless little pearl, Minna. So what did your sodding teacher do to you, Bas?'

'What did he do to her? Katrina, I told you not to get this again.' Minna looked disgustedly at the white bread which was all she could find, and started stroking on the margarine.

Basil rocketed into Katrina's arms, sobbing noisily. Minna rolled her eyes.

He had· hardly settled himself in his mother's lap when the coughing began, a deep gasp rising from his chest. He sounded as if he was suffocating.

'Stop.' Katrina shook him. 'Stop crying, you're making yourself sick.'

He burrowed his head against her. In the next room Sharna began to cry. Basil's coughing subsided, but his breathing was loud and spasmodic.

'Jealousy,' said Minna. 'Here, have something to eat.'

Basil shook his head.

'Okay. I don't know why I bothered in the first place.' She opened the rubbish tin.

'Minna, don't.'

Minna's foot paused on the pedal of the bin, her hand poised. Basil's face was beseeching as his mother interceded.

The child stretched out his hand, taking a sandwich, his throat working in small swallowing convulsions before he had bitten into it.

'Did you give him some of the syrup I got?'

'Of course. But it's a bit early for it to do any good.'

'Maybe you shouldn't have sent him to school.'

'The doctor didn't say. Anyway, he's home now.' Katrina nuzzled into Basil's neck smelling him, her mouth hovering over his skin in open-mouthed kisses. 'He tastes like tears,' she said. 'Like salt.'

Minna was still, her eyes glittered. She walked over to the chair where they sat and picked up Basil's hand, licked it.

'It's somebody who knows me very well,' Rose said. 'Someone who's known me for a long time.'

'You're saying that it's someone in the Party.'

'What's left of it. Yes.'

'It could be anyone in the electorate. Not necessarily a member at all.'

'You mean one of the suffering masses? One of the marchers?'

Morris Applebloom uncrossed his legs, and recrossed them, leaning his head back on the wall of the motel. 'The march is off,' he told her. The room smelled of both old and new disinfectant, and cigarette smoke; the television with the sound turned off stood winking in the yellowish embossed corner; outside the sign clinked on a chain that suspended it from a crossbar. Only one other unit in the motel appeared to be occupied and already its light was out; Rose's unit glowed like an aquarium in its isolation.

'Where have you been for the past two days?'

She shook her head, looking around as if not quite believing what she saw, although it was she who had arranged the meeting here.

'You know the police are out looking for you?'

'Why?'

'Don't be naïve. You make me angry when you behave like this. You're living very dangerously and you want me to do the same. What do you think it's cost me to come here?'

'How much?'

'I wasn't talking about money.'

'No. Does Sarah know you're here?'

'Of course she doesn't. She thinks I'm in Wellington . . . seeing Kit. I think.'

'You're playing double games, Morris. You're a fucking hypocrite.'

'So's everybody who goes near this Government. But we still have to live. Rose, the economy's stuffed, the regions are being squeezed to death. The Minister of Finance thinks they can survive without employment. Every damn thing that anyone's tried to start round Weyville has been stymied by junk imports. I know, because the bank carries the can for them. How many unemployed do you know that could run a small business? Could you?

'Shut up, I know. I bloody know.'

'Okay, so what are you doing holed up in a plastic and candlewick motel this side of Taihape? Waiting to flag the trains through? Writing jokes for sweatshirts? *I Spent the Afternoon in Taihape*? They've done that, Rose, you're too late.'

'Shut up.'

'Don't shout. I don't want the management in here.'

'I'll bet you don't.'

'I'll stop them too, so don't try it on with me, Rose. I don't want to be here.'

'Then why did you come?'

He scratched his nose, examined a nylon carnation in a container, and appeared to consider the matter.

She really did want to know. She supposed it was because she had put him on a spot. It seemed as absurd to her that she had rung him, now, as it must appear to him. The further she drove, the more she wished that she had not. All day she had driven this way and that, down the Desert Road, branching off at Waiouru, back towards Ohakune, then doubling back, always with Mt Ruapehu in sight.

She had almost encompassed the mountain since she left home. When he arrived at the motel, she had tried to explain how frightened she had been in the hotel the night before when she had stood holding the dead phone. It was harder to explain why she had thought of him as the safe person whom she might call, a sort of old reflex. Perhaps he would know.

By the time she arrived at the motel she had convinced herself that he would not come. Even so, as she waited, she could not help picturing him gliding through the countryside towards her at a hundred and fifty kilometres an hour in his smooth and silent Renault Turbo.

Eventually, almost jubilant, she had decided that it was definitely too late. When, finally, he did knock on her door, he had been angry.

'What are you doing about the state of the nation?' she asked now, to break the silence. 'Playing the right hand off against the left? Or is it the other way round? You always liked to please everybody, Morris.'

'Trying to work the system, what's left of it. And if that means milking Kit Kendall, and paying him off, that's too bad. I didn't vote for Thatcher's New Zealand, but that's what we've got. And the rest of the Government sits and tells us it'll be all right tomorrow and tomorrow and tomorrow and it never is because they don't know what to do. So I do what I can. I'm even sorry for people I don't like. God help me, I'm sorry for Larry Verschoelt.'

He got up and poured himself a glass of the wine Rose had chilled. She had offered to make a meal. 'I can cook up a steak,' she had said, knowing he wouldn't want to be seen eating out with her even if there was anywhere to go, but he claimed, impatiently, that he had eaten. He walked over and poured wine into the motel tumbler she was holding.

'And what does Kit do?' He stared into the wine without expecting her to reply. 'He sits on the backbench and wrings his hands and says how sad it is and jumps when the whips tell him to jump, and votes the way he's told. And when caucus meets he moves whichever way will most easily save his hide.'

'Is there a plan to stop him getting selected again?'

'Does it matter? Yes, I suppose it does, you wouldn't have any good works to do any more, would you Rose? Not that it matters, the Government'll go down the tubes anyway.'

'Well, that'll be a relief for everybody.'

'You know it won't be. That's not what we wanted. Or would it be for you?'

'The only relief I'll get is when these phone calls stop.'

'Oh yes. Back to the subject of Rose.'

'You don't know what it's like. You can't even begin to imagine. I've even wondered if it was you, Morris.'

'Me? That's ridiculous.' For the first time since arriving at the Sparkle Inn he looked genuinely astonished.

'The phone goes ping when I'm making dinner, just like it used to, that winter when I was seeing you. Only this time there's no reason for the person at the other end to hang up. I don't have to hide from Kit who's thinking of me, because he's not there. This person doesn't want to talk to me, he only wants to frighten me.'

'How do you know it's a him?'

'You sound like Toni... Did a woman slit my dog's throat? What woman? Hortense? Is it Hortense? Belinda?'

'It's not Belinda.'

'Oh, so you know something about Belinda? Have you got something going with her?'

'No I haven't. She's got other things on her mind.'

'Like who?'

'Lyle Warner.'

'You're kidding? Well...how about that. Poor old Toni.' She considered the matter. 'Then again, it could be Toni herself... Is she that good an actress?'

'That's, oh, that's stupid too. Preposterous.'

'Why is it? She knows me well enough. In fact, Toni was the only person who even knew I'd left town. Well, there was a boy that came to the house.' She broke off. She had forgotten Jason. Her head couldn't accommodate so much confusion. Things had seemed clearer during the day; now the muddle was coming back, as bad as ever.

Morris was watching her. He looked troubled, less angry. 'I don't think it's Toni.'

'Nor do I. Not really. Morris, nobody in the world knew I was at that hotel.'

'You're sure of that?'

She hesitated again. 'Well... I don't know. A man called Ellis Hannen saw me down the road. You don't know him. He used to know us, my brother and sister and me, when we were young. He might have seen me go in there. But it wouldn't have been him.'

'Why not?'

'Because...oh, because I know Ellie Hannen.'

'So do I. He runs a bank account.'

'It's too big a coincidence.'

'Although I don't know him well enough to call him Ellie.'

'I haven't talked to him in years. I hadn't really talked to him since the night I met Kit. God knows how many years ago that was.'

'So he does know Kit?'

'Morris, it isn't him.'

'But it might have been, just that once. He might have seen you go in, and thought, I'd like to see Rose Kendall again, for whatever reason, though I must say he doesn't seem your type Rose, and given it a shot just that once. You see what I'm getting at?'

'That it doesn't have to be one person all the time? But it was the person who rings me. I know.'

'You know the silence he makes?' He pushed his fingers into his forehead, tired. 'Or Hannen could have told your brother he'd seen you. An innocent remark.'

'It doesn't add up. Not a random meeting like that.'

'Maybe there are some people you just don't want it to be.'

'So you think it's in my family? As simple as that?'

'What do you think?'

'I've thought till I'm going crazy.' The refrigerator's motor lurched into life, startling them both. She saw him glance at the phone, as if it might ring. She half-wished it would. But somehow, tonight, she did not expect it to, as if the caller would know that she wanted to prove a point. She shivered, recognising that not far from the surface the thought floated that she was being watched, even now. But how could she be? This time nobody, except Morris, could possibly know where she was.

As if reading her thoughts, he said, 'Did you let Kit know where you were?'

'No.'

'He knows the house was broken into.'

'What break-in?'

'Shit. This is too complicated for me.' He hesitated. 'Look, you should let the cops know where you are, anyway.'

'You didn't tell me my house had been broken into.'

'I thought you'd know. Though I can see now . . . well, I didn't think of it, that you wouldn't know.'

'Who told you?'

'Toni.'

'Toni. Jesus, Morris. Did you hear what you just said?'

He stood up. 'Okay, it could be Toni, but maybe it's not, maybe it's not your brother, but it could be either of them, or any of a few hundred other people. I don't know who it is. I grant you've got a problem.'

He put his hand on her shoulder. 'I'm sorry about all this. You could go unlisted.'

'I can't. The electorate.'

'I'd better get going.'

'I know it's not Toni. You see what I mean, though?'

'It's okay.' His hand had stiffened on the nape of her neck; she didn't know why.

'You're not going back to Weyville tonight?'

'You don't want me to stay here?'

She smiled, a wan glimmer in the motel room's ugly light. 'We've stayed in worse.'

She could analyse the exact moment when their affair began to end. I want, he said, after reading The White Hotel, *to go away with you to a place as beautiful as that and sleep with you all night. I want us to throw our rings away and pretend we were never married to anyone else. The trouble was she believed him. Love was an affliction, like dying, something sensible people never wanted to happen to them, but it had happened to her. Conniving and telling lies and making arrangements which he seemed increasingly reluctant to fall in with, she had planned a weekend when they could go away and stay in the same town together. They would stay by a real lake. Their business would be legitimate, thanks to the machinery of the Party. Afterwards she would see how odd it was that she had made all the arrangements without his contribution.*

When it happened, it was not at all like he said. He clung resolutely to his wedding ring, did not tell her that he loved her, and left her near dawn, creeping out into the thin light of morning like any other adulterer. They did not part then, but later when their lovemaking had become at once more energetic and less kind. She had joined him in Auckland where he had gone on business. This was before Kit was elected. She had gone to his room and they had ordered room service, eaten and had a great deal to drink, and it was she who had left by midnight. In the morning he had woken with a hangover and been appalled by the squalor they had left in their wake—trays, dirty plates, bottles, strewn glasses. He rang her at her hotel before she returned home to tell her that he could not handle the worry of it all for the moment, perhaps they should leave things for a little while. The guilt was palpable in his voice.

Of course, as a lover, she did not see him again, although for a long time they saw each other almost every day, at meetings, at parties, or when she visited the bank. Saying goodbye was a pre-emptive strike in a town like theirs. It had been an aberration of the tour, she told herself, when people fell into each other's arms because they were frightened and their lives were in chaos and because, at the same time, there was that dangerous edge of excitement always there, the feeling that anything could happen. She wrote herself lists to comfort herself, steps to get through each day; at first instructions to fill the day between breakfast and lunchtime. Later, lists to run an election campaign. Then lists to run the electorate. One day she wrote a list headed: Factors influencing crisis of guilt (the woman — Factor X — hereafter referred to as she)

the hotel's exit was not clearly enough marked
she wanted to have his baby
his wife had got him to promise they would be buried together
his dick might fall off
(and/or he might catch thrush)
his wife had started vegetarian cooking
he had claimed to have seen Citizen Kane *four times at Film Society and his wife wouldn't wear it a fifth time*
she still wanted to have his baby
he's sensitive to condoms
his wife's sister had married an influential stock market analyst (Rose had seen Maud's marriage in the gossip columns)
his wife wanted to have his baby
she had told her best friend why she was so thin lately
she could see how it was her fault

They both led exemplary lives as far as she could tell, certainly she did. If anyone had asked her, and nobody, not even Toni, did, she would have said that their affair ended not when he woke ashamed in a hotel room, but when he had first promised her a glimpse of something lovely. Not just of pleasure, which was relatively simple, but of that certain danger. Of something Katrina had understood, but she could not.

'We've been drinking and it's late. There're two beds.' She indicated the twin beds in the long concrete-walled room.

'There are three,' he said walking to the door of the second room.

She sat with her hands in her lap. She had already examined the double bed, turning the sheets back and running her fingers over the linen to make sure it had been aired.

'You stayed in my head longer than you were meant to.'

'You never left mine,' he said.

'I was never in it.'

'Oh yes you were.' They looked at each other. He looked away first.

'Sex is a very moral concept for you, Morris.'

'No, love is. You couldn't share it, you're not that kind of person. You want everything.'

'You're talking shit, Morris.'

He was loosening his tie so she guessed he would stay. She continued to sit still. If love was an affliction it was beginning to seem like a pale one. It occurred to her that she could sleep in one of the single beds under the same roof with him. Great step forward for womankind. She tucked that away for future reference.

'I've got a red in the car,' he said.

Not bad, if I can say no she thought while he fetched the wine. A pity the body felt more feeble, more full of longing, than the head. She wished she had given herself more time to decide what she wanted. As if all these years had not been enough.

'We should be watching *Casablanca*,' she commented on his return.

He smiled without replying and opened the wine.

She said, 'Then you could say, *Play it again, Sam* or something like that.' He had brought cheese and some grapes. *Just like a travelling fucking deli* she thought. *Mind your language Rose Kendall it's too much you're just too tired for any more.*

'It's a cult, did you know, like old-time Gothic, how many times you watch it. Some people see it hundreds of times, did you know?' Her voice seemed to babble on from a long way off.

As Morris handed her her glass, he said, 'I have to ask Kit's help to arrange something for me when I see him next. Oh it's nothing much. A building permit, actually.' He smiled, self-deprecating. 'But you must see that I couldn't.'

'Couldn't what?' She heard herself laugh. 'Oh that. Whatever made you think? As if I would. A misunderstanding.'

He sat on one of the twin beds unlacing his shoes. 'God, I'm sorry, I'm so sorry Rose,' he said.

'He thought he was doing himself a favour but he did me one, Ellie.'

They were sitting at a table in the trucking caf at Bulls. 'I tell you what, I'm starved.'

'I've ordered for you.' As Ellis spoke the proprietor, red-eyed from the early morning start, put plates covered with steak, two eggs each and chips in front of them.

'Jeez, Ro, you get yourself tied up with some weirdos. Kendall, and now Applebloom.'

'I'm not tied up with Applebloom.'

'You were, it was all over town a few years back.'

'And Kit's not weird, he's my husband.'

He shrugged. 'That banking chap foreclosed on me once. While ago now. Dunno what he thought he was going to do with my trucks. Asked him once, he said mebbe he'd drive 'em himself.' He polished his knife against his overall and began eating. 'Tell you, Ro, I wouldn't let that joker drive my pig in a perambulator.'

'What happened?'

'Ah.' He sliced an egg and inserted half in his mouth. 'Saw the error of his ways. Think he just wanted to cut me down to size. So much for the working man's friend. He set me back though.'

'Is that why you sold the trucks?'

'Sorta. Less hassle driving for other people.'

'Screw him, which as it happens, which Ellie, as I have mentioned, I did not. Recently,' she qualified.

'I wasn't asking.'

It was easy sitting here in the Manawatu where the shining grasses stretched away from the edges of the town into distance, to laugh at Morris's expense. In the night, though, she had got up and walked through to the kitchenette to get a glass of water. Her mouth tasted like dirty newspaper. He was asleep in one of the single beds. She had looked down at him sleeping. His face was neat and composed, no different from when he ushered clients into his office at the bank. Even his beard hadn't begun to show on the smooth surface of his skin. From the beginning she had admired the way he confounded her expectations of his role, his busy sturdy sexuality, the compact perfection of it all. This was what she had wanted. He stirred in his sleep—*What is it?*—turned over, looked at her, his eyes open. *You can't play the system if you don't believe in it.*

That's no better than Kit, she said. He closed his eyes again. *It's all chaos*, he said then, as if he had been talking in his sleep, as if he were dreaming. *Actually it's a joke*, she replied, although he couldn't hear her. She put the jar of pickled bums where he would see them when he woke up.

In the morning when he was leaving she asked, 'Is it you who's to be the alternative candidate, then?' He was closing his briefcase in the back of the car and appeared not to have heard her.

Now she sat turning her hand towards the light so that it caught reflections on her topaz ring, unearthed from the drawer before she left home. What she had never told anyone, not even Kit, was that she had taken the ring once to get it valued and the jeweller had laughed in an embarrassed regretful way when he returned it to her. Although the gold filigree was good, and certainly antique, the stone was glass, maybe even beer bottle glass, although it was a cunning imitation. Maybe, about the time of the Depression, someone had had the stone removed and this put in its place. It seemed like the kind of joke Ellis might enjoy but she decided not to tell him.

'I think there's a plan afoot to get Morris selected in place of Kit at the next election,' she said instead.

'They're really taking the right on board.'

'They think they'll move the Party back to the left.'

Ellis looked incredulous, then he began to laugh. 'If that's Weyville's version of the left wing, God help socialism.'

'What do you know about politics?'

He stopped laughing. 'About as much as you do.'

When she looked injured, he grinned. 'Think about it,' he said. 'Anyway, you know I'm right.'

A woman hurried in and sat at a table nearby. She glanced at her watch with annoyance as if she was running late for an appointment. Her hair was sleek and shiny brown and she wore a wedding ring. By the cut of her suit Rose would have said she was a businesswoman of some kind, although it was hard to see her in the context of the Bulls caf. Rose thought she might be twenty-five or so, although when she studied her in what she hoped was a covert fashion, for she had almost run out of things to say to Ellis and what there was left to ask was difficult, she decided she was closer to thirty. Maybe even older. The woman ordered breakfast and took some notes out of a briefcase. She studied them as she waited for her meal and when it came she continued to look at them, frowning as she did so, putting her fork down between rapid mouthfuls in order to scribble on the papers. Rose wondered how she could be so thin and eat so much. A folder on the table bore the words VISUAL DISPLAY UNITS. Everyone seemed to be into computers these days. Rose wondered how difficult it was to learn about them. Toni said they were a living and strictly to be ignored if you could. Technological, unfortunately essential, high-tack. She left them all to Lyle.

'How did you find me?' Rose asked Ellis, losing interest in the woman. It was the question she would have to ask sooner or later.

'Heard the cops were looking out for you. Bit hard to miss you on the main road south in that piebald contraption of yours, seeing I'm on the road all the time. Followed you on down here from the motel.'

'You going to ring the cops?'

'Figured you'd do that yourself.'

'I already have.'

He nodded, drank some of the rank hot coffee they had been served.

'So you are running away?'

She introduced a note of caution. 'I'm going to Wellington. To Kit. My husband the weirdo.'

'Taken a long time getting there.'

'I'm not running away. Just moving on. I've had some scary times. I'm taking charge. Um, Ellie, about Morris.'

'Applebum?' He drew a line across his throat with his forefinger.

Part II

★

7

The Minister clasped his hands and swung around in his swivel chair. Beyond him lay Wellington Harbour. Below were the docks and a tangle of railway lines leading out of the city towards the faultline. The bronze-tinted double-glazed glass of the Beehive window glinted with wintry sun. Rex Gamble considered his tastes aesthetic; the walls of his office were covered with a mixture of paintings from overseas as well as leading New Zealand artists while the wall of books behind him reflected an interest in Florentine architecture. A tall slim man, he swam six lengths of the Beehive pool each morning. If he could only stop smoking he would consider himself an example to his colleagues.

Still, he comforted himself, this single vice kept him lean, protecting him from the ravages not just of State banquets but the insidious daily intake of a Bellamy's diet. He wore an unadorned white shirt, a neat lemon tie, black shoes and black socks with his light grey suit. He joked to press photographers about getting his 'good side' in such a way that nobody believed (at least, at the time) that he was serious. Usually they aimed for the left which had a serious, just discernible crease. Once a week he walked up the Terrace to get his slightly longer than fashionable hair and his very blond beard trimmed at the Razor's Edge and marvelled each time that this was a country in which Cabinet Ministers could walk around the streets to the barber of their choice without a bodyguard. But recently he had been going in late afternoon when the crowds were thickest and he could mingle less conspicuously amongst them. Or so he hoped. There was a general twitchiness around the corridors these days. Unfortunately the public always recognised him; there was a price to pay for his appearance. And the Press Gallery had him down for a marked man, especially when he dined out.

He looked at his watch. He had meant to ask his secretary to order him a table for two at Le Petit Lyon but on second thoughts there was a delegation in town which could be eating there tonight. Il Casino was his preference, but his ministerial colleague Mike Moore ate there too often for comfort. In the end he would almost certainly have to settle for wine in a BYO canvas carrybag and throw himself again on the mercy of his newest girl—he corrected himself mentally, newest woman friend's cooking. She cooked well, that was not the problem, but his driver had parked outside her house for three nights out of the last four and the ministerial car was becoming obvious in the street.

In the meantime, he awaited Kit Kendall's visit with growing impatience. Until that was over he could make no private phone calls. As a second-fiddle minister in a Government already eyeing others with constant suspicion, he was not about to give indications of clandestine communication, personal or professional, to back-benchers. He was not at all certain how he would fare in a Cabinet reshuffle. His portfolio was small enough as it was.

★

Kit had, in fact, delayed the meeting simply by dawdling. He more or less knew why Gamble wanted to see him, and he had no answers. He excused himself from the rimu-panelled debating chamber, turning to bow to the Speaker, and retreated down the gangway. A debate on estimates was adequately covered; the Press Gallery was almost empty. Kit took the marble staircase, forgoing the clanking lift, stopped to chat with the tour guides and a messenger, and finally made his way to the covered access that joined the old Parliament Buildings and the Beehive area. He crossed the balcony above the Calvert mural. A party of some kind was going on in the foyer below, perhaps a book launching, the sort of gathering that had been popular when the Government first took power. Every minister was jumping on literary bandwagons then and launching anything from atlases to slim volumes of poetry; the place crawled with women dressed in downbeat black, sporting Katherine Mansfield haircuts, and middle-aged men in jeans who called on embossed accents to order their drinks, a sprinkling of suits, a panama hat or two, and a number of greenstone pendants. It was a similar scene today. The gathering gravitated towards trays of sausage rolls cut in half, club sandwiches and marinated drumsticks of No. 9 Tegels. There was rarely enough alcohol for even the most ambitious drinker to start falling over, but a younger man than usual, with multi-studded ears, was trying to climb the marble stairway on the opposite side of the foyer. As Kit leaned on the railing watching a security guard restrain the unruly visitor a wave of envy swept over him.

He had written a book once, a textbook on *dothistroma pini*, a disease which attacked pine trees; its presence had been noted in

New Zealand by a scientist in the 1960s. Kit's book was intended to be definitive; it had taken him years to write and he reckoned on new discoveries about the spread of the disease along the way, but the topic was exhausted by the time he finished the manuscript. Sometimes, although he did not mean to, he blamed Rose for the length of time it had taken him. There were so many family commitments and obligations to fulfil, so much parent togetherness with the children to be honoured. He had almost wished they had not been so bright, so able. It would have been a relief, perhaps, to have had average hard-working children who made their way through the system and got steady average jobs at the end of it. Instead, he and Rose were saddled from the beginning with the knowledge that their children were university material, would go places, demand sacrifices beyond broken nights and hardship. Or, knowing what Olivia's and Richard's potential was, that he could have hidden it from people like his parents, who hung with delight and pride on the achievements of their grandchildren, as they had once done on his and his brother's.

His brother had never married. These children were 'all they had', as they reminded him, not just now and then, but constantly, in letters and phone calls and on visits. Cherish these creatures who are our hope of immortality. Let them be free spirits but make sure they are spirits in our own image. He remembered how daunted they were by Rose on her first arrival. She had worn too much make-up and too-pointed brassières and stiletto heels and she was so nervous she could hardly speak, just sat turning a large ring which if he hadn't known better he would have said was paste (and the gold looked good). If she had not had a teacher's certificate his mother might not have made such a determined effort to be nice, and then to her surprise she had found that she liked Rose, and before long the idea had taken hold that she would be the ideal person for Kit to marry, as if it was she who had discovered her and not him. She had never been disappointed.

Now they, his parents, were dead and he was richer (or at least he had spent their money on assets), and so were the children, and they had gone, and when he went home, after first getting elected, Rose would cry at night. He sometimes wanted to cry too, not for them, but himself. He would never write another book, or save another tree except as a Sunday horticulturalist. It was impossible to tell where the time had gone. If it was personal achievement which he craved, he supposed that he must be fulfilled in this as a parliamentarian, but his parents had missed even that, and anyway, they had been astute enough in life to have heard the victory turn hollow had they lived (his father had asked at least once a month when the book would be coming out up until a year before he died when he stopped without warning and did not mention it again).

Kit went to Weyville much less often now that Rose had come to live in Wellington and refused to go back north with him; a situation which was making his life both difficult and embarrassing. His electorate 'surgeries' were virtually boycotted; he had cut them down from once a week, when first elected, to once a fortnight; he paid Harry Ryan a retainer out of his own pocket to open the office in between times — he slept at Harry's place, too, now that Belinda had left him. Even though the filthy mess in the Kendalls' house had been cleaned up after the break-in, he didn't have the heart to stay there. 'People are saying you've left me,' he complained to Rose. 'How can they say I've left you, when I've come to live with you?' she said, smiling.

Rose didn't cry at night any more, or, in fact, at all. She gazed with seeming serenity at him each morning across the pottery coffee mugs she had bought at Clayshapes. Sometimes she seemed like a still centre that he could not penetrate. At other times she looked around her with an appraising eye. He knew that she was thinking how small their Hataitai flat was, and she was quite right; it was suffocating him.

Without her it had been idyllic.

Gamble believed in monetarism; the more the Minister of Finance's policies came under fire as the second term of the fourth Labour Government staggered on, the more enthusiastically Gamble embraced them, or so it appeared to observers. But the unease on the Government benches had not escaped him. Backbenchers, who never, in their wildest dreams, had believed that they would be sent to power by their blue-ribbon electorates in 1984, saw their constituents turn against them with lightning speed. Many had given up jobs which would have progressed satisfactorily had they stayed in them; now they saw themselves facing unemployment after the next election. Kit Kendall had, reputedly, been a competent scientist who 'got on' with people. Rex Gamble supposed he would have been the head of a minor branch of a government department by now. Four years later it was unlikely that he would ever be re-employed by that department again.

Gamble had been, and still was, a businessman. The sharemarket crash had left him shaken but intact. His interests were widely spread. Any shrewd operator, he believed, could have covered himself against the inevitable. He called it business acumen. Political commentators called it being in the know, observations he shrugged aside. But he was uneasy, worried about the infighting in caucus, and within the Party itself. With enough support he was certain the loony left, as he thought of their opponents, would renege on the deals the Government had in place. The Prime Minister was waivering on sales of the nation's assets; there was talk of more benefit handouts, and the country was still in the grip of the unions. Gamble shuddered to think of spiralling wage rounds. And a change in direction would inevitably spell the end of his own political career, in much the same way that Kendall and his like already faced ruination. It was a fine line they all walked.

He leaned across his desk, favouring Kit with a long scrutiny, as if inviting an exchange of candour. 'Where was your wife for those two days?'

'Taking time out. Well, that was how she explained it to me.'

'I see.' He looked sad. 'I understand the Prime Minister is having second thoughts about you sitting on the Select Committee on Internal Security.' He tapped the file on his desk with meaning.

'I'm not a security risk.'

'I don't think you are. I'd like you to sit on the committee. It would be bad news if you didn't.'

'It would be a public scandal. I might as well resign. You don't need to tell me.'

'I don't want you to resign.'

Too right, he didn't, Kit thought, seeing it all.

'If your good lady wife could just explain a few details about those missing days,' Gamble was saying. He opened the file. 'You see, there were these people she met along the way.'

'She was upset. Someone had been giving her the hang-up treatment rather a lot.'

'No voice phone calls. The weapon of the 'eighties. Well we all get those.'

'They were driving her . . . well, she couldn't take much more.'

'Do they bother you much?'

'I don't get them.'

Gamble looked pained.

'And then our dog's throat was slit,' said Kit hurriedly. 'She was pretty frightened. And our house was broken into.'

'But that was after she left, I understand.'

'What are you saying? Look, there was paint stripper thrown on her car. She couldn't have done that. I know she didn't do that.' But his voice was uncertain.

'Then there were the marchers.'

'Oh, the marchers. Well, you know that didn't come to much. It was full of crooks, that march.'

'A handful of them did turn up in the end, as I recall.'

'Half a dozen. I saw them in my office.' Stung, he said, 'But there were some good people amongst them. Wiki Muru is a fine person.' It eased his heart to say this.

'Mrs Muru, oh yes. But she didn't finish the march.'

'Well no. Her son was up on a charge at the time.'

'What did he get?'

'Three years.'

The silence deepened. It was getting dark out in the city. In the outer offices the secretaries were putting on their coats, preparing to descend the circular tower by the lifts and pour out into the street towards their buses and trains, their families and bedsits.

'Your wife met some people on her way south. She spent the night with . . . an old friend of hers.' Gamble hoped that his voice was suitably compassionate.

Kit flushed scarlet, turned away until his blush had subsided. He had never coped well with embarrassment. 'I cannot afford to antagonise Applebloom,' he said carefully, wishing to hide any trace of surprise. He was not even sure that he was correct but it was a guess that rose instinctively to his lips. The worst thing would be that he was wrong and that she had found someone else.

But Gamble was nodding sympathetically. 'I can see that. Very sensible of you, old chap.' Kit noticed that he did not close the file. 'Really, it confirms my opinion that you're above reproach as far as this committee is concerned. I would hope that I could handle such a . . . delicate matter as, well, as decently as you.'

Fat chance that he would need to, Kit thought. Gamble always cut and run from his marriages before they turned messy.

'There's just one other matter to clear up.' Gamble looked back at the typed-up notes in front of him. Soon it would be too dark to see, but the Minister made no move to turn on the lights. 'She met a communist on that journey. An infiltrator of the old school.' He smoothed the sheaf of paper.

Kit shook his head. 'No. That can't be right.'

'Not once but twice. A truck driver.'

'Hannen? Not Hannen.'

'She went straight from her... I know this is painful, her tryst at the motel—I must say I thought Applebloom could have afforded better, your wife paid, incidentally, in cash—to a meeting with Hannen just over an hour later.'

Kit stood up and walked over to the window, although this was not entirely protocol. He looked out across the harbour where a swell was developing and rows of whitecaps marched across the edge of the wind. 'I wouldn't have thought it.'

★

The office was on the fifth floor of the old DIC Building, now trendily renamed Harbour City Centre, on Lambton Quay. The lift was lined with a pale greenish carpet that spread beyond to the floors in the building. There was often a man with a dog in the lift. When Rose stepped out the only sound was the steady rustle of water behind the varnished door marked Men's Toilets. Arched windows admitted filtered light. Lilac and sepia tiles lined the passage walls to shoulder height for what seemed like miles. Rooms leading off bore a strange anonymity, although the doors were discreetly lettered with the names of doctors, dentists, gem dealers (she saw destitute women in the latter offering to trade their engagement rings), opticians and accountants. And Buff Daniels.

It was like going to an analyst.

'I've made some charts,' said Buff Daniels. The private investigator did not look like Colombo, or Jack Nicholson in *Chinatown*. In a city of civil servants the small gingery man would have passed for one.

'See, critical path analysis.' He had lined up papers that had fed out of a computer. They were covered with names.

'We line up the possibilities. Match events. Take this one... your former students.'

'I really don't think... it's so long since I taught.'

'Grudges can resurface when kids get older. Especially with your connections. We've been through that.' He looked at her as if she was being recalcitrant. He had been famous for divorce cases when adultery still mattered, got famous tracking a runaway company director to Port Moresby in the 'seventies, and specialised in high-class family feuds. He was reputed to be able to smell who sold the family silver by the time he drove up a tree-lined driveway.

'You're really keen on this line?'

Buff walked around his charts. The names of Rose's family and friends and all the people she could think of whom she had ever known stared back at her.

She stood shaking her head. 'I can't make the connections,' she said.

★

'But that's what I've done,' Toni said. She was kneeling on the floor of the Hataitai flat surrounded by paper.

The spread sheets didn't look much different to the ones Buff Daniels had made, but they listed some names Rose had forgotten.

'How did you do that?'

'Nick did them.'

'Nick Newbone? You told him?'

'He was the only person I trusted to make up the charts.'

'It seems like you've told everyone in Weyville, Toni.'

Toni shot her a look. Perhaps, Rose thought, she will say something about the Appleblooms, but of course she didn't and Rose couldn't ask.

'Stick to the point,' said Toni. 'Look, my charts are better than his. We've arranged them by streets and occupations.'

'How did you do that?'

'With the electoral rolls.'

'Toni, you're clever.'

'I know. Then we've broken them down into shift workers.'

Rose studied the charts. 'Yes, so you have . . . we talked about that, didn't we?'

'There *are* patterns in the times they ring.'

'Have you worked them out?'

'Consistent for a week, maybe two weeks, then there's a break.'

'A nurse?'

'No nurses in Power Street. Where the phone box is. The one they traced the call to.'

'It wouldn't be the same street,' said Rose, catching on. 'Surely he wouldn't make the calls in the street where he lived. Maybe when he's passing on his way home from somewhere. Wherever that is.'

'I think it's the same street. Or very close. It's miles to another phone box.'

'A nurse would know how to slit a dog's throat. It was a tidy job.'

'Mill workers live over there.'

'Newspaper workers do shifts. Association of ideas, huh?'

'You mean Matt or Hortense?'

'No I didn't. Did I? I don't know. Let's have some lunch. Let me dress up and we can go out. We'll get a taxi so we don't have to park. You look good already, Toni. You look a million dollars.'

She did too. She was dressed in a green frock that hugged her hips and flared out around the knees. Her black hair was cut even shorter. Her energy permeated the tiny flat. She had flown from Weyville the day before to attend a conference on school boards—'not that I'm sure they'll work,' she muttered darkly to Rose, 'but we've got to get into them, not that I'm talking politics, don't get me started.'

Though they had spoken of the Prime Minister's illness, with the same intense fascination that was sweeping the country. 'Do you think he'll die?' Toni had said even as she stepped through the door. 'He'll be a martyr like Norman Kirk, I wonder if he'll have a state funeral.' 'He's getting better,' Rose had said, 'he can't die now,' and Toni had retorted, 'Well, maybe it would be better if he did, he doesn't seem to be doing anything else, does he?'

'I don't mind staying here,' Toni was saying. 'Honestly. Anyway, I'm booked on the 1.30 plane. Lyle minded the kids yesterday after school.'

The flat consisted of a living area, two very small bedrooms and a bathroom. Kit and Rose slept in one of the bedrooms in a bed that almost filled it. Some nights Kit came in late and slept in the other bedroom on a stretcher. He had installed a desk in this room. In the early mornings, when Rose brought him tea after one of these late sessions, she would find him sitting at the desk, apparently working on papers that were piled on it. Quite often it looked as if he was moving them from one side of the desk to the other. She remembered her neat little piles in the desk she had commandeered from her daughter. She wondered sometimes if Harry was answering any of the letters these days. Kit never asked her to answer any mail. Once she had found a card from a psychiatrist propped against the teapot on the breakfast bar where she would find it. She had wrapped it up with the potato peelings.

The living area opened through sliding doors on to a tiny balcony. All around the flat they could see the sea below them: Evans Bay where the yachts were moored lay to their right; the city stood across the water to their left, the lights shining in tracks over the waves at night like the raiments of priests. Over the bay a white luminous monument to a dead prime minister loomed on a headland jutting out to sea. Some days the sea was the colour of hydrangeas, on others—like today—it was salad green and stirring all the time under a grey sky. There were days when it was as much as she could manage to contend with the sky. The flat stood in the flight path of planes landing and taking off from the airport, depending on the wind. Today it was a northerly and the roar of jets taking off into the wind drowned out their conversation every few minutes.

'Okay, so I'll ring someone to pick up the kids.'

'Sarah would do that for you.' Testing the water. Sarah would confide in Toni if she was unhappy or worried or thought that Morris had acted strangely. But then, she reminded herself, it was months since his mysterious absence. Knowing Morris it probably hadn't caused a ripple.

She tidied up the bench with her back to Toni. They had been drinking coffee ever since Toni turned up unannounced on the doorstep with her computer printouts. Rose had asked Toni where she had stayed the night before, but she was evasive. Now Toni consulted a notebook.

'So why didn't you get in touch?' Rose asked, pursuing the silence. 'We could have gone to a show. I tell you Toni, I'm not going to let the grass grow under my feet here.'

'The meeting took ages to wind down.' Toni put on a black jacket and walked through to the bathroom to admire the effect. 'I like it here. It's quiet, apart from the planes.'

'Eight minutes to the middle of the city.'

Because they were calling out to each other over a jet, it took both of them a moment to hear the phone. Rose had finished the dishes and gone into the bedroom to change.

'Let it ring,' Rose called. 'I've left phones behind.'

But the phone kept on. On the seventeenth ring Toni said, 'Rose that's driving me crazy,' and picked it up.

Rose came out of the bedroom wearing pantyhose and a slip.

'I shouldn't stay,' Toni was saying. 'But why not? Why don't we? Rose wants to go out. We'll meet you at five . . . at the Oak Bar, okay? . . . I'll make her.' She looked at Rose. 'It's Nick Newbone, he's in town too.'

Rose shook her head violently, but Toni said goodbye and hung up. Rose said, 'Are you seeing Nick?'

'Don't be small town, Rose. That's what you said you'd left Weyville for.'

'Sex is pretty universal, isn't it? The only difference in this town is condoms. They tell me they're making a comeback.'

Toni's hands shook slightly on the page she was running her finger over. 'Let's say it's political wherever it happens.'

'Problems on the home front?'

'Everyone's got problems. No, I'm not seeing Nick, as you so delicately put it. Speaking of problems, why did you let that phone ring? Rose, tell me? Can't you answer phones any more? Hey, are you telling me the phantom's moved down here? Rose, I've been doing all this work...'

'The phantom moves around. The phantom was here for a week, and he's gone away again. I thought I was safe.'

'When? How long ago?'

'It stopped ten days ago. He knows my address, of course. He sends me a letter now and then.' She opened the cutlery drawer and slid out a pile of letters from underneath the plastic compartment tray. 'Weyville postmark. Auckland postmark. And in the week he was phoning up again, no postmark. Dropped by and put one in the letterbox. Next day I was in the village at the hot bread shop and he popped it under the windscreen wipers while I slipped in and bought a French roll, a farmyard loaf and six doughnuts because I thought Kit was coming home that night and he likes doughnuts so I bought him some. I remember itemising everything in that brown paperbag while I sat there, and the piece of paper, which I had thought was a parking ticket, looked through the glass right back at me. Then I saw that handwriting, very careful plain writing, almost printing. Sometimes he uses a typewriter, but he can't have had one here, so he printed in the same writing that he uses to sign the letters. A Friend. Someone Who Keeps An Eye On You. Oh, by the way, Kit didn't come home that night. I ate all the doughnuts myself.'

'What does Kit say about these?' Toni turned an envelope over with distaste.

'I haven't told Kit. You could say Kit's and my relationship is on the big dipper.' She pulled her dress down over her head and slipped her feet into a pair of shoes that had been lying under the sofa.

'You were humouring me.' Toni gestured at her charts.

'It's being taken care of, okay?' Rose bundled the papers up into a rough ball and threw them in a corner of the room. 'It's not happening, Toni.'

'But it is.'

'Not to you. To me. I don't want to see Nick Newbone tonight, either. He happens in Weyville, not here. Now what are you going to do?'

Toni hesitated, deciding whether or not to walk out. 'We've always been friends, you and me.'

'Yes.'

She gestured, not wanting to make the break. 'We'll have lunch and I'll catch the 5.30.' Her mood changed and she laughed. 'There, compromise.'

'You'll stand Nick up.'

'Stand him up? No, I won't. It was you he was ringing.'

Across town in his office, Kit was talking to Alan Smart. Smart was a senior backbencher whose father had worked on the wharves and been locked out during '51. Alan had been twenty then and marched with his father. Diligent, and unswerving to his socialism, it was difficult to see why he had never been elevated to Cabinet. Some said he was of more use as a prod to straggling consciences where he was. The other view was that the new right had blackballed him.

Smart said, 'The Prime Minister's going to need all the support he can get when he comes back to the House.'

'If he does.'

'He's not dead yet. Where do you stand?'

'I don't think I need answer that.'

'Why not?'

'I would have thought my loyalty was obvious.'

'Yes, that's what I'm getting at.'

'Look, there isn't going to be a showdown with the Finance Minister.'

'You're sure of that?'

Kit hesitated. 'If there was, he'd win it hands down.'

'And if he does, the Government loses the next election.'

'That's simplistic.'

'Aren't you reading your electorate, Kit?'

Kit yawned and looked at his watch. He was due to meet Rex Gamble for lunch.

Toni wanted to eat Italian but La Spaghettata was booked out with a crowd from the university. They walked up past James Smith's and Toni spotted a canary-yellow felt stetson with a black band round it displayed in the window and declared it was exactly what she had always wanted. She went straight in and bought it. On the track of Italian now, they fought their way along Courtenay Place, planning to turn right up Cambridge Terrace to Ferruccio's. The wind buffeted them from behind and sideways.

'I should have bought a piece of chin elastic.' Toni clutched the hat.

'We should have caught a bus.' Rose huddled into her coat. But she lengthened her stride. She liked it here, this end of town in particular: New Season's Muttonbirds, the Women's Place bookshop, the urn with the child's face over the Bar-B-Q-King Restaurant, the green and red Shanghai, even the Courtenay Place bus shelters where the pay phones hardly ever worked and the drunks hung out and slept on mattresses and fought. These were people and things she could see. Fashion and violence, which seemed more dictatorial than even Auckland's self-evident hedonism, left her more uncertain. 'The constellations are falling apart,' someone had said at a party the week before, 'Odd things are happening, people are slitting each other's throats for leather jackets, there's traffic jams composed entirely of left-hand drive brothel cars, we spend our lives talking to each other on our answerphones and never hearing the real voice.' (It had occurred to her then that what she needed, had always needed, was an answerphone; Kit said it was an unwarranted expense when people could always leave messages for him at Parliament. But that was not what she meant.) The people she met owned futon beds, bidets, personalised number plates, told stories to themselves aloud in public, talked about the decline of kiwifruit, deplored the rise of the white backlash and the numbers of Greeks who drove Rollers, belonged to the Diet Clinic, made excuses for sending their children to private schools, and believed that couple togetherness could cause stress. Well, amen to that.

Beneath it all ran the ongoing fear of the big one, the earthquake that would kill them all. Sometimes as she walked she thought she could see the lurch in the shining earth coming towards her but then she would decide that it was simply her own unstable heart.

When Rose and Toni were seated in the restaurant, dense with Chanel No. 19—grassy perfumes were in this winter—Rose saw Alan Smart's wife, Mary, at the next table. She was lunching with the wife of an Opposition member who played Tag war games at the weekends. They were holding transistor radios to their ears. That was another thing Wellington people always seemed to be doing, as if they could not bear to go without their fix of news. Mary Smart looked grave. The other woman gave a slight excited squeal. 'He's having an operation on his *heart*,' she cried.

'Did you hear that?' Toni muttered. 'They're talking about the Prime Minister.' Mary Smart caught Rose's eye.

'A meeting of the political wives' support group,' she cried when Rose introduced Toni. 'Do join us.' A waiter opened their second bottle of wine.

'Some other time, but thanks.' Rose studied the menu.

At another table a young woman with neat brown hair sat alone trying not to look conspicuous. She studied a folder of notes from a briefcase. There was something familiar about her.

'Alan Smart's all right, isn't he?' Toni said, when they were eating pasta. 'What's wrong with his wife?'

'Nothing. I think she's quite straight. It's who she's with. You can never tell for sure who stands for what in this town.'

'I don't know if you can anywhere.' For a moment Toni's voice was bitter.

'What's the matter? Why are you really here, Toni?' She thought Toni was going to tell her something, the way her eyes clouded.

Toni shook her head backwards and forwards as if denying something to herself. 'Nothing,' she said at last.

Later, in the women's room, the Opposition member's wife came in behind them, her complexion glassy.

'How long is it since you've been sick at lunchtime?' she said to Rose in passing.

★

'So where does Kit stand?' Rose had collected the Metro, now sleekly navy-blue again, and driven Toni out to the airport.

'Why don't you ask him.'

'We have. He just waffles. The branch is split right down the middle.'

'I know there's a plan to get rid of him,' said Rose.

Toni looked away, embarrassed.

Now was the moment for her to speak of Morris. Rose waited.

'They did ask someone. But I'm not sure that he'll do. The person's an opportunist, just like all the rest.'

'You mean, no better than Kit?'

They were talking doublespeak. Rose was about to say, forget it, when Toni added, 'The branch is like all the rural electorates, you know. They thought they were going with the left, but now that it's turned out to be the right and they're running scared, they'll simply run further to the right. They don't know what they want.'

'Well thanks for telling me, anyway.'

'So where do you stand, Rose? Have you decided yet?'

'On my own,' said Rose.

Toni leaned against the wall by the airport bookstall. Outside, they had seen the Friendships rock dangerously on the tarmac as they passed the wire; wind, still rising, had snatched their breaths in the carpark.

'Remember the tour, Rose?'

'All the time.' And for a moment that seemed true. Maybe it was true. You clasped one moment of history, she had thought, and it became your yardstick, your touchstone by which you measured all the rest of your life. Sometimes she could hardly remember the time between, from 1981 till now. That unity had carried her for years. But it hadn't lasted, and she and Kit were to blame. It was the loneliest feeling in the world.

Toni's voice was quiet beside her. 'Rose, when you left town I got scared. I had this crazy feeling I wasn't going to see you again.'

'Well there you are. You've seen me. Shows how crazy you can get.'

Nick Newbone ordered his second beer. He hadn't intended to stay in town for the evening. He had meant to go home to his wife Hortense who, to their mutual sorrow, remained childless. Well, he supposed it was still mutual, Hortense no longer discussed the subject with him. She denied the need for comfort and he had almost come to believe her. The soft toys in the spare bedroom had been put away in Kleensaks in the garage. There were so many other things one could do without children, he heard Hortense say.

Still, Nick always went home.

It was six o'clock and he did not know why he had been so easily persuaded to stay in Wellington overnight. The Oaks was filling up with out-of-work actors, underworked stockbrokers and a cross-section of rebels without a cause. He smiled at himself. Showing his age, he supposed. He brushed at his shoulderpads and wished he had worn a better jacket. But it seemed clear that he was going to spend the evening alone.

He looked at his watch. Once he would have phoned up his local Member; maybe they would have gone out on the town, or he would have gone down to the House if it was in session and listened to the debate. It was no longer appropriate. Besides, Kit Kendall's wife was supposed to be here.

A woman with a briefcase smiled pleasantly at him. She had straight shiny brown hair. He felt the old familiar panic which possessed him when the unknown presented itself. Certain that he could not refuse the overture, he motioned to the chair beside him, resolving not to get picked up.

★

At the Cobham Drive/Evans Bay Road intersection, with the traffic built up in four directions, Rose turned at the lights to head past the boat marina and home, but the ministerial car heading towards her failed to stop on the red. Even as she felt the impact she had seen Rex Gamble seated in the back.

She found a place to park through the intersection and waited for the beige car with Crown numberplates to pull in behind her on the next change of lights.

The daylight was almost gone and the streetlights had just come on. In the dim light she examined the driver's side where the limousine had hit. The damage was not great. Thank God for heavy traffic, she thought, even a speeding chauffeur could hardly have driven her off the road. But the Metro's paint job was another write-off.

The Minister's car pulled in; it had a broken headlight.

The chauffeur got out of the car. 'Silly bit of driving, if you ask me.' His voice was high and nasal.

'I had the green.' She looked for Rex Gamble, but he was nowhere to be seen. It occurred to her that he might be injured and was flooded with panic.

'Is he all right?'

'Is who all right?' The chauffeur was becoming querulous.

'Rex. Mr Gamble.'

The chauffeur looked mutinous, and took out a pad. 'I've got your number,' he said, writing quickly. 'It'd make it a lot easier if you gave me the details now. We can just send the bill.'

'The bill?' Glancing across his shoulder she saw movement in the back of the car. 'I'm not paying for anything.'

Stalking along the path, she wrenched open the back door of the ministerial car. A hand shot up to push down the lock, but she was there first.

Rex Gamble was lying the full width of the car floor. He looked up at her and giggled.

'Rose, how lovely to see you. I was taking a nap.' He called out to the driver. 'Lennie. What seems to be the problem?'

He uncurled himself from the floor and peered out across the front seat at Rose's car.

'What a pity, Rose. Send the bill to the Public Service Garage will you. We'll attend to it.'

'Thank you, Rex,' she heard herself say.

'Lennie, be a dear boy and hurry, I must get that plane.'

Lennie jerked the car door out of Rose's hand and slammed it shut. Rex Gamble pulled his knees up under his chin on the back seat of the car. As Lennie prepared to take off at speed, one headlight swaying wildly, Gamble crooked his forefinger from under his chin and wiggled it at Rose.

8

The mail was late but then it often was in Hataitai. Rose supposed it must be the hilly terrain that made it hard for the posties to deliver early in the day. Anyway, the mail services seemed to be a shambles. Everyone said so.

Well nearly everyone. She did not deliver this opinion in the company she kept with Kit. They dined frequently with the heads of the new state-owned corporations, usually men with glossy faces who wore a lot of gold and commuted almost daily between Auckland and Wellington, business class. Only one or two, like the head of the new forestry corporation, were older men who had survived the shake-up. They were prone to long silences that appeared to hide a yearning anxiety about the social cost of their activities, and rushes of conversation to cover what in other company might pass for conscience. Kit avoided this latter breed, if he could, but sometimes Rose would find herself seated by one of them at dinner.

She probed, without much success, over the obligatory chicken breasts. Persistence sometimes paid off. By the time they got to the mousse, there would be dreary admissions. Yes, some people were out of work in Kaingaroa, and yes, Murupara, and well yes, Weyville too. But it was a challenge. It was up to the people to meet it. Then, over coffee, the conversation would move on to prospects for increased privatisation while Rose fell silent or engaged in discussion with the woman nearest to her about children and exam prospects or successes. Failures were seldom mentioned. She had yet to meet one of the new postal bosses, but when she did she thought she might raise the subject of postal deliveries.

For the second time she walked up to the gate in the drizzling rain. Olivia had not written for a fortnight. The last time her letter had been full of complaints about where she was going to stay in the August holidays if Rose was not at home in Weyville. As her daughter had spent the minimum possible amount of time at home in the past three years, this came as a surprise. Now, she said, the prospect of Wellington did not appeal to her and anyway Daddy had said that there wasn't really room in the flat. This was the first Rose had known of such an exchange between them, but so far she had not commented on it to Kit. When she wrote back she had told Olivia that they could probably make room in the flat, but if she was quite set against Wellington then there was no reason why she could not stay at home in Weyville, provided she had a friend with her.

After she had sent this letter she had worried about it for days, feeling certain that Olivia would interpret it as a suggestion that she was not responsible for herself. Three times since then she had tried to phone her at the flat in Dunedin but she was never in. No doubt she would decide her mother was neurotic (if Kit had not already suggested this) if she said she was worried about her being in the house on her own, but at least if Rose voiced her fears in so many words, it might convince Olivia that her mother was not treating her like a child.

There were two letters and one of them was from Olivia. What she said, in effect, was that she had spoken to Daddy on the phone and he was sure that her mother could be persuaded to return to Weyville with her for a few weeks. She got the impression, Olivia wrote, that Daddy thought it was a really good idea and might give Mum a break from all the engagements that political life imposed on her there in Wellington.

Point to Olivia. She was always the better of their children at playing one parent off against another.

The handwriting on the second letter was vaguely familiar, a childish scrawl, different from the Phantom's; the postmark was Weyville. She made coffee before she opened it. It sat on the breakfast bar like a time bomb.

Kit, at that moment, sat crying on the sea wall at Oriental Parade with the rain trickling down the back of his neck off a Norfolk pine. A full tide lapped at his feet. An air hostess called Violet Rumgay stood under the tree wearing her teal and white uniform. Her regulation wide-brimmed black hat was tilted over her brown eyes so that passers-by would not recognise her. Her public was all around her, she often said.

Violet was fed up with not being able to ring Kit at home any more. 'I come in from an international flight and I'm dead beat,' she said, above the waves. 'The first thing I want to do is to talk to you. You've no idea how lonely it is.'

'I know. I'm sorry.'

'I'm doing an overseas tour next week. I'll be away for a month.'

'I'm trying to get leave from the House for a study tour.'

'You're always saying that.'

'Perhaps we should give this all away. It's too hard.'

Her eyes were suddenly frightened. He noticed the shadows like bruises under them. Once she had told him that she crossed her fingers when the planes were coming in to land. 'I think I've had it in the air industry,' she told him, 'it's just a matter of time.' Her mouth was like a fuschia, quite perfect, and he wanted to hold her and tell her she would be safe.

Rose's second letter was from Larissa. It read:

Deer Auntie Rose

I don't now weather my mother, your sister, has told youse down there that her little boy Bas is real sick. It doesnt meen nothing much to me as hes not my brother reely but I thort maybe you should now about this.

The wethers not too good here. Me and Gary and his frend Jason were going to go off for a bit of a cruise round the North island but Gary reckons we should stay put until the wether gets better.

Yours faithfully,

Larissa.

PS I have not told Gary that I am written you a letter.

PS agen I have not told my mother I am written you a letter.

When Rose rang Katrina's number Minna answered the phone.

'She's not here,' said Minna.

'Where is she?'

The voice at the other end was guarded. 'I'm not sure right at this minute.'

'Did she say if she was going to be long?'

'I really don't know, Rose.'

'Are you looking after Sharna?' She had heard Sharna call out in the background.

'Rose, who's been talking to you?'

Rose checked herself. 'Nobody's been talking to me. Katrina's my sister, remember.'

'I *know* that.' There was a pause. 'Basil's got cystic fibrosis. He's having tests at the hospital.'

'Jesus. Are you sure?'

'Of course I'm sure. That bloody doctor should have picked it up long ago. I knew as soon as she said she tasted salt on Basil's skin.'

'It wouldn't make much difference,' Rose said, amazed at her own brutality. Minna evoked something unpleasant in her. 'He'll die anyway.'

'Sooner or later. There's things they can do to help, though. It's called quality of life.'

'Is Mungo doing them?'

'Mungo. Mungo. You're all the same, you're all mates.'

'Minna, don't hang up. Doctor Lord, whatever you like, I hardly know him.'

'Well . . .'

'He's not my doctor.'

'. . . who cares? He speaks to people like dirt round here.'

'She should change her doctor.'

'Oh listen to you.' Rose could hear the plums rattling in Minna's mouth. 'You don't change your doctor here. You haven't been away long enough to forget that.'

It was true, Rose thought, standing on the end of the phone, reduced to helplessness. She doubted if she would ever have had the courage to change, and she didn't live in the Blake Block.

'I'll come home,' said Rose.

'There's nothing you can do.'

'Maybe I could talk to someone.'

'Who? Are you going to save his life Rose?' Minna's voice was cutting.

'Katrina needs family around.'

'She has. Jim's here, him and his wife come in nearly every day. I'm here. Ellie drops in most days.'

'Ellis Hannen?'

'Why not? He's kind. And Larissa's even been in, not that that's saying much.'

'Does Katrina need money?' She knew it was the wrong thing to say straight away.

'Sure,' said Minna in a drawl. 'Send some money, that's a really good idea.'

★

Toni said, 'We could discuss this. Like reasonable people.' She was standing at the kitchen bench cutting up ingredients for ratatouille, a mound of purple eggplant already cubed lay on the board, another of sliced zucchini. She scooped the seeds out of a brilliant red pepper and began chopping it.

Now that certain decisions had been made she felt empty and

quite unemotive. While Lyle had shouted for the past half hour, her thoughts had flowed above what he was saying like clean water over a dirty stretch of riverbed. She thought suddenly: *This is how Rose must have felt.*

At the time she couldn't have understood. She was too young and she and Lyle loved each other so much. Even then. Even when he got angry and couldn't understand her passion and how she got tied up in causes.

'What are you thinking about now?' he shouted. 'Speak to me. Say something.'

'Rose. I was thinking about Rose.'

'That silly bitch.'

'That's so like you, Lyle.'

The garlic bulb separated under her fingers. She began stripping a clove. It was very strong garlic, maybe it would cure them both of whatever ailed them. Above the bench she caught a reflection of herself in the glass, and Lyle standing behind her. We were so handsome, she thought. Perfect in every way. She smiled at their reflection. She could afford to admire them both from afar.

He sneered. 'You've got plenty in common with her.'

'It's over,' she repeated for perhaps the twentieth time.

'Then why are you leaving?'

'I would have thought you'd be pleased. You're free. Belinda can come here.'

'You're taking my children.'

'They're our children, I don't feel like giving them to Belinda.'

'I don't feel like giving them to Applebloom.'

'You're not. I'm just taking them away for awhile.'

'You're not taking anything anywhere.'

He had hit her before. She didn't want it to happen again. Carefully, she said, 'They'll be home soon. Let's stop shouting, don't let's argue any more. We can eat dinner together, like we always do.'

'What do you see in him?'

She paused, selected a knife for the onions. 'Did. Did see in him.'

'What could he do that I couldn't?'

'Nothing.'

'Tell me. I'll do it to you too.'

'Don't be disgusting.'

'Is that what you call it, disgusting?'

'It wasn't anything, well, not much to do with sex, Lyle.'

'Politics. Trendy wanking bloody politics.'

'Not even politics. You wouldn't understand.'

'Of course not. I wouldn't, would I? That's what they say, isn't it?'

Her hands trembled as she measured olive oil into the pan. It had been a mistake to tell him he didn't understand, the worst kind of insult.

'Don't upset the children,' she pleaded. She was suddenly dreadfully afraid.

'Fuck the children.'

'Don't say that.'

'Come to bed.'

'No, Lyle, not now.'

'Why not?'

'Because.' She gestured helplessly around her.

'Because you can't wait to get to him. You and him, you can't wait to get into each other.'

'No.'

He snatched the knife off the bench. 'Bullshit.'

The door handle seemed to stick under her hand in a way it never had before, and then she was running towards the drive, blundering over the paving stones and across the pruned-back daisy bushes, like moths around her legs. At the gate she saw the children walking along the street together, one from her ballet class, the other from his cricket practice.

'No,' she cried. 'No.' She turned back to Lyle as he came down the driveway. She looked at him advancing upon her. She began walking back towards him as if the shining blade were a magnet. When she had nearly reached him she put her hands in front of her face and waited.

'I'm so tired, Lyle,' she whispered.

'Ellis Hannen goes to see them,' said Rose later, when she was telling Kit about Basil. Or some of it. She had not mentioned yet that she was sending money.

'Hannen. He's a communist.'

'Ellie? Kit, who told you that?' She began to laugh, in spite of herself and the gravity she had felt all day.

'You'd better believe it,' Kit said, pushing away his plate.

'Who?' She was still not taking him seriously.

He stood up abruptly, went to the window. Fog horns moaned across the bay. He leaned against the glass.

'Rex Gamble.'

'Rex . . . what does he know about Ellis Hannen?'
'You shouldn't see him.'
'Who said I was . . .? Kit, who's watching me?'
'Who's watching *me*?' He flipped a worn business card out of his pocket. It bore the name of Buff Daniels and his security firm.
Her hand shook as she picked up the card. She had wondered where it had got to. 'He's not watching you. I've been talking to him. I wanted to tell you but you leave psychiatrists' cards around for me.'
Kit straightened and threw himself into an armchair. He picked threads in its fabric as he looked at her. 'Keep your hair on. I just meant that you should avoid Hannen when you go up to Weyville. If he's going to see Katrina. Well, you know what she's like, the sort of company she keeps.'
There was an air of suppressed excitement about him, as if something was going to happen, or he could actually see her getting up and walking out the door already.
'I'm not going to Weyville.'
'You can't stay here for ever.'
'Why not? Why can't I stay here?' Rose walked over to the armchair and touched his shoulder tentatively.
'I've got leave for a study tour. I'm going to Europe for a month. I've decided I should keep up in the field. I might get a portfolio in science if there's a reshuffle.'
'Is that what Gamble says?' She left her hand where it was; maybe they could break this impasse.
He moved restlessly, brushing her hand aside, got up as if she wasn't there. It was a long time since she had stood beside him like this and he seemed taller, or different, as if he had grown a dimension while she wasn't looking.
'It's what I'm saying. You can stay here while I'm gone if you like.' He shrugged. 'Though I thought you couldn't bear to be on your own these days.'
'I could come with you.'
'Rose!' His alarm was palpable.
'Of course I could. Is it the money? We're not short, are we? Kit, I've been thinking, we could sell the house in Weyville, we don't need it any more.'
'It's in the electorate, are you crazy?'
She was silent for a moment. 'I know, I've thought of that. Of course we need a base. But it could be a smaller one than that.'
'No. That's my home, Rose. That's what I wanted, all those years in that little box. That's what I thought you wanted. I'm not going

to sell it just because now I've got it, *you* don't want it.'

'So if I won't, who will?'

She was thinking, *This is it, we really haven't got much left*. The truth of this hurt her more than she expected.

Stalling, she said, 'I'd like to go to Europe again. We've had such nice times when we've gone away. I could sell the Metro.'

'Fat lot you'd get for that. It's spent more time in the panelbeaters than it has on the road.'

'I suppose you're right.' She was unhappy with the latest paint job on the Metro but it hadn't seemed appropriate to take it up with Rex Gamble.

'I'm in love,' he said, 'don't you understand, it's love I'm talking about.' And then ashamed, he looked at her, saying, but not saying, *Oh for Chrissake it's you I'm telling this to, I wish it were anyone but you.*

It was a relief to her that he had said it, and she thought that now was the time when she might tell him that this was not the end of the world, and that one day they might both recover from this, that it might take a long time, but if they were careful and treated each other as if they had shared an illness, it would be all right again. But she was not sure whether she could sustain that effort now for herself, and she felt bone-tired. Only sleeping alone for a long time would cure her weariness, she thought.

Kit said, 'So you see it's impossible for you to come with me.'

She might have agreed, only at that moment the phone rang. Kit answered it. It was Denise Taite to say that Lyle Warner had stabbed Toni to death in the driveway of their home. Toni had started to run away, and then she had turned and gone back, 'almost as if she wanted him to'. Rose could hear Denise's high hysterical voice crackling over the line, past the lakes and over the Desert Road, across pylons and down the Sanson straights, as her heart froze around what she was hearing.

'Why?' she asked, when he hung up. His face heaved. 'Was it because he wanted to go off with Belinda?'

He looked at her strangely. For an instant, she supposed that he was thinking that it might have been her, might have been one of them lying slain in the driveway. She could see the cloud of white Michaelmas daisies that flowered alongside the Warners' drive all through the autumn, massed like the flurrying feathers of a White Orpington.

But he shook his head; answered with a note of venom: 'It was because of her and Morris.'

'Morris? Morris Applebloom?'

'Of course. Didn't you know? Didn't you ever know?'

9

The children's ward of the Weyville Hospital was a long annexe to the main building, with a glassed-in wall like a porch running down its length. The linoleum was still that dark and institutional brown which achieved a high polish and squeaked when the nurses walked on it in their soft-soled shoes. 'Everything will be different when the new children's ward is built,' the hospital board had promised for years. Only it never happened. Lately, in the wake of new recommendations to cut the health vote, a rumour was circulating that the whole ward might get closed down and the Weyville children would have to go elsewhere for treatment. The threat was enough to quieten complaints about the state of the old hospital, at least for the moment.

There was nowhere for parents to room-in with their children, but a blind eye was turned towards those who brought in a mattress or a folding chair to sleep by a distraught child.

Katrina slept in such a chair by Basil for nine nights in a row, although she couldn't exactly describe him as distraught. If anybody had asked her, she might have said that she was, but nobody did. Basil's cough was deep and hacking. He was not in any danger, Mungo Lord said, when he called on his rounds, but they would keep him under observation for a few days.

The first week wasn't so bad, or at least Basil didn't seem worse. If anything, he was better than he had been for months. The children who could get out of bed ran wild during the day and Basil usually led the charges down the passage. The nurses looked fraught whenever Basil was in sight and during the day Katrina had been slinking out, not wanting to admit that the monster on the prowl was hers. The pit was the day he taught the other boys to look up the nurses' skirts while they attended bed patients. Basil lay in wait by the beds; as soon as a hapless nurse bent over he and two or three others would be up the back of her legs and clutching at the tops of her panties. It wasn't like school where the kids could be expelled, but there was talk of Basil being sent home as soon as possible.

Katrina could not quite fathom why he was being kept there anyway. When she asked for information she was referred to Mungo Lord who always looked vague and said that it was better to be sure than sorry. 'It'd be a good idea for you to get in touch with the cystic fibrosis organisation, help you cope a bit better.' He glanced at his watch.

Basil was receiving medication, though Katrina wasn't sure what it was for; as far as she could see, that was the only treatment. 'I don't quite understand what's happening,' she said to Mungo Lord when this had gone on for seven days.

'My dear Katrina,' he said, 'don't worry.'

It annoyed her that he called her Katrina, though she had not dealt in formality since she wore chiffon ball dresses. Minna said she should demand that he call her Ms Diamond, seeing that she had gone back to her maiden name. Minna had moved in with her at the house in Blake Block. It had all happened very suddenly. Life was much easier with her there and Katrina enjoyed the luxury of tidiness and routine that Minna imposed on the household. Sharna cried less and there were times when she almost liked the kid.

She liked being treated tenderly too, and thought, oh yes, if Paul, or Wolf, or even George (not that George had seen her for more than a day in his entire life; she wondered what he'd say if she ever came across him and presented him with evidence of those twenty-four hours *ha ha* he'd have to believe that red hair) could see her now. But sometimes she felt she could never live up to Minna's expectations of her. She couldn't hear herself telling Mungo to call her Ms Diamond. But she might just call him Mungo one day and see how he liked it.

When she didn't move out of the doctor's way he ran his hands through his hair in an exasperated way. 'Look, you don't have to bother about understanding things, you've got better things to do.'

Presuming, she supposed, like looking after Basil and keeping him out of the nurses' hair, or their pants.

Later, she heard him say to the charge nurse, 'I feel like wringing that woman's neck till her eyes pop out sometimes.' She guessed there must be some difficult mothers around and was sure he couldn't be talking about her.

Another day, speaking to the same nurse, who was nice as pie to him, she had noticed, and a bad-tempered bitch when she spoke to junior staff, he said, 'She's thick as an A-rab's armpit, if you ask me.'

Coincidence, Katrina told herself. He couldn't have been talking about her.

A day or two later Basil was listless and did not want to get out of bed. Nobody objected to him staying there.

It was nearly midnight on the tenth evening when Katrina touched Basil's head again, feeling a dry restless temperature beneath her hand. His breathing was uneven.

She was so tired she couldn't think, couldn't sleep either. She dragged herself down the passage to the coffee and television room. The coffee dispenser had a notice on it requesting that coffee not be taken into the ward, but at this hour of the night she figured nobody would notice.

In the passage another mother, in with her son, leaned against a wall, smoking. An older woman, she could almost have been the child's grandmother.

'Makes you think a bit, doesn't it?' she commented to Katrina. 'Place like this.' She held out her cigarette pack, and flicked open a lighter when Katrina accepted.

'How long's your kid in for?' Katrina dragged smoke down and held it.

'Just overnight. What about yours?'

'God knows.'

'I never wanted this little bastard, but I don't like seeing him in here.'

'How many have you got?'

'Six.'

'Jesus. What happened?' As if she didn't know, but there you are, you asked questions like that in hospital corridors at night.

'There was a young man from Matterhorn, who wouldn't have been born, if his mother had known the letter was torn.'

'Yeah. Tell me about it. Fucking birth control. Fucking pill.'

'Fucking everything. I've got a drink, d'you want one?' The woman opened a shopping bag slung over her arm, producing a bottle of Malibu. She unscrewed the top, handing it over.

'Ta.' Katrina swigged, feeling the rum and coconut slide through her, leaving a delicate trail of fire all the way to her gut.

'Have some more. It's benefit day.'

'So it is. I'd forgotten.'

'How could you do that?'

'Easy.' Katrina gestured towards the ward where Basil lay. After awhile she said: 'I've gotta see Bas. See if he's okay.'

'All right. Come back, will you?'

Katrina looked down at Basil. He wasn't coughing but his temperature was high. His head was turned on the pillow, then he rolled over. She visualised his father, the turn of his head and how she had been stunned by the full frontal beauty of it the first time he turned and looked at her. Her eyes prickled. The enormity of what was going to happen to Basil filled her, threatened to topple her. He had been her biggest gamble, and it was a goof-up. She would have him for a few more years while he got more and more sick and then he would die. The room felt claustrophobic; the row of sleeping restless kids made her want to throw up.

A light was on in the office. The senior night nurse was filling in charts.

'My kid's sick,' she said.

'He's doing all right. His temperature's up, but we're keeping an eye on it, Mrs Diamond.'

'Ms Diamond,' Katrina said, too loud, feeling foolish. Her head floated gently somewhere about level with the ceiling.

'Ms Diamond,' the nurse replied, watching her.

'I want you to ring Dr Lord.' Katrina spoke carefully. *I'm not drunk*, she reminded herself, *I'm exhausted out of my mind, and a couple of nips have gone to my head.* Reassured, she spoke more boldly. 'I want you to ring him right now and tell him to come and look at Basil.'

'I'll ring him in the morning. Why don't you get some sleep?' There was a note of steel behind the words.

'I'll ring him myself. I'm being messed about.'

'Then I'll have to have you removed from the hospital if you do that.'

In the coffee room Katrina's new friend had filled an ashtray while she was gone. She was listening to the all-night programme playing quietly on the shelf radio. When Katrina arrived she looked up, half asleep. 'What's up? You look crook.'

'I feel crook.'

'Hey, I've been trying to place you. Didn't you used to teach dancing?'

'That's right. How did you know?'

'Used to teach my cousin.' She mentioned a name but Katrina couldn't place it.

'Always wanted to learn. I never did.' The woman sounded dreamy. 'You'd think I'd have learnt, everyone danced in those days, real dancing not hurdy gurdy stuff like they do now. But not me, number one came along when I was fifteen; they let me keep her if I kept outta sight until I was sixteen when I could get married. The father stuck around. Something to be said for him, I suppose, but I wish he'd buggered off before he left me with six. Ah well.'

She stubbed out her cigarette and got out the bottle. 'Here, have another one.' This time she slopped some in styrofoam cups from the coffee dispenser. 'Go on, it'll help you sleep. You've gotta get some rest.'

Katrina drank and the radio started playing old-time dance music.

'Teach me.' The woman stood up, holding out her arms to Katrina.

'You're crazy', But the woman was pulling her by the hand.

'C'mon, a few steps. Please.'

'Okay, just a few then, I don't feel too much like standing up.' They stood poised together. 'Put your hand on my shoulder, okay, and I put my hand on your waist like this, I'm being the man, see.'

They both giggled, stumbled a little against the passage wall as Katrina manoeuvred the woman along. 'Right, point your toe a little, foot together with mine, and one two, here we go, follow me.'

The woman smelled comfortably of cigarettes and booze, and after a moment Katrina put her cheek against hers. 'All right? Is that okay?'

So it was that while Katrina and the woman whose name she never learned danced in a corridor and while Minna took care of Sharna, Mungo Lord lay sleeping and Basil died.

★

The early shift had just begun. Jeffrey Campbell viewed the day to come with unease. He often found himself thinking about early retirement options; he and Lola could take a trip. In the meantime, they both needed a good holiday to tide them over. The girl would like that. He smiled fondly to himself. The feminists would rap him over the knuckles if they could see into his head; only he was not planning to give them access.

A travel brochure was spread out in front of him. The white coral of Raratongan beaches gleamed, beckoning under the station light. Perhaps she would want to go somewhere with more shopping? What he would really like was to choose exactly the right place and present her with the tickets. That way she wouldn't be discussing it with all her customers before they made a decision. Campbell sighed. He knew his wife's weaknesses. If possible, he would like a holiday that had not been decided by half the female population of Weyville.

Teddy O'Meara walked in and threw his hat on the desk beside him. 'I'm glad I'm going off duty. They're burying the Warner woman today.'

'You've been recalled for it.'
'Ah shit.'
'A pity the body couldn't have been released sooner, there's a few people out there who've had a chance to work up a head of steam.'
'Preserve us from ranting females.'
'They've got a point.' Campbell stopped short of condemning fair comment.
'Yeah? Warner's lawyer's going for provocation. I reckon he might get it, too.'
'D'you happen to know whether Mrs Kendall's coming back for the funeral?'
'Wouldn't have a clue, Sarge. I haven't seen the lady in months.'
'I gave you a copy of that last letter about her?'
'Oh, yep, Daniels. The Lambton Quay sleuth. The letter's on file.'
'I thought you might have heard something. We seem to have drawn blanks all round.'
'You'd be the first to know if I did. Anyway, there's not much we can do about her while we're here and she's in Wellington, is there?'
'If Mrs Kendall's coming back to town we ought to know about it. She might need protection.'
'Have you mentioned it to CIB?'
'Well. I'm thinking about it.'
O'Meara lifted an eyebrow. It was so light it almost disappeared into his skin. Then his face widened in a disarming smile. 'She is a couple of sandwiches short of the full picnic, don't you reckon?'
'Sooner or later that turkey has to make a slip,' said Campbell grimly. 'I'd like to be there when he does.'
O'Meara shrugged. 'Yeah, I guess.'
'You ought to get some rest before the funeral.'
Campbell got called out after that to investigate an overnight break-in at the Blake Block School. On his way back to the station, along Blake Pass, he stopped at the filling station to look at some spanners. He knew he was dawdling, wouldn't have tolerated it in other staff, but anything rather than the station was irresistible today. He had no special use for spanners but he thought he might eventually do a little tinkering on some old motors. Retirement again; he would have to make a decision soon.
He listened to petrol gushing in the background while he chose a twelve-inch crescent, feeling the weight of it in his hand. The attendant took it without comment and dropped it in a container bag.
In the background a man was sweeping the yard, bending and shuffling along like someone much older than his years. Campbell

recognised him as the attendant who had been beaten up and robbed months earlier. His neck had been injured.

'I thought your mate was still on compo?'

'I thought your mates might have caught the bastards who did him.' The attendant handed him a Biro to sign his credit slip.

Driving through the Block, Campbell looked for clues, as if he could somehow sleuth the air. It occurred to him that the reason he stayed in Weyville was, in spite of all he said to the contrary, because he loved it. All his life he had heard people slamming small towns as if lesser beings lived here. His father, the Irishman, was a Dublin man; he said that the heart died before the body in places like this. Why did you stay, his son had asked him, to which his father had shaken his head and asked where else a man was to find a bite to eat to feed the hungry mouths. Which was a lie, because there were only the two boys to feed. At the weekends his father had worn string around the tops of his pants and pissed himself after he had been to the pub; during the week he worked on a factory floor. His son had disappointed him, a boy with an absence of music in his heart, he said, too quiet for his own good and a straight and narrow kind of lad at that.

Now he knew, as he watched the town shaking itself into gear for another day, that he had always wanted to die in a place like this. There were empty streets and filling stations, motels that nobody went to any more and lawns littered with old cars and flightless wooden butterflies on houses and rusting railway tracks, and cold blue lights which lit the vacant shops at night; there were houses where people slept six to a room and beer bottles piled on the verges in this part of town, and up the road there were neat suburban boxes with clipped edges and blinds which lined up with each other right around the sides of the house and milk bottles out on the dot and hair nets and cold cream and letterboxes with gnomes on them waiting for letters that never came from children who had escaped (he thought of his wife's son then), and there were sumptuous places like Orchard Close and Cedarwood Grove where he was now heading, and all of them he loved. For, as well, there were children playing outside the schools, and Queen Anne lace growing in the gardens, there was a library where all the attendants knew what all the borrowers read and put books aside for people, and art exhibitions where everyone who went to see the pictures understood them, home-baked bread and pot-luck dinners, flower shows and horticultural demonstrations (he and Lola went to the rose pruning at the garden by the lake once a year) and a cemetery where the dead were buried beside their relatives.

He needed to remind himself of all of this because a scandalous killing had taken place in a town already full of random violence and it was the responsibility of the police to stop it and still it kept on. An image of a ball bouncing up and down assailed him; it hit the ground and a force propelled it upwards and if you were quick you caught it but if it eluded you it bounded off into space and you might well lose it in the undergrowth. There was no one simple way that you could keep the ball under control, but the mystery that surrounded Rose Kendall seemed to be at the heart of the problem, almost the force itself.

He shook his head, tired. Too simple. Blame politics for everything. That was what people were doing. Only he couldn't get it out of his head that politics was people; it was like diets and what you put in your mouth. We are what we eat, fat, thin, healthy, unhealthy. That was how it looked to him. People had done politics to themselves.

Campbell turned the car into Cedarwood Grove, heading towards the Kendalls'. Emerging from the driveway, Teddy O'Meara's off-duty Laser picked up speed and passed him.

Teddy drove on, sliced to a halt as he caught sight of Campbell and did a fast U-turn.

'Place looks dead quiet to me,' he called when he was alongside Campbell. 'I've checked right around, snug as a bug in a rug.'

He gave a thumbs up, letting his motor idle. Jeffrey Campbell studied the dead windows. Trees were growing in a wild unchecked way across the driveway. Someone had collected papers from the letterbox, but items of junk mail had fallen out and were strewn along the path.

'I heard you up here, Chief.' O'Meara tapped his skull with his forefinger.

'Yep, good one, Teddy.'

'And I called the Newbone woman, the one who works on the paper . . .'

'Hortense?'

'The Kendalls aren't coming. Skedaddled.'

'You're kidding?'

'Nope.'

'Know any details?'

'Not yet.' The young man spoke with triumph and with the

pleasure of someone who has been seen to do well in such an obvious manner.

'Thanks. Well done, O'Meara.'

Campbell drove down Cedarwood Grove. Glancing back in the rear-vision mirror, he saw O'Meara hesitate, but it was only to put on sunglasses in the early morning light.

A hearse bore down on him travelling away from the hospital. A small coffin was carried inside it. Its smallness and bareness affected him. He pulled over to the side of the road, thinking how important it was that he sort himself out before he went back to the station. After awhile it occurred to him that O'Meara had not passed him.

★

When Larissa saw the line of cars winding through the hills that led to the crematorium she could not believe so many people would be coming to Basil's funeral. The sun glinted on their roofs and fenders, and their headlights blazed on full beam in the midday light.

She glanced at her mother's stony face beside her. Katrina had not addressed anyone directly all day.

'That's amazing,' Larissa said, to nobody in particular. She rather wished that she had let Gary come now. 'It won't be your scene,' she had told him, 'and anyway my mother doesn't like you.' It was getting easier and easier to be nasty to him these days, partly because he didn't really notice. He was out of it a lot of the time or else he was away working at the greenhouse. It would have been all right if she could have asked Jason.

Of course she could see that would have been a mistake.

But she felt that he would have understood more about life and death. He had been very nice to her since this had happened. 'It doesn't matter too much, he was my half brother and I hated his father's guts,' she told him. But she had a feeling that it did matter, that the death of a brother could not be so easily dismissed; nor could she discount the enormous role he had played in her alienation from her mother. What lay before them both, now that Basil was dead, was a mystery that Larissa could only guess at. Maybe nothing would happen. After all, death was about nothingness, so why should she expect it to deliver solutions and answers, to her in particular.

Her uncle, Jim Diamond, was standing on her other side. He looked puzzled too when he saw the cars coming towards them. He flicked a look at his watch. Now Larissa could see that there were family station wagons and a sprinkling of Volvos in the procession.

Perhaps, after all, there were only twenty or so, but that was twenty more than they expected to come to their funeral.

'We're early,' he said, to Ellis Hannen rather than to her.

'I don't understand what's going on. Perhaps we should just go in.'

'The coffin's not in place yet,' Jim said. 'I'll ask the funeral director.'

The funeral director, one of the new school with a chubby face that positively renounced lugubriousness, was looking unusually perturbed. He hurried forward to speak to Jim, drawing him to one side and whispering.

Jim shook his head, and shrugged. 'It's the Warner funeral,' he announced to Katrina when he returned. 'They weren't due for another half hour, but the police have had a problem with the families. Some of his turned up and her family wanted to get stuck into them plus there's a radical group of women who went to the service and Mrs Warner's old mother from Hawke's Bay can't understand what they're doing there, so they're coming up earlier here than they were expected.'

'They all ought to migrate to the Blake Block, don't you think? Such behaviour, we could sort them out.' Minna was actually wearing a dress, an embroidered caftan which had seen better days, but looked as if it had been starched-up for the occasion. Her blonde hair swung against it like spun glass as she moved. Sharna was sleeping in her arms, her head against Minna's shoulder.

'They'll just have to wait,' said Ellis.

'That's the point, they want them to go first, so they're not all hanging round while we have our service.'

'But that's not on.' Minna was genuinely shocked now.

'Well we're still early, you see.'

'It's all a mix-up, I am so sorry.' The funeral director was close to wringing his hands. 'Special circumstances, it's very awkward. They'll only take a few minutes, having had their main service at the church. This is just a short committal.' Beads of perspiration stood out on his forehead. 'It would be so sad if... if your service were to suffer any disturbance. For your sakes, I am thinking of.'

'I don't care,' said Katrina, speaking at last. 'It really doesn't matter.'

'Oh thank you, Ms Diamond. So kind.' The funeral director bobbed his head. 'Most unusual circumstances. Most understanding. Perhaps if you would care to sit in your cars. Or I could provide a little place for you to retire to at the back of the chapel.'

'We'll stay here and watch them, thank you,' said Katrina.

An uneasy silence fell over the group. A small red-complexioned man in an unremarkable suit with a raincoat thrown over his arm and a briefcase in one hand had joined them, or was at least standing near to them. It was difficult to tell exactly where he had come from. His stance was distant but respectful. For all that, Larissa did not like the way he was looking at her. She was trying to work out where he fitted in when he moved towards the incoming group of mourners.

Larissa recognised some of the local cops trying to look inconspicuous. They were a laugh really, they stood out like sore thumbs. Though O'Meara looked kind of cool, you had to give it to him, he was a bit of a dude. He did not let on that he had seen her as he walked on into the chapel. Apart from them the cremation was supposed to be private, so the mourners consisted of tearful relatives and another group whom Larissa remembered from the days when they visited her aunt's house. Presumably classed as 'close friends', they appeared strung-out and desperate to the point of incoherence. Matt Decker and Nick Newbone and Harry Ryan (who looked as if he was going to faint) carried the coffin with some other men. Larissa was glad they weren't having pallbearers; she couldn't think who they could have got to make up the numbers.

'That's Mungo Lord,' said Katrina, making a little darting movement in the direction of one of the pallbearers whom Larissa had not recognised on the far side.

'Leave it.' Minna put out a restraining arm. 'Not now.'

'He wouldn't see me.' Katrina's voice traced acid into space.

Mungo, preoccupied with the sorrow of the moment did not, indeed, see Katrina.

'You'd think Rose Kendall would be there,' said the reddish man with the raincoat, to Jim.

'You'd think Rose Kendall would be *here*. She's my sister.' Jim's voice was grim.

The man swallowed, looked as if he was about to take his own pulse, Larissa thought. She wondered who was going to say first what a phoney this guy was, pretending to be one of them, when really it was like he was spying on them.

'Name's Daniels, just call me Buff,' said the man, extending his hand to Jim.

'It's like Jim's sister not to be here,' her Aunty Fay said. Fay was a washed-out person who had started to cry as soon as she saw Toni Warner's coffin topped with a spray of red hothouse carnations.

Larissa tried to read the card as it was lifted out of the hearse. It said something like, 'In memory of our beloved Toni, from the Weyville Branch of the Labour Party': then the funeral director came back and took it off the coffin and replaced it with a similar one which was from Toni's mother and father and children, and put the Labour Party one on the table in the foyer. Another bouquet which was as good as identical to these two remained in the hearse. The card on it read; 'To my darling Toni, love you for ever, Lyle.' Only no one moved to bring that inside, and Lyle, being locked in jail, was unable to deliver it himself.'

'Rose always leaves things to other people,' Fay said.

'That is not exactly true,' said Katrina, surprising them, and again silence fell over the group.

Jim was turning to the sandy-haired man to make conversation, which was the appropriate thing in Jim's eyes to do at a funeral, and Larissa was getting ready to denounce him as a spy when she was distracted by the sight of her own father, Paul, emerging from a V12 Jag. She watched with a kind of wonder as he sprinted across the grass towards them.

'Am I too late?' he panted.

'We'll be starting in a few minutes.'

'But...' He gaped around the group, seeing Katrina now.

'My former husband,' said Katrina loudly to Minna. Inside the chapel heads turned, mouths pursing and shushing them. 'My son is dead,' she said to Paul.

'I heard that, gee I'm sorry, I didn't know yours was today too. Kind of coincidence, eh.' He ran his hand over his thinning hair, then gestured towards the service, embarrassed. 'I thought I ought to come, you know, the firm's gone computerised. Well. I did business with Mr Warner's firm.'

'Gawper,' said Minna.

'This bit's private,' said Larissa, 'so you'd better come to ours.'

As the mourners from Toni's service filed out, a car started up in the parking lot, driving away at speed.

'Applebloom,' said Ellis Hannen. 'I wouldn't have gone in either if I'd been him.'

Finally, at exactly the appointed hour, they walked into the chapel to confront the fact of Basil's dying. Larissa had no way of knowing, of course, but she suspected that the same fire would consume both Basil's and Toni's misadventures.

★

That night the weather changed and fog lay in dank streamers over the town. Buff Daniels, returning to Wellington, was driven off the road in his car. At first he did not believe it was happening. The following car commenced overtaking and slowed down two or three times alongside him as if the driver was uncertain, then fell back.

Then on a shoulder of hillside the car drew level again, holding the road until an oncoming car approached, as if on a signal, and Buff drove towards the only place left for him to go, over the bank. Listening to the wheels spinning, the gathering wind whipping the sides of the gully where he had landed, and his own heart racing, he heard too the cars turning and coming back to the spot where he had gone down.

That might have been an end of it, but a truckdriver called Ellis stopped, attracted by the unquenched beam of his headlights, and pulled him back on to the road. The cars which had pursued him accelerated off into the night. Daniels was grateful for a passion for numbers which printed them like photographs in his brain. The world was swirling around him, but when he woke up he was certain, sooner or later, he would remember.

10

Katrina Diamond wore black leather pants bought from an op shop and a denim jacket that Minna had given her for a present when she went to see Mungo Lord. The pants fitted her beautifully; she could not imagine why anyone would give them away for next to nothing unless they had got too fat for them. Every now and then she stroked her bottom as if she was stroking a live animal. As well, she wore Shadze so that he couldn't read her eyes, not straight away.

For a week she had stalked him. It amazed her how careful it made you, following someone. Her shoes were soft-soled, she did not wear scent, or smoke near him, and when she was sitting in his orchard as she had done the day before, she moved very stealthily so that birds did not flurry or get agitated. But it was there that she had nearly been caught when his dog got wind of her. It was a large dog, a Dobermann she thought, and it came at the hedge where she sat half frozen in the frosty August air. Minna had been teaching her a mantra and she said it, hoping that if she did not respond to the dog it would go away.

Mungo, inspecting the way the buds were setting on the stone fruit, cultivated for a hobby and because the orchard gave him a little extra space (as he was fond of telling people), called the dog. The mantra worked. She did not scream or move, continuing to sit cross-legged amongst the bushes until the dog loped away.

It was no good going to Mungo's house, of course. One of those houses like the Appleblooms' and the Warners' (and look what good it had done Toni Warner, poor bitch, poor cow, poor dumb broad, getting done in over a man for Chrissake), or her sister Rose's (and she'd never heard her have a good word to say about her borer-ridden dump), only newer, it was bristling with children and his wife looking beatific and earth motherish with her hair pulled back from a middle parting and a bulge under her handwoven putty-coloured dress. Katrina had actually been up to the door one day earlier in the week when he was out, to case the joint. The woman did not look at all surprised or ruffled when Katrina said that she must have come to the wrong place, it was the address someone had given her where there was a chest of drawers for sale. Even the dog was quite calm about her appearance on the scene, perhaps thinking it knew her now. No problem at all, the wife had said, would she like to use their phone to check out the number, and stood chatting easily while two small children stared at her from behind her skirts, like something in a Bergman film. Only when she smelled a pot boiling over in the kitchen did the woman excuse herself, by which time Katrina was getting frantic in case Mungo turned up and saw her.

After that she was more careful. Neither the orchard nor the house would be suitable.

Instead she watched the surgery, noting the times that he came and left, and when his receptionist arrived and went home. This was more difficult because it appeared that the receptionist was there a great deal more than he was. When he came out of the rooms (and she had sat on a bench seat on the street outside for so many hours she felt as if her backside was welded to it in the black leather pants) he slid into the Range Rover, throwing papers into the back seat along with children's toys and brightly coloured rugs. She had watched him glide away a dozen times already, always with one hand casually manoeuvring the steering wheel and the fingers of his right hand carelessly curled around the top edge of the car roof. His stereo would start playing even before he moved off, usually some Mozart, sometimes cool and soulful jazz. When he turned towards her, never seeing her, she was astounded by his good looks. He reminded her a little of Wolf. There was a time when she would have considered it a privilege to get laid by a man like Mungo. It was satisfying to think how much she had changed.

'I hope you're not going nuts, I don't want to be the one to put you away,' said Minna at the end of the week. Sharna was sitting on Minna's lap acting as if she was her mother and not Katrina. Katrina didn't think she cared much. She cared less for this child than she had for the others and her funny eye gave her the creeps.

'Of course I'm nuts, what do you expect?'

'It's not healthy, you walking round day and night like this.'

'I never fucking asked to be happy, did I? Just to have Basil.' Any moment she knew she would cry if Minna did not leave off. The memory of him running in the door and grabbing her breasts assailed her. As she remembered him, and already that's what he was, just a memory, he was the sweetest little boy. The scent of him was in her nostrils. She turned away, and a tear and some snot did trickle down, hitting her tongue. Salty, just the way Basil had tasted that first day that they had known there was something wrong. Sometimes she hated Minna for having alerted her that he was ill, as if through not knowing, nothing might have happened.

'Where are you going, anyway?' Minna asked for what must have been the fiftieth time.

'Just out.'

'You sound like a kid.'

'Don't. Don't fuckin' hassle me Minna or I'll turn you out.'

'Oh yeah?' She glanced at Sharna.

'Okay, okay, just leave me, all right? I have to get out of here a bit. It'll come right.'

'Are you seeing someone?'

'Oh give over.'

'Are you?'

'Minna, I didn't give up seeing men to get heavied like I was.'

'But are you?'

'Jesus, Minna, my kid's just died. Remember? Gentle Jesus, loving father of thy flock, and all that. It's a week since I was in that crematorium and thank Christ Jim Diamond coughed up with the money for the funeral or I'd be up shit creek without a paddle. Even if we did have to sing hymns.'

'His wife's going to Memphis to see Elvis Presley's grave, did you know?'

'Well, fine, she's doing something, isn't she? It's more than just sitting round on our backsides in Weyville doing nothing.'

'Trust you, there's a very unsavoury side to your nature, Katrina.' Minna's voiced was prim.

In the end Katrina settled for the hospital car parking lot. She knew what time he did his rounds; from her observations she would say that it was the most deserted territory that Mungo Lord traversed.

When he came out to the Range Rover it was exactly as she had planned. Not a soul in sight. It was the moment she had been dreaming of. His shirt was pale blue under his red tie and it was as if a slash of blood was already cascading down him. She could see the shape of his mouth contorting into agony and she almost laughed before she stepped up to him.

'Dr Lord,' she said, smiling.

'Katrina,' he said, and she was grateful to see that he was disconcerted.

'Ms Diamond.'

'Well sure. How're you getting along?'

'I wanted a word.' She inserted herself between him and the vehicle.

'Sure. How about fixing a time with my receptionist, and we can have a chat. You've got our number?'

'Now.' He was such a big man and she had to get the ribcage lined up just right.

'You've had a tough time.' His voice was quiet, almost sexy, she thought. The steel was warm from lying against her body. She had come to like its feel and could almost understand how Toni Warner went back to collect it. You touched steel once in a certain way and there was a kind of dizzying pleasure in it. Like looking up at the sky, the great clean bright sky, into the eye of God.

Hesitating. Just long enough for him to scent danger. Turning swiftly to catch her nimble wrist and taking the brunt of the blade on his arm. But wounded all the same, and calling out for help.

'You can help put these letters in envelopes while I feed the baby. Then we can have something to eat. That's what you'd like, wouldn't you, honey?' Joylene spoke with a slight assumed American twang while she spooned food into the mouth of a pert child called Angel who sat in a high chair.

'It's up to you.' Larissa was sitting on her hands and trying to keep her fingers crossed at the same time.

'And your daddy'll be home for his lunch real soon. What would you like me to make for you?'

'It doesn't matter, Joylene, honest, I'm not that hungry.'

'Why, honey, you just said. The Lord's work is hungry business.' She stopped feeding the baby long enough to flick through a pile of the folded circulars, counting at speed. 'Only another hundred and three to go.' Larissa couldn't take her eyes off her cleavage. It was a wonder she didn't get cold in this weather, though the central heating in the house was turned up high.

As if reading her thoughts, Joylene touched her breast. 'Paul and I do sunbathing by electricity regular twice a week. We're into massage too, he has such beautiful hands, your daddy. I can't think of any better expression of married togetherness than a little massage. When you're a big grown up girl and get a husband of your own you ought to keep that in mind.'

'How long do you think Paul's going to be?'

In fact Paul had just arrived and on his own Spanish hacienda, circa 1980, was more in charge than the last time Larissa had seen him.

He stood, allowing the door to frame him, and surveyed the scene of domesticity. 'Well now, if that doesn't beat everything,' he exclaimed. 'Praise the Lord.'

'Actually, the good news is, I'm not staying long.'

'She will,' said Joylene. 'We're going to have something nice to eat, and see, Larissa's been helping me with the circulars. Oh the Lord moves in mysterious ways His work to perform.'

'Oh Jesus.' Larissa threw down a pile of folders, knowing she'd made a mistake as she spoke. 'I mean, cut the crap will you, Joylene?'

Paul stepped up so close to her she could smell his aftershave. She felt like throwing up.

'You can leave right this minute if you speak to your mother like that.' He raised his palm sharply, holding it close to her face.

'She's my stepmother.'

'You better do what your daddy says to you. He is the head of the household, you know.' Joylene's voice was satisfied as she lifted Angel from her chair, purring into her hair.

Larissa took a deep breath, longing for a cigarette. She needed something to help her through this. Jason had offered her a joint before she came, but she told him no because she'd be sure to blow it if she was too loosened up; Gary had told her she was out of her head anyway coming here, and for once he was right. She sat very still and Paul dropped his hand.

'Sure,' said Larissa, addressing Joylene. 'I'd like something to eat. Can I hold the baby for you?'

The tension eased. Paul sat down opposite Larissa. The baby didn't want to sit with her, but climbed on to Paul's lap instead. It suited Larissa, though sitting there with nothing to do except keep on stuffing the stupid envelopes she felt exposed to his stare. She folded faster.

'It gives my heart ease seeing you do that, Larissa.' He was wearing a gold chain on his wrist and a heavy gold signet ring on the little finger of each hand.

'You sell any cars this morning, hon?' Joylene sounded just like an advertisement for second-hand cars Larissa had seen on television, where the mother asked a question like that and the baby squeaked excitedly when the father said yes.

'Did I what? Two cars. Both in the twenty-five thousand range. We are going to have ourselves a holiday soon, baby.'

'God is good,' Joylene sighed.

'When are you going to start dressing like a Christian woman?' Paul asked Larissa.

She tore the corner of the envelope trying to stuff the paper in too fast. This was too much; she had washed her hair three times trying to get the rinse out, and ironed a blouse. Herbert had nearly had a heart attack when she asked for the camp iron. It was the jeans, she supposed, but they were decent. Definitely decent, and no tighter than Joylene's bodice.

'Paul, I've come about Sharna. Dad,' she corrected herself, because it was too important to give it away now, having come this far.

Nobody said anything. Joylene was defrosting frozen muffins in the microwave; Angel sucked Paul's golden bracelet.

'Who's Sharna?'

'You know.'

'Lighten our darkness, Larissa.' She remembered, incongruously at this moment, that he and her mother had called her Larissa after the heroine in a Russian film . . . *Some day my love you'll come to me, some day we will be fre-ee.* Her eyes filled with tears.

'My sister,' she mumbled. 'She's in social welfare. They took her away when Mum went in jail.'

Paul sat stroking Angel's hair, his eyes thoughtful. *It's going to be all right*, Larissa decided. *He's going to come across, fix it up, make things okay this time.*

Maybe.

'That seems like the proper place for her. Your mother never had rights to a child that has no father.'

'Dad. Stop.' Larissa put her hands up to her ears.

'Who would look after the child if she was not taken into care?'

'Her friend Minna. She really loves Sharna. If you could just see somebody, tell her that it would be all right for Minna to look after her. Sharna must be real scared where she is.'

'Hmmm.' He looked at Joylene. The microwave pinged.

'She is a child innocent and beloved in the eyes of God.' Joylene buttered the muffins with a slick and practised hand. 'We could save her.'

'I don't want you to save her,' Larissa cried. 'I want you to get her back for Minna to look after.'

Paul looked back at her with his hard prominent blue eyes. She was grateful she had never taken anything from him, not even his looks.

'She's unfit to look after a child.'

'You don't know her.'

'I've seen her.'

Joylene put a plate of muffins in front of her. 'You eat up now and don't worry about a thing. The grown-ups'll take care of everything.'

Larissa stood up angrily. 'You can't do this to me, Paul. It's the only thing I've ever asked.'

His lip curled. 'There's always your Auntie Rose. I thought you only had to snap your finger at her.'

Larissa wished she had brought Gary with her. He carried a knife these days which was kind of fashionable in Weyville.

'You don't know where she is, do you?'

Larissa said, 'So. Are you still pushing, or is the free market getting to you?'

He jumped out of the chair then, letting Angel slide, wailing, into a heap, and before she could duck smacked her hard across the face the way he had wanted to in the first place.

'I'm clean, damn you.'

She rolled away to avoid his flying foot and climbed off the floor. 'Now.'

'Whore.'

Hate filled her in a pure sweet wave. Her head was spinning but it was great, like flying, a great buzz of joy, to hate anyone as much as she hated her father. What a charge.

'You don't know where she is.' His voice pursued her towards the door. Joylene's muffins gleamed in buttery clusters on the plate, turning soggy. Faster than him, now the action was on, she picked up a handful and threw them at Angel.

Out on the street the elation passed. The cold sang in the telegraph wires and bit her cheeks like wasps. It had been a tough winter and she never seemed to have enough clothes. The wind bit through her thin jacket. The op shop was out of dufflecoats. Lately she had been thinking about getting a job. Gary was hardly ever at the camp nowadays. He had 'business'. When he was there he was stoned, right out of it more often than not. Sometimes she spent time with Poppy, but she couldn't make sense of half the things she said and she had had her cup and her hand read so often by her (she never told her the same things twice, and nothing ever did come true) that it was boring. Poppy made her go through the camp putting plastic bottles of water round the caravans to stop the dogs from shitting. Larissa couldn't see how this would work. She mentioned that it could be a hoax but Poppy said it was a scientific fact, it was all in the papers. Other times, when Jason was there, though that wasn't often either, because he was usually off with Gary, he would sit and talk to her, or just sit. The shape of the blue hills she had always known but never studied before were imprinted on her brain; she wished she could climb them.

That was on the same scale as getting a job. Pigs might fly. More than once it occurred to her that nobody wanted her much, except perhaps Jason and she didn't fancy him. Even if she did, it would be like doomed love. Gary would do one of them, maybe for good. Like the Warners, only there wouldn't be lots of flowers and mourners for either of them. Probably less than there had been for Basil.

Paul had struck a bitter chord when he spoke of Rose. It was true, Larissa did not know where she was. She had tried to find her and failed. Even the letter she had so painstakingly written had gone unanswered. Not that she could have changed things much, she supposed: not her brother's death (she had taken to thinking of Basil as her brother) or her mother's despair and subsequent imprisonment. But she might have saved her flawed pathetic sister from vanishing. That, at least.

Her footsteps led her toward Cedarwood Grove. Gary had told her to keep away but she couldn't today.

★

Neither could Jeffrey Campbell.

Cruising slowly in that direction for the third time this morning, he looked again for the Studebaker. It had headed up here early and then he had lost it. For more than a week he had tailed it. That, and three other cars. Buff Daniels's note had given him the four combinations of numbers which his scrambled brain had come up with. As well as that he remembered the shape of the old car which had run him down; it was like a bomb, he said, or a bullet.

The match was perfect when the numbers had been checked out. A Studebaker '51? Campbell had asked him over the phone.

Daniels couldn't remember what they looked like, but he went to the library that night and matched a picture with the blurred impression in his memory.

Yes, he had said in the next call, that's what it could have been.

It was fitting into place. Well, something was, but Campbell did not know what just yet. He asked Teddy if he had checked the Kendalls' house recently.

'Every second day. Not a sign of life.'

It seemed that O'Meara had missed something. The Studebaker had gone up that driveway not once but five times that week.

Campbell had watched it from a driveway at the bottom of the street.

Mostly it reappeared a short time later, but today it had not.

'Are you sure that nobody's been into Kendalls'?' he asked O'Meara again. He could have insisted that the visits be logged, but it had started out as a simple favour so that he didn't have to go out of his way. He couldn't help wondering if O'Meara called him an old woman behind his back and simply humoured him by appearing to make these visits. But it was beginning to look as if the Kendall woman's complaints were making all of them look foolish.

'Why don't you take a look?' O'Meara had been terse.

Very slowly, Campbell drove up Cedarwood Grove to the bushed-in driveway that led to the Kendalls' place. He parked, and just as O'Meara had suggested, walked around the house, peering in at the windows.

The house was as desolate as before, abandoned but intact, furnished with ageing chairs and tables all in their place. There was no damage that he could see and all the doors held fast. It was very still around the garden. The swimming pool was full of leaves and debris. A wrought-iron chair was overturned, but it looked as if it had been lying on its side for a long time. Campbell righted it, and saw that rust was setting in where the paint had chipped.

Nevertheless as he got back into the patrol car he could have sworn that he was not alone. He could not understand it. The Studebaker had disappeared but it was not here, or it did not seem to be.

Then in a flash it came to him: the car was inside the garage with the automatic doors.

Shaken, he drove back again to the driveway at the bottom of the road and pulled in. If he was correct, he would need help. But was this the right time to go in?

He was so close to knowing, but still it eluded him. There were still too many pieces missing. He was afraid of moving too quickly and finding one thing only to miss some other, more important, clue.

As he sat there he was alerted by a young woman, so slight she looked like a child although she carried herself as if weighed down with ancient care. She walked hurriedly, casting anxious looks over her shoulder, until she came to the Kendalls' driveway, then she vanished. Campbell knew he was right, that indeed the Studebaker was inside the property.

★

She sprigged herself on the holly bush and swore softly. Even though she had been here once before she could not find the glasshouse at once amongst the ngaios and the broom at the end of the garden. When she did, its windows, covered over from the inside, reflected her face back at her, frightening her as if she had been confronted by someone else.

She knocked, even though she knew she had been seen. After a moment or two the door was opened by Jason and she was admitted into the warm and sumptuous smell of growing plants.

'I told you not to come here, fuckwit,' Gary said. 'There's been a cop snooping round. You want to lead him straight down the path?'

'I thought you had the cops sewn up.'

'Jesus you're dumb.' For the second time in the space of an hour Larissa was hit.

Rose dreamed as she lay sleeping in a cool room at Delphi while the midday sun blazed down outside. She dreamed that she was in Wellington, dancing on a marble table top in the foyer of Parliament Buildings.

When she woke, her pillow was wet as if she had been crying in her sleep for a long time. Not that this was immediately clear to her for at first she believed what she had dreamed was true, seeing it all with an absolute and terrifying clarity. She saw Kit standing beside her and his face was dark with rage. 'I'm sorry, I'm so sorry,' she whimpered. 'Please Kit, I didn't mean to make you angry.'

'You made me look stupid, you promised that you wouldn't ever do anything like that again.'

'I was dancing. I felt so *gay*.'

'Everyone looked.'

'They were all having fun too.'

'Funny, yes. They were laughing at you.'

'They'll have forgotten by tomorrow.'

'I won't. I won't ever.'

'Here's my ring. Take my ring, it's all I've got.'

'It's all you've got on.'

'That's not true, Kit.' She sat straight up in the bed, angrily denying such a falsehood, pulling her swirling peasant dress down over her knees and adjusting her bodice. 'That's Katrina you're looking at.'

Then she looked down at the glittering sheet fallen away from her and her robe drawn in modestly round her waist and glancing about saw that the room was empty. Her ring lay on the dresser beside the pitcher of water. She slipped it over her finger, staring down at it. Keeping up appearances. Sometimes she had thought of throwing it away because it was false. But it was her mother's secret, she would keep it for her. She wondered if her mother had ever known or whether it had been handed on as it was and she had believed in it too. It occurred to her that her mother had died keeping up appearances. Perhaps it was a case of dying or going on pretending to be happy with Tom Diamond (though that was romanticising her death, her mother had simply died of cancer). But she could not remember her mother being happy. There were no servants and no frangipani and no cucumber sandwiches, none of which was Tom Diamond's fault.

It was still too hot to go outside but she did anyway, opening the shutters on to the balcony and sitting on a chair which had been provided. From there she looked down into a grove of olive trees and the Gulf of Itea shining beyond. A woman in blue sat on a rock below her gathering up flowers into her skirt, then stood up, brushing herself down and stretching in a voluptuous way, wandering away inside, unconscious of having been watched. The stark hills sheltered narrow streets and the white houses with their shingled roofs clung to the hillside. Early that morning she had stood in the Stadium in front of the terraces before the crowds came and there wasn't another living person in sight. The night before she had met some Americans at Stamatis' and joined them later at the bar of one of the larger hotels, drinking margaritas and exchanging extravagant travellers' tales; she had not told them that she was the wife of an antipodean politician. Late at night as the conversation exhausted itself and the Americans began talking more to each other she smiled at the barman who propositioned her straight away. 'It is lonely here, my family live in Athens. Why not you talk to me and be kind to me?' he had asked. 'We can talk later in my room.'

She had shaken her head, smiling to soften the refusal.

'But yes, why not? It is little thing.'

'Because I have much family in New Zealand who love me and trust me to travel alone. Kalinikta.'

He spat, and the Americans looked away from her, embarrassed. She knew what they were thinking; she asked for it.

Nor had she exactly spoken the truth, for only the night before that she had visited the same hotel and sat in the same room with her son Richard, to whom she had said goodbye at the bus station the next day; the barman had not distinguished the mother as the woman who now travelled alone. Or perhaps he had assumed that she had a beautiful young paramour who had now deserted her. After all, Richard had held her hand.

'Come back to Athens,' Richard had said.

'You can board an international flight on your own,' she said. 'You're getting good at it.'

'I don't want to leave you here alone, Ma.'

'I need a little bit more time amongst the ruins.'

'Most people only stay here for a day. D'you think the Oracle's going to speak to you?'

'You never know.' She made her voice light, mocking. Since he had arrived in Greece a fortnight before she had been happy. Travelling had been safe and easy for her in a way that it had not been when she was alone. He had grown taller since she had seen him last, and in his manner was taking on the assurance of an adult. From time to time she would put her arm through his, without thinking, in a way that she would not have done when he was younger, and certainly not in Weyville. He accepted the gesture as if it was perfectly natural and they had strolled along companionably through ruins and on the edges of bright seas. In a way, she supposed, she was in love with him, as mothers were said to be with their sons. Definitely, she reflected, the proceeds of the battered Metro's sale had been well spent, bringing him over from America, not to mention paying off Buff Daniels before she left.

'I wish Olivia was here,' she said once.

'I don't,' he had replied promptly.

'You two, you'll get on some day, you wait and see.'

'Like your family?'

'That's different.' Her retort was sharp.

'Is it really?'

He took up the matter of her staying in Delphi again, the night before he left.

'Is it because you don't want to see Dad?'

She hesitated. 'We're having separate holidays,' she said carefully.

'Is he with someone else?'

'Richard, don't be silly.'

'He is, isn't he? What's her name?'

'I don't know.'

'Please. Go on, tell me.' He was a child again; it was a bad moment to confide in him.

'Violet.'

'Jeez. Aw shit, Ma.'

'Forget it.'
'He doesn't mean it. Come to Athens and we can have a good time together. Anyway, she won't be staying at the Espiria with him, will she, not when he meets me?'
'I've no idea.'
'I won't stay there if he brings her. What's she like?'
'I haven't met her.'
'Shall I write and tell you?'
'No. No, please don't do that.'
'When will you go back to New Zealand?'
'Soon, I expect. My money won't last much longer.'
'Get some from Dad. He owes you.'
'It's not like that.' It was on the tip of her tongue to say that Violet had paid for Kit's trip but she stopped herself in time.
'Will you go back to Weyville?'
'I don't think so.' She laughed. 'It'd be a bit hard getting round Weyville without a car. Anyway, I like Wellington.' She wanted desperately to ask him if he would come back to New Zealand, only she had promised herself that she would not. She guessed that he would not return for a long time, maybe never, if he could find a way to stay abroad. It had been important to her that she see him, to tell him in a way that did not threaten him with her need, that it was all right, that she understood. Now she longed for him to go home with her. If she went to Athens she would be lost.
'Are you leaving Dad?' he asked her at the bus stop. It was on the roadside, beside a steep bank. Their backs were to the sea, and the port of Kyrrha. The gilded dome of a church gleamed in the morning light. Rose shivered in the sun; she wondered if she would ever come here again. Yesterday she had bought a kilim to remind her of it. It had exhausted the last of her funds.
'Maybe we'll leave each other. It's too soon to say.'
His kiss was quick, his voice grown-up and brusque as he said goodbye; she knew he would cry on the bus.
She remembered her conversation with the Americans. The women all had jobs. They were resting up from being lawyers and doctors and corporate executives. This was clear even without them saying so in so many words because they gave her their business cards. I've run out, she had told them, but actually I'm a film director.
'Telephone for madame.' The woman dressed in blue stood behind her.
As she trekked down the stairs it occurred to Rose that hotels with

telephones in the rooms were not her strong point, even accepting that in Greece they were a rarity. For a dreadful moment she thought she might pick up the phone and discover that the line was dead, or that the caller would hang up, like the other time.

Instead, the operator asked her to hold for a call from Naya Zeelandia, and then Jeffrey Campbell was talking on a static-laden line from Weyville.

'Your glasshouse,' he shouted. 'They're camped in your garden.'

'What? Who?'

'Your niece. Larissa, and her mates.'

'What are they doing?'

'Growing dope.'

'They're not, oh, they're not.' Suddenly she began to laugh.

'Mrs Kendall.'

'I'm sorry, it's just so funny. Right under our noses. I can see the headlines. Politician cultivates pot plot. It's good, isn't it? Who knows about it?'

Campbell's voice was stiff. 'At the moment, just me . . . er, and your investigator, Mr Daniels. I thought you ought to know.'

'Larissa.' Rose was wary. 'I've thought about her but I didn't think so. She's got an awful boyfriend though. What are you doing about it?'

'Nothing.'

'Why not?

'There's a problem.' He was anxious to change the subject. 'I've been watching them since the funeral.'

This was something Rose did not want to hear. She was tempted to hang up, pretend the line had cut out. The laughter in her voice fading, she said, 'What have they got to do with Toni?'

There was a pause at the other end. 'Not Mrs Warner's funeral.'

Then nothing at all was amusing any more. 'Basil,' he shouted, and she shouted the name back. He was trying to tell her something else but the satellite started to echo and she could not understand.

Kit rang later, from Athens. He knew about Katrina. He had been briefed, he explained: Katrina was in jail and they were disgraced.

'Where's Sharna?' she asked.

'Sharna? How should I know?'

The last bus for Athens for the day had left. She went to Stamatis' and ate skewered meat and tzatziki and drank retsina and thought about Richard, already somewhere over the Atlantic heading for La Guardia and a connecting flight south, and how easy it would be for a woman like her to make her way to lonely Greek barmen and how like a movie scenario her life was becoming.

When she slept, briefly, before dawn, it was neither Larissa nor Basil's name that echoed in her head but that of the child Sharna.

11

Rex Gamble's ministerial car was waiting at the airport for Kit and Rose. So was Gamble himself.

Kit said, 'I wasn't expecting this.'

He looked drawn from the flight. Rose had suggested that he follow commonsense procedures about drinking and eating in the air, but he ignored her advice in a pointed way. She guessed that an idyll was over for him. It bothered her when she first met him at the airport in Athens, that his stricken face and sense of loss might be due to some misplaced sense of conscience on her account. But it soon became clear that if Violet had been relinquished, or Kit relinquished by Violet (and it was all rather unclear), little had altered between herself and Kit. The hours passed in silence. Anyway, she had not much to say either. The sheer catastrophe that had befallen her family in her absence, and the fact that such momentous events could transpire without her being there to prevent them or, at least, supervise their outcome, had rendered her still and apart from him.

Now, despite his pallor, Kit was coming to life in the back of Gamble's car, as if undergoing an adrenalin charge.

'Have you kept up with the play, mate, or shall I fill you in?' Rex Gamble leaned over from the front seat of the car as it picked up speed along Cobham Drive.

'Run through the essentials,' Kit said, and Rose gave him points for that.

'RSL's collapsed.' He pulled a face.

'Shit.'

'Bad news all right.' From the tightening of his knuckles along the back of the chauffeur's seat, Rose guessed that this was personal as well as political.

'And SLU's are up.'

'What are SLU's?' asked Rose.

'Surplus Labour Units.' Gamble was brisk.

'Unemployed people?'

'Something like that,' Kit said.
'How many?'
'Six thousand this month.'
'Je-siss.' Kit drew a sharp breath. 'It can't go much higher.'
'Courage.' Gamble blew a long stream of smoke towards the car's roof. It curled over and fell, gently engulfing Rose. 'Sunshine, wait till you see our inflation figures. We've knocked them for six.'
'What's Prebble up to?'
'The dear boy is in strife with the risen Messiah but what's new about that? The Prime Minister, incidentally, still bears a remarkable resemblance to Billy Bunter in spite of all the health foods. They say he's eating them as well as.' He tapped the side of his nose.
'What's going to happen?'
'Oh, he'll have to go.'
'Who, Prebble?' Rose could hardly contain her eagerness. She felt Kit lean against her, wishing to restrain her without being seen to.
'No, dear. The Prime Minister of course.' Gamble chuckled.
They were coming up alongside the boat marina at Evans Bay, and would soon turn up to Hataitai where they were to be let off at the flat.
'Oh, yes. And they've found some mining prospects in a bit of scrub up the back of Weyville. Your electorate, no less.'
'What bit of scrub?'
'A bit they call the reserve, I expect you know it. It's nothing serious they tell me.'
'They can't touch that.' Kit's voice was tense.
'They can't not touch it.'
'Who says?'
'Market forces. The pickings could be rich. No room for greenies in territory like that.'
'Kit's a forester,' said Rose. 'You must know that.'
'And your sister's in jail, I hear.'
A hard lump choked Rose's throat. As if she had not always known what politics was about.
Hadn't she?
Always the trade-off. And her family were playing straight into it.
The car had pulled up. 'Attempted murder, isn't it?'
'Aggravated assault, I believe,' said Kit.
Their luggage was following by taxi. As they stood in the road waiting for it to arrive, Gamble's Crown car did a U-turn and he wound the window down with an electric flick. 'Don't get wet, my children,' he said, 'it looks like rain.'

★

They found Larissa sitting on the step as they struggled up the steep path with their luggage.

'It's a bit late for confessions, isn't it,' Kit snapped when they were inside.

'Oh shut up, Kit.' Rose shot him a warning look, reminding him that, in theory, they did not know of the presence in their garden in Weyville.

He subsided, sullen, hemmed in by the place already.

There was no food in the flat and the air smelled stale.

'How long have you been waiting for us?' Rose asked, opening windows and turning on the hot water.

'Three days.'

Rose looked properly at her niece. The spiky hair was flattened out, streaky blue and darkish at the roots, the eyes huge and hungry.

'I slept at the shelter at nights. Come back here in the mornings.'

'Haven't you got any money?'

The question was greeted with a shrug.

'Did they feed you?'

'Yeah. A bit.'

'Get some fish and chips. There's a place round the corner. And get some biscuits and milk at the shop next door.' Kit was pulling out money from his wallet.

'You don't want to know why I'm here, do you? Go and get some fish and chips, go and do the messages. That's all you know.'

'We know.' Rose put her head down in her hands. 'We do know.'

'Then why didn't you say? I've been waiting here three days.'

'Give us a chance. We weren't expecting to see you. We flew back straight away.'

'You did?'

'Yes.'

'So who told you?'

'It doesn't matter.' Treading through the minefield. 'Where's Sharna?'

Larissa began to cry then, not real crying, not weeping, just short puffy gasps as if it was so long since she had cried that she had forgotten how to.

Rose said, 'You go to the shops, Kit.' He turned and left without speaking.

'He hates me and my family, doesn't he?'

'He hates himself, I think.' It surprised Rose that she had said this, but as soon as she had it sounded true. 'So tell me about it.

How did it happen? How did Basil die?'

Larissa stared at her. 'That was ages ago.'

'Two weeks, three weeks.'

'A month. He was dead and you were gone.'

'A month, well then, yes it must be all of that. Tell me about Sharna.'

Larissa stirred restlessly. Probably she was as tired as Rose. 'Can I use your bathroom?'

She took a long time, running taps, and then there was a long silence, almost as if the flat was empty. When she emerged, she sat down on the floor by the window, staring at the sea.

'That's where Gary and me should go, somewhere by the sea. That's where the housetruckers go.'

'Larissa, where's Sharna?'

'Oh yeah. Sharna's in welfare and they won't tell us where she's been taken. Mum's friend Minna wants to look after her, and they says she's not a fit person.'

'Do you think she is?'

'She's okay. She likes Sharna.'

'What about you? Could you look after her?'

'Me?' Larissa was shocked. 'You must be joking, they'd never let me look after Sharna in a caravan.'

'You could move out of it.'

'And leave Gary, you serious?'

'I don't know what I'm serious about. I haven't slept properly for forty-eight hours, I couldn't get sleeping pills for the plane in Athens, I'm nearly out of my head.'

'Nah, you're just like, talking off the top of your head, aren't you? Not thinking, but you are thinking underneath. You're just not being careful the way you usually are. I'll tell you what you're thinking— here's another chance to reform Larissa. Get her away from the gypsies in the wood. Well, I'm not going to leave Gary.'

'Not even for Sharna?'

Larissa's face crumpled again. 'All right then, I've asked them. I've promised them anything, and they've said no. Satisfied?'

They would say no, too, Rose thought. How could they hand Sharna over to Gary's accomplice? Or whatever she was. For all Rose knew Gary's crimes were Larissa's too. Some of them, if not all of them.

'And I asked Uncle Jim, who was at least kind enough to bury Basil for us, and he said get stuffed, and now he's gone to Memphis, and then I asked my father if he'd ask them to give her to Minna and he chucked me out.'

'And now you've come to ask me?'

'They'd give Sharna to you.' The tears that had been so hard to shed were falling fast. Rose moved to put her arms around Larissa, as if, at last, something she had lost was about to be returned to her.

Kit pushed the door open and put a bundle of groceries and a hot parcel of fish and chips on the bench. 'I called a taxi from the shops.'

'Where are you going?'

'Down to the House. To my office. I need somewhere I can think.'

But for a moment his face softened as he looked at Larissa's head bent over her arms. He shook his head and turned away. The loss between him and Rose was not Violet, or Morris Applebloom, or even politics; it was the loss of this girl. The loss lay between them, a vacuum in Rose which she had never been able to fill. It was so easy to blame someone else, Rose could see, but in the end it came down to oneself. Loss, and guilt, and the belief that she could have done better in redeeming Larissa from what had befallen her, had numbed her, paralysing all her best intentions and coming between her and Kit and the children.

She let her hand rest on Larissa's arm.

'Don't touch me,' said Larissa, pulling away as if she had been stung. 'Don't ever fuckin' touch me.'

Nick Newbone had also been looking for Rose for the past three days. He hadn't come to Wellington just to see her but when Kit's office told him that the Kendalls were due back he stayed on. He made more appointments and hung around. Probably Rose wouldn't want to see him after a long flight, but what he had to tell her could not wait any longer. For more than a week he had carried the information which he had picked up from Toni Warner's lawyer. It was contained in a sealed envelope with his name on it. The police had supervised the lawyer handing it over to him in case it should provide evidence for their case against Lyle Warner.

'It's nothing,' he had said to the detective-sergeant and to Tippet, a young officer new to Weyville. The force had been supplemented from out of town to help with all the inquiries that had been taking place over the past months.

'It's just some material for me to print out for the Labour Party. Street names.' He held it out for them to look at, but his heart pounded.

'Do we need a copy?' the constable was asking.

The detective-sergeant crinkled his nose. The Warner case was open and shut. 'Just for the records.' His attention had already moved on.

Nick had been careful not to open it until he was out of sight.

The Oaks bar had become too familiar to him. He had a second beer and wished he had not. It was still his intention to drive to Weyville that night. He allowed what he considered to be a decent time after Rose and Kit's expected arrival home and dialled their number. When there was no answer, he rang Parliament. Kit was in a meeting already, a secretary told him, but if he was looking for Mrs Kendall, there was a message here from her saying she had left on a plane for Weyville.

He picked up a hitchhiker on the way, a straggly childish-looking woman with blueish hair, trying to shelter from the intermittent rain beneath a makeshift pack. He could have sworn he had seen her before. It was hard to tell what she looked like behind the freshly applied layers of black mascara and kohl.

'I could have got a ride on a plane,' she said, 'but I like hitching.'

'You turned down the plane for a night on the road?'

'See, there's this woman offered me a ticket, but I don't trust her.'

Liar. 'What did she do?' he asked, amused.

'Tried to get too close. You'll hit Weyville by ten if you step on the gas.'

'You're an expert?'

'Nope. I never come down here before. I can figure things out.'

He didn't doubt this. But he was suspicious of her cultivated roughness. She seemed smarter than her cover suggested.

At Hunterville, she said, 'You look stuffed, man. Like me to drive?'

'What sort of a mug do you take me for?'

'I'm a good driver.'

'Have you got a licence?'

'Yeah, sure. It's tattooed on my bum. Do you want to see it?'

He slowed. 'Don't start anything, eh. I can drop you here at the shops.'

'Relax. I only said I'd like to drive.'

On impulse, he pulled over. 'You're right, I'm stuffed out of my tree.' All the same, he held on to the keys while he walked round to the passenger's side and she slid into his place. What the hell, life took some funny turns.

As the car gathered momentum he sat taut, ready to save them if it turned out she couldn't drive. But as they glided into the night he felt that he didn't have to worry, only a slight hesitation on the corners giving away the driver's inexperience. Her confidence built and he dozed as the road sped beneath them, shaking himself awake now and then with a question flickering through his head. Why was Rose Kendall coming back to town?

Towards Weyville, the silent girl intent at the wheel, and as he could see, happy in some contained way like an aquarium fish that has seen the open sea, turned and broke the silence of hours.

'Was it heavy?' she asked. 'Was Mrs Warner heavy? We didn't have pallbearers.'

Instinctively, he put his hand on his breast pocket where the wad of papers was stored. After awhile, he said, 'Let's say it was a heavy scene.' They cruised down the hill towards the lights of the town. He knew who the girl was.

Rose thought it was about fifty-two hours since she had slept and her lids felt gummed to her eyeballs. She had not been to bed since she left Delphi, however long ago that was.

Larissa had stormed out of the flat.

'I'll do whatever you want,' Rose had cried, seeing her anger. 'No strings attached.'

'That's what you always said,' Larissa shouted as she backed down the path.

Rose could not remember ever saying any such thing, but the argument was pointless. Larissa still went.

Sanity suggested that she wait until the morning to go to Weyville, but she faltered at the thought of her return. By morning she might not be able to go at all.

The plane was delayed by fog and it was after six when it took off. The woman in the seat beside Rose had a young child. Masses of pretty fluffy brown hair surrounded the woman's face; her trim body was encased in tailored slacks and a baby-blue button-through cardigan. She released a torrent of information which included details of what the child's name would have been had she not been called Chloe (it would have been Alice), the number of women in the nursing home who had given their child the same name, and how many teeth the girl had. She leapt on the seat to play games with the baby, paraded its toddling footsteps the length of the plane by fingertip control, and sang 'Old MacDonald Had A Farm' in a high penetrating voice as the plane came in to land, to protect her from turbulence, she explained. As they trundled along the tarmac towards the terminal building she burst into 'Jingle Bells'.

Rose viewed this remarkable performance with wonder. She had hoped to sleep. While they waited inside the plane for the steps to be wheeled into place, the woman, still fussing over the child, turned and said in the loud silence of the waiting passengers, 'Now I've got you. I've been trying to work out who you were, all the way up. You're that horrible politician's wife.' Her look of triumph flashed around the plane's interior. 'We vote National anyway, but you might stop him having the trees cut down in the reserve. That's the very least you could do. But I don't expect you care.'

Inside the terminal building she was accosted straight away by Hortense Newbone. For a moment Rose did not recognise her. Hortense's hair was dyed persimmon and cropped short over her ears; she wore a very brief tunic clasped at the waist by a huge leather belt, red stockings and Doc Marten boots. Altogether she was not unlike an older version of Larissa in one of her various guises. Actually, much older. Her white face with its wine-red lips was taut and lined.

'I wasn't expecting you,' she said.

'Who were you expecting?'

'I took a chance on Kit being on board. Matt heard he was back in the country. We thought he might have come straight up to see the electorate about the mining issue.'

'He's being briefed at Parliament right now,' Rose lied. Though it could be true.

'Can I quote you on that?' The pencil hovered above the note-book.

Rose shook her head. 'Get it from the horse's mouth.'

'You look dreadful.'

'Thanks, I feel it.' She opened and shut her mouth, trying to say more. 'It's awful about Toni,' she said at last.

Hortense sniffed. 'Oh, Toni. She was very man-orientated.'

'Hortense, she's dead.'

'Obviously. I'm telling you what the jury will say when Lyle goes on trial. The woman's always wrong.'

'You sound as if you believe it.'

'Me? I'm for women. But I'm just a journo, very impartial, don't you know. They'll crucify her.'

'How can they if she's not there?'

'That's what makes it so easy.' Hortense gave a superior smile as if she thought Rose was pathetic.

'Don't be a media hoon, it doesn't suit you.' Hortense was making a horrible kind of sense.

Hortense picked her ear with the end of her pencil. Her look said it all: *You weren't even there, you didn't even come.*

'What do you think of your sister?' she asked.

'Look, lay off Hortense. And put that damn pencil away.'

'C'mon, you must have something to say about that.'

'What do you expect me to say?' Ever since Kit had filled her in with the details about ten million light years ago in Athens she had been putting off thinking about Katrina.

'I'd say she was great, that's what I would say if I were you.' Hortense slammed her notebook angrily into the canvas bag she wore over her shoulder. Then Rose saw the billboard of the evening paper behind them. I DID IT FOR MOTHERS, it blazed, and underneath there was a photograph of Katrina.

'She's a heroine,' said Hortense. 'Anarchy rules, okay?'

'Going to the airport,' said Jeffrey Campbell, picking up his hat.

'Visiting celebrity?' Teddy O'Meara's voice bridled.

'Mrs Kendall's arrived in town,' said Campbell evenly. 'I'm escorting her home.'

'You don't tell me. I thought she'd beggared off for good.'

'It seems you were wrong.'

Since O'Meara had been taken off the Kendall inquiry he mentioned it more often than when he was on it. As if the honey drew him. Still, Campbell thought, he need not have told him that he was going to meet Rose Kendall. O'Meara had been given no reason for his withdrawal from the case; if he knew he was being watched he showed no signs of it.

'I always said . . . ' Teddy stopped.

'Yes, what did you always say?' Campbell paused in the doorway.

'That she was a lettuce or two short of a green salad.'

He heard Teddy's laughter follow him out the station door and into the spring night.

He explained to her that the shed was empty when it was raided the previous day. It was impossible to tell whether it had been left in the same condition as when the Kendalls lived in the house, given that they did not use the shed, but it was remarkably clean for an outhouse that had been in disuse for so long. The ground around it had been disturbed and shovelled over; the branches of a tree broken back. But nobody except him, and Buff Daniels, had seen it in use and he was at a loss to prove what he had seen.

'Do you want to go and look for yourself?'

'In the morning, perhaps. I don't know what I'll be doing. I'll probably have to find somewhere else to live.'

'Would you be better to stay with a friend for tonight?'

He was right of course, but who? There was no Toni. She might once have gone to Mungo Lord's but her sister had tried hard to kill him, so that was out. And Hortense, well, maybe, at a pinch, but her encounter with her this evening hardly promised a restful night.

'Maybe I'll ring Matt and Nancy Decker. At least if they know I'm here . . . but I've got some things to do . . . I want to make some toll calls, my daughter, you know, she doesn't know we're back in the country. And I want to get a rental car delivered. Maybe it would be best for me just to go to bed.'

'I'll send a patrol car round a couple of times during the night. And I'll come past on my way home.' He picked up the phone and dialled a number. 'Just testing, thanks. Your phone's working.'

'Will Teddy O'Meara come round?'

'Probably not. Did you want him to?'

'It makes no difference. I've dealt with him in the past when you've been around, that's all.'

Campbell sidestepped. 'I don't think he's working tonight.'

'I can understand that the case is peculiar.' She was remembering her outburst in the station months before. 'I expect you get fed up with me.'

'We're here to help.'

'I know that, of course.'

'But you hired a private investigator?'

'True, how did you find out about that?'

He hesitated. 'Perhaps we could talk about it tomorrow. You're tired, if you don't mind me saying so. You'll need some rest, especially if you're going to collect the little girl in the morning.'

'Thank you. I'm grateful for that. I was afraid you might not want me to have Sharna.'

Campbell had contacted a welfare worker and arranged that she pick up Sharna first thing in the morning. 'It seemed like the right thing to do,' he said.

When he had gone, she considered how easy it was, if you were just a little important, to pull strings in the system. How much easier it was for those who were very important. And how totally impossible if you were Minna or Larissa, or indeed, if you were Katrina. Perhaps Katrina was a true heroine. Stunningly, she had done something. For the moment it hardly mattered whether or not it was right. She couldn't tell.

The house was clean, if dusty, and barer since the break-in. Broken items had been tidied up and taken away. She turned on heaters, shivering in the cool spring night. Outside a frog squawked near the swimming pool. She tried the door on to the patio; it was fastened. After that, she checked each window on the ground floor again, although she had watched Jeffrey Campbell do that once already. When the hire firm delivered her car she signed for it and parked it in the garage, noting that the mechanism for the automatic door was missing. It would turn up she supposed. Then she checked the doors again. Afterwards she rang Olivia.

'I'm sorry I went away at holiday time,' Rose said.

'I was happy here, after all,' Olivia said. It sounded slightly quaint, a little reproving.

'I'm glad. What did you do?'

There was a pause.

'Met a man and lived with him.'

'Oh. Um, that's nice dear. Where is he now?'

'It wasn't long-term, mother.'

'Well. I hope he was a nice boy.'

'He was fifty. His wife came back from sabbatical.'

'That's nice,' said Rose again.

'Yes.'

'Greece was nice too.'

'Oh Greece, yes.'

Taking a plunge to break this impasse, Rose told her daughter about Katrina and Basil and Larissa and Sharna, rattling on into the silence. In the end she said, 'I'm going to pick up Sharna in the morning.'

'That's your decision,' said Olivia, and hung up.

When at last she went upstairs and climbed into bed, Rose lay awake for a few minutes. I'll manage, she thought. Then she fell into a dreamless sleep.

Towards two the phone rang.

'Hullo. Hullo. Hullo,' she cried into the silence. The familiar click greeted her at the other end.

As she reached to phone the police it rang a second time.

She screamed, 'You're being watched!'

There was a click, a button pushed, coins falling through a slot.

The voice at the other end was muffled. 'I'm coming to burn your house down.' The line went dead.

So, there was a voice. At last. How he must have missed her, her secret caller.

The policeman in the watch house was business-like. No, Sergeant Campbell was not there, he had finished hours before. So had Constable O'Meara. His voice was courteous but brisk. 'Is there a problem, Mrs Kendall?' he enquired, clearly alerted to the possibility of her call.

'I'm sorry,' she said. 'Maybe I just heard a noise. It was probably nothing.'

It would be fatal to crack now. They would never let her take Sharna.

'A patrol car cruised past less than half an hour ago, would you like someone to come round again?'

'It's all right,' she heard herself say. 'I'll call you if I'm really worried.'

She sat by the heater, dozing a little, pulling herself awake from time to time. Between naps, she thought that her head was quite clear, as if the short sleep had restored all her senses. Only once when she dozed she was back in Delphi, and another time she was dancing on a marble tabletop which turned into the flat tray of a truck.

The phone pinged. On her feet in an instant, she picked the receiver up and slammed it down again before the rings began.

She sat with her hand quivering above it. It pinged again. She took the receiver off its cradle and lay it beside the instrument. I can live with that, she told herself. It would be daylight soon.

Perhaps twenty minutes passed while she sat rigid and upright.

The house creaked. Or so she thought. She heard her heart beating, a steady bang of terror.

The next creak was more definite. At first she did not recognise the noise for what it was. It was a slow soft slipstream of sound. But then she picked it, the garage door rolling upwards.

She willed herself to stand up, walk to the window, look out, but she could not. Any minute she expected to hear the rental car being jump-started. But instead, all she heard was the door roll downwards again.

Now she did not know if there was someone in the house or not. It could be entered through the garage.

Shakily she picked up the phone's receiver. Almost immediately, as she reached for the dial, it began to ring.

'I've been trying to get you, Mrs Kendall,' said the muffled voice. 'What a long time you talk.'

She slammed the phone down.

The house was very still now, more still than she could ever remember it. But then, in the distance, a dog began to yap. It sounded like Roach. She could have sworn it was him.

'Roach,' she called. The constriction in her throat was painful as if something was breaking. If she could touch the dog now it would make so much difference. Instead, an image of his slit throat flashed past her. Outside something splashed in the pool. A hedgehog drowning, perhaps.

More splashes followed, as if something heavy was being thrown in. This was no hedgehog.

But at least the noise was outside. If there was only one of them, that was where he was now. It occurred to Rose that there was more than one. There had to be. One here, and one somewhere in a phone box.

The phone rang again.

'Yes,' she said dully.

'Rose.' The voice was intimate beneath its filtered sound. 'You shouldn't have done it.'

'Please, don't . . . do this to me.' She was ashamed of the whining in her voice, and dropped the phone this time.

Crying now, she pressed herself against the wall, edging to the window. Below her the garage door rolled up again. Down in the kitchen she heard something land heavily, as if thrown. She crouched down, waiting for the explosion, the smell of burning, or for the stranger to emerge from the top of the stairs.

But there was nothing, not even running feet.

Dawn was streaking the sky. She willed herself to move again and looked down on to the path below. As she moved, as if the person was moving when she did, the garage door rolled down again. Then it happened several more times, down and up, as if whoever it was was simply having fun. She couldn't see anyone and cursed the way the bushes had been allowed to run riot.

Firmly she picked up the phone, determined this time to ring Campbell at his home. Too bad if Lola objected.

The line was dead.

The noise below stopped. She walked back to the window. In the shadows a figure made its way unhurriedly along the driveway, sloping off towards the gate that led to Cedarwood Grove.

When the light filled the sky she could see where bricks had been thrown around the pool and into it. There was one in the kitchen too, but nothing was broken, no sign left of the intruder's entry.

★

Katrina was in Mt Eden jail. Ellis Hannen had offered to put up bail for her but it was refused. They thought she might try to kill Mungo again. It was a possibility, she admitted. She would still like to. More than that, she would like to crawl around hedgerows on the edge of fields, sniffing clean air and earth and rubbing tangy leaves between her fingers, the way she had when she followed him. This place was full of the smell of shit and Lysol and food so badly cooked it made you dry-retch before it reached your mouth.

It was nearly breakfast time. She would have to face it or die, she supposed.

The night before they had asked her if she objected to her sister uplifting Sharna. At first she was inclined to say yes. Rose had never done Larissa much good as far as she could see, though there were signs that Larissa was improving. In the end she said she didn't mind. 'I'd like her to take her to Minna,' she added. Fat chance, but it was worth a try.

★

At 7.45 Rose knocked on the door at the address she had been given, No. 10 Power Street.

For awhile there was no answer. A woman over the fence at No. 12 was pegging up a row of black regulation socks on a clothesline. She looked across at Rose.

'You needn't bother coming here,' she called. 'I could never stomach your lot.'

'It's all right, Mrs Marment,' said a young woman appearing round the side of the house, 'it's just a visitor for me.' Her arms were full of unfolded napkins. 'I didn't expect you so soon,' she said, leading the way inside.

Other children, preparing for school, stared at Rose. The air was thick with the smell of hot milk and burnt toast.

'I'll help you fold,' said Rose, speaking in what she hoped was an unhurried way.

'It's all right, I'll get Sharna for you. Come in. Why don't you sit down and give her a cuddle while I finish fixing her things?' She shooed her children away. 'They've been playing with her, they don't want her to go,' she explained.

'I can help you, really,' Rose said. She half-snatched the napkins.

The woman shrugged, turned away.

'I'll get her.' It was clear she thought Sharna was in for a bad run.

'I'm sorry,' said Rose, trying to sound calm. 'I've got a rental car that I have to return. I hired it especially to fetch her things.' It was a thin excuse but she could think of no other. 'I didn't mean to hurry you.'

'She's a good kid,' said the woman when she returned with Sharna. She appeared to be a little mollified.

Sharna seemed to smile for a moment, and Rose thought *She knows me*, but then the child was distracted, turning her one good eye to follow the movement of a cat in the room.

After what felt like a long time the woman had all her things gathered together and Rose was able to leave. She drove carefully and slowly down Power Street. There was no harness for Sharna.

At the corner of the street she saw a telephone box. It was an ordinary battered phone box covered with the usual graffiti and scarred paint. Slowing down still further she glanced over her shoulder, seeing down the whole length of the street. It was the only phone box.

But it was like a living presence. This was where, just once, a call had been traced. Whoever the caller was, it might well have been here that he had stood in the last few hours and spoken to her.

A police car cruised along in her direction from the far end of the street. She wondered if it might be Campbell, come to supervise her uplifting of Sharna, or perhaps wanting to see if she needed help. He would think of something like that. In a panic, she accelerated away, one hand holding the child in place. She had no wish to see Campbell this morning. The time for that was past. With a surge of relief, she realised that he would not know what the car she was driving looked like. She risked another swift glimpse behind her as she turned out of Power Street. It appeared that the car had stopped near where she had just been. She thought she recognised the driver. She thought it was O'Meara. Maybe Campbell had sent him instead.

The car showed no signs of following her.

★

This time the plane was nearly empty. Sharna lay sleeping in Rose's lap where she had collapsed as soon as they sat down. The child showed no signs of noticing the journey, or her change of company. The plane's engines seemed very loud to Rose, as if she was hearing them for the first time, as Sharna would. She didn't budge. It was as though she didn't notice what was happening. Or if she did, as if it no longer mattered. Rose wondered how early a child's sense of wonder could be abandoned.

Looking down at the sleeping child she touched her cheek with her finger. It was the first moment she had had to reflect upon Sharna. The bizarre sequence of events which led to her sitting on a plane running away with her sister's child had not fallen into place. Although she had known since five o'clock that morning, with seemingly steady logic, that she must leave Weyville by the first possible means, that logic was faltering. She doubted that it had ever existed. The Phantom had won again. It wasn't logic that had possessed her, it was the same old madness. Only there was a difference; the terror had been so close she believed she had all but felt his breath on her cheek. And now he had multiplied like a poisonous plant breaking off and rerooting itself wherever it touched the ground. It had felt as if nothing would save her if she stayed.

But she could understand quite clearly now that she had no right to take Sharna with her, though for hours she had seen it as essential to protect them both.

At the airport she had written a note to Campbell and asked the reservations clerk to ring and tell him that it was there. She prayed that he would get it. It said: 'I'll be back in a few days. So will the baby. Please tell anyone who needs to know.' Only she didn't mean to go back, not ever. Welfare might intervene, though she doubted it, not immediately anyway. Then she would have sorted things out.

Or would she? She put her finger in the child's hand, expecting the fingers to curl, as Larissa's or her own children's would have done. But nothing happened. She appeared almost to shrug Rose aside.

Of course, this was not Larissa. It was Sharna.

As the plane rose she saw a convoy of buses heading along the south road. There was a purposeful, organised look about them.

Wearily, Nick Newbone prepared to leave for Wellington again. He had missed Rose by inches everywhere. He wouldn't have known where she was going now if his wife, Hortense, had not reported seeing her at the airport with a child. Rose had hurried on to the plane, almost as if she were running away from something, Hortense told him over lunch.

He was grateful, both for the time she had deigned to spend with him for once and for the information. But he didn't trade with her.

12

'It's the least you can do,' cried Kit.

'Why?' He hadn't been home the night before and Rose hadn't tried to find him. But she had left another message, this time advising of her return to the capital.

'Because this party's important. Don't you understand? Gamble's asked us to his house.'

'Well you can go.'

'He asked specially for you. I *need* you. Look, there's a bloody great army of protesters on its way to Wellington, it's going to be a rough day.' He sounded almost tremulous on the end of the phone.

'Mining rights in the reserve?'

'Yep. I've got to weather this one, Rose.'

'Who with? Gamble or the electorate? You can't have both, Kit.'

'Your chum Applebloom sees the sense in it.'

'He would, there's money in it. Instant cash. Is he coming down?'

'I thought you'd know.'

'You've got it wrong, Kit.'

He hesitated. 'No, well he's not.'

'Staying clear today, is he? What about Harry? Matt?'

'Yes, and I hear Nick Newbone's on his way, although it was only yesterday he said he was keeping clear.'

'Five busloads of protesters, eh? They must have stayed somewhere overnight. I saw them from the air,' she added by way of explanation.

'They'll be here about two. What were you doing in Weyville, anyway?'

'Collecting Sharna.'

'I don't believe I'm hearing this.'

'You are.'

'Where is she?'

'Here. Asleep. She sleeps a lot. Or else she eats. She's like Larissa. Remember?'

'Rose, you've got children of your own.'

'But Sharna hasn't got parents of her own. She's family, Kit.'

'She can't stay in the flat. Or if she does I'm moving out of it.'
'Well maybe. I thought we could talk about that.'
He sighed. 'Yes, I suppose we'll have to. But I can't now. Not today. I'll tell Gamble to expect us this evening, all right?'
'But I've got the baby.'
'Well, you'll have to get a sitter won't you?'
As Kit hung up Nick Newbone banged on the door of the flat.
'I'm the enemy, don't you know?' she said when the coffee was poured. 'Depending whose side you're on.'
'I don't know whose side I'm on. I don't think anybody does. Whose are you?'
'Buggered if I know, Charlie.' She grinned, playing it dumb. She hoped he would not notice how much her hands shook. Until Nick told her why he was here she would not give much away. His crumpled appearance and awful clothes seemed more touching than she remembered. He was a bit overweight, always had been, and today he needed a shave. But he had the cleanest fingernails of any man she knew. They shone in rows along his clasped hands like rims of pale cheese. And his looks were deceptive; she knew he was extraordinarily competent at whatever he did and, as well, he was one of the people she had trusted. As Kit had. Perhaps Nick felt betrayed by Kit too — she supposed he must do, thinking back to the night when he had failed to appear at the Party meeting. It would be like him not to come, rather than stand as one of his accusers after what they had been through together. But she wasn't going to ask about that.
'I really didn't come to talk politics,' he said, as if reading her mind. 'Look, Toni had some stuff she meant to give me but she died before I could get it from her. It was really for you.'
'Toni's stuff? What're you talking about, Nick?'
Suddenly awkward, he said, 'It's all right. I know why you didn't come to the funeral.'
'Do you really?'
'Of course.'
'How many other people knew?'
'Everybody that mattered.'
'God, that's just about as bad.'
'It doesn't make any difference now.'
'I ran away, you know. It's turning into à habit.'
'It was best that you didn't come.'
'She mattered more than he ever did. In fact, I mean, you know, I ask myself, did he ever, though it seemed so clear at the time. It was

all such a long time ago.' The sea in Evans Bay was bleak. Windsurfers fluttered on the waves, breaking the grey surface. 'It's hard to walk away from mistakes. I'd like to have got closer to Sarah, d'you know? We were friends in that tidy suburban way that pushes everything under the rug, but it never went far enough. I wish she was my friend now.'

'She didn't go to the funeral either.'

'I wouldn't have thought so. So what did Toni leave for me, a pair of his unwashed socks? Surely Sarah could have had those.' Her laughter sounded like a dog bark to him.

'Rose, stop.'

The coffee cup rattled in her hand against the saucer. Not for the first time the foolishness of their lives struck her. She could see how their group had turned in on itself. They hadn't achieved what they had hoped. In the end they were devouring one another. She tried to see them as they all saw themselves in 1981, but it was like looking at a blank screen. At last she wanted to cry for Toni, but she was afraid Nick would think it was for herself.

'So what is this about anyway?'

'All right then. You remember giving Toni the time sheets you'd kept on your caller?'

'No, not that, I don't want to talk about that.'

'Please. Just for a minute. I might be able to help.'

'All right. But I don't think anyone can.'

'You know I'd been feeding the computer for the electoral rolls?'

She nodded.

'Toni asked me to help her do an AI.'

'What's that?'

'Computerspeak for artificial intelligence. She knew more about computers than she let on. AI's a bit crude — the computer doesn't actually think for you, but it does help to sort out your ideas and set up a path, or a number of paths that you can explore. It sorts out possibilities, if you like.'

'That's what she showed me when she came here?'

'That's right.'

'What my investigator calls critical path analysis?'

'Quite. After she'd seen you, we began to take it further. We made a complete list of each person who worked within a ten-street radius of Power Street. These are what I did.' He opened his briefcase and produced sheets of computer paper. 'Then we tried to match them alongside the people you might know.' He took an envelope out of the briefcase and opened it. Lists emerged, written in Toni's elegant old-fashioned copperplate which had always amazed Rose. It was headed up 'Known', 'Probably Known', 'Maybe'.

'That means, "known" to you, of course. The bottom of the scale is "maybe" because in a sense you know everyone in Weyville because you've lived there all your life and she hadn't. Then there's a list of ticks, indicating the ones that are shift workers. None of the shift workers get past "probably known"—to you, that is, meaning they've been Party supporters, they've come to functions, things like that, but not people we thought you'd know really well. But it doesn't eliminate them. After awhile, gaps began to show up. There were gaps in the Power Street roll, for instance, that we couldn't work out.'

'This is where the telephone box is, the one where they traced the call?'

'Yup.'

'I told her it wouldn't be anyone in that street. He'd have been caught when the police put a watch on the phone box if he lived in the area.'

'Are you sure they watched it, or were they just humouring you?'

'Surely they wouldn't do that?'

'The police are too busy to take harassment seriously. The chances are, they looked sympathetic and did sweet f.a.'

'Campbell seems all right. He's been kind.'

'So I gathered. I wondered why. It took me a long time to work it out.'

'Why?'

'Because kindness was all he could offer you. Let me take you a bit further. After that call was traced, didn't your caller start ringing mostly in the middle of the night?'

'That's right. Because they don't monitor in the middle of the night unless it's life and death, it costs too much. And nobody's ever been certain that I was telling the truth. It always happened when Kit was away.'

'Do you realise what you just said? Look, how did the person know that the trace was on your phone?'

'I suppose... well, I did suppose, because you can sort of tell. You hear clicks on the line. So if you're watching out for them, you know.'

'All right, but if your caller was afraid he was being watched, would he have known that the trace was taken off at nights?'

'Well, it depends on who he is.'

'Exactly. It's somebody who knows about these things. And it's somebody who always knew when Kit was away.'

'So it's someone close to me. That's been obvious for ages. Look Nick, I'm sorry to disappoint you, but there's more than one of these people.'

He looked crestfallen. 'Are you sure?'

'Yes.'

'That's not what you thought when you told Toni about it.'

'Well. I thought it was one. But I know differently now.'

Nick reflected on this information. 'All the same, short of your immediate family, who knew just when Kit came and went?'

'There were a number of you in the Party who were close to us. You, Harry, Matt, usually Toni herself, which meant Lyle too even though he wasn't what you'd call in the Party. Only of course, it's neither of them. It's happened since . . . well, you know . . .'

'Since you came back?'

'Last night. Long story.' Rose shuddered.

'No wonder . . . well, you don't look great.'

'I'm not.' Briefly, she told him what had happened the night before. He listened intently.

'I swear there has to be more than one of them,' she said when she had finished. 'It changes things, doesn't it?'

'I don't know. One person behind it, perhaps?'

'That's possible.' She rubbed her hands across her eyes. 'It's true it felt like one person up until last night.'

'Let's go back to thinking of it as one person for the moment.'

'To fit your theory?'

'It's too good a theory to give up. It doesn't wipe out what we discovered.' He looked grim. 'Bear with me a bit longer?'

She nodded.

'Well, you're right, that we'd narrowed the range. But what would any of us be doing in Power Street in the middle of the night, often night after night? I mean, we'd have done it from somewhere more convenient, closer to home.'

'He's rung in the daytime too.'

'But always in batches of time. At certain times?'

'I knew it had to be a shift worker, yes. I did wonder quite a lot about Matt. Or Hortense, for that matter, if it was a woman. Oh cancel that, I didn't mean it.'

'Didn't you?'

'I could have, I suppose. But it seems unconvincing.'

'You see, we were looking for one perfect profile. Somebody who always knew where you were. One person who could be everywhere and not be noticed. The same person had to understand what made people frightened. Calling at your house and cutting your dog's throat, throwing paint stripper over your car, throwing things at your house, making phone calls from telephone boxes. Perhaps he didn't do it all himself but he had to have the capacity to do it if he needed to. That's one person at work, I'm sure. After all, he turned up in Wellington. Surely a whole gang of them didn't turn up here together?'

'They could have. Kids on the move.'

'You don't believe that, do you?'

'Why shouldn't I?'

'Because...' He balled up his hands, impotent to make her understand. 'They wouldn't have all that information that I've just been talking about. It's too sophisticated.'

'All right. So what? Tell me who it is.'

'Wait. Toni and I went over and over it. We spent so much time going through the rolls that Morris got jealous. Of me, for God's sake.' He gave himself a downward deprecatory glance. 'He started going on at her about it.'

'Was that how Lyle found out?'

'Oh God no, somebody told him.'

'Nice of them.'

'That's what I thought. But it did make Toni look differently at Morris, him carrying on about me. It was so kind of... silly.'

'So was it still on between them when Lyle killed her?'

'No. Pretty wasted effort. If you see what I mean. Except I think she'd had all of them, so she'd have left Lyle anyway. She was planning to move out for awhile and sort something out. She rang the afternoon she died and said she couldn't do any more, but she'd give me all the information we'd collected and I should get it from her as soon as possible because she might go away. She was very nervous. She had the idea that her phone was being tapped. Everything had got to her, much the same way as it had got to you. And Lyle was always lurking round listening to her phone calls as well.'

'Poor Toni.'

'Yeah, that doesn't say half of it.' His glasses misted over and he was silent.

'Well, anyway,' he said, 'as far as your mystery caller was concerned, I thought I had every house matched—but there's always the chance of one or two slipping through. Somebody converts a few rooms into a flat and the tenant doesn't register on the roll and you've got a mystery spot. There isn't a record of where every person in the country lives, it simply doesn't exist. You can get close but not that close. And it's a long time between census counts.'

'I know. Remember how we canvassed people who swore they were Labour one week and the next week you had the dogs on you because tenants had shifted or a house got sold?'

'All of that. Well, Toni went out canvassing in Power Street.'

'Off her own bat? It's out of her area.'

'She wanted to check the register. She only called where there were gaps.'

'She did that for me?'

'And she found a place just like the one I've described. It's just rooms really, at the back of a house, not even a flat. The woman who owned the place wouldn't tell her who lived in them, she said the tenant had very important work and didn't want his identity revealed. But she told her one thing, just before she threatened to call the police — she said it was no use coming round here looking for him because he worked odd hours.'

Rose glanced through the names on Toni's list again, nodding, paused, her finger stopping at a circled entry with a red exclamation mark alongside it. In the next room Sharna was stirring.

'And this one has the shift worker in the rooms at the back of the house?'

'Right.'

'It says "Maybe"?'

'She had an idea. I did another print-out of the area by occupation.'

'You could do that?'

'A hack-out. Oh never mind. Look, I don't know for sure . . . I might still be pissing in the wind.'

'Nick, please.'

'I think a cop lives there.'

In the stillness of the room, she thought, *It has to be.*

'Turn the list over, Rose. I nearly lost that bit of paper when the cops had it. They held it in their hands but they never turned it over.'

Lightly pencilled on the back of the list were the words: 'Shift worker absent on leave in Wellington, July 9 — 20.'

'Does it tie in?'

'I've got the dates written down somewhere. I think that's about the time I got pestered after I came down here.'

'That's what I expected.'

She said, 'He wouldn't have had a typewriter when he came to Wellington.' It sounded stupid, ordinary. She couldn't think of what else to say. She shook her head, dazed. 'How would she have found out these dates, d'you think?'

'She bought a lot of dresses.'

'*Dresses?*'

'Sergeant Campbell's wife runs the dress shop. She knows when everybody takes leave.'

'My God. Lola Campbell. So Toni probably knew who it was, as well.'

'I should think so.'

'Why didn't she tell you straight away?'

'Because of being scared about the phone. She would have told me that night when I collected the envelope.'

'Yes, I can see that.'

'Do you have any idea who it is, Rose?'

Glimpses, so quick that they seemed almost subliminal, switched on and off in her brain.

'Oh yes. It's Teddy O'Meara, of course.' She couldn't understand why she hadn't seen it right away. 'Every shift, coming and going, he went to that phone box. All that time.' She shook her head, trying to clear it of what she saw. 'He was supposed to be helping me. Oh, Nick, how could he have done it?'

Beneath the glitzy towers that line Lambton Quay marched the Weyville protesters. It was a curious assembly. When the people piled out of the buses it felt as if there was a crowd of them, but against the new buildings and the high glass walls they appeared just a handful. A small group at the front carried a banner protesting mining rights in the reserve, which was what the march was supposed to be about, then there was a crowd of farmers, the ones who had set out earlier in the year and never made it, and behind them a group of the unemployed who fitted the same description, and behind that a larger group of people who had lost their jobs since then.

Nobody paid them much attention, although a couple of tomatoes had been lobbed at the front of the march near Kirkcaldie and Stains and a few motorists banked up down Grey Street sat honking.

Those of the marchers who had not visited Wellington for some time gazed up in wonder at the high empty rooms that flanked the street, wondering where the people were who were supposed to occupy so many of the buildings.

'No mining rights, leave our trees, keep out blights,' yelled the first group. *'Jobs, we want jobs,'* the tail end of the march was chanting.

'Get your act together,' a bystander shouted.

'Make up your minds.'

'Get back to work.'

'It's all right for you jokers,' Henare Muru shouted, but it wasn't and he earned an egg for it.

Sharna was enjoying the ride in her pushchair. For the first time since Rose had taken charge of her she was laughing, in little yelping grunts. Nick pushed her along, dodging ruts in the street.

'You're doing a great job,' Rose panted, half running to keep up with him.

'Great kid.' Sharna gazed up at him with adoring eyes. It had been love at first sight of his hand-painted tie.

Behind them the crowd was beginning to swell. Bystanders were coming off the pavement and getting mixed up with them, apparently not caring much what the demonstration was about. It was a long time since Rose had marched; the sight of the police coming towards her made her stomach lurch for an instant, but smiling and courteous they directed the group to the side of the road to let traffic edge past and seemed not to notice them unduly, or if they did, not to care about their presence.

'Why O'Meara? Why would he have done it?' she said, jogging along beside the pushchair. Nick appeared oblivious of the crowd, he was enjoying the laughing child so much.

He looked round them briefly. 'Think about it,' he said.

It was almost as if he had forgotten about O'Meara. But she couldn't. Nothing could alleviate the sense of rage and betrayal she felt.

Outside Parliament ropes had been slung up hurriedly to keep the group off the courtyard. The group was cantering now, hardly believing that this was the last obstacle.

And it wasn't. The police appeared in a steady stream from the side entrance and formed a phalanx across the steps.

'We want Kendall, give us Kendall,' the marchers shouted.

He emerged at last, a thin tired man with a greying beard whom Rose hardly recognised, although it was less than two days since he had walked out of the flat leaving her behind with Larissa and the fish and chips. At his side stood Harry Ryan, apparently still the loyal lieutenant. Matt Decker followed a few paces behind, not aligning himself with Kit, even though he advanced with the group.

Kit raised the megaphone. 'Friends, welcome to Wellington,' he cried, his voice crackling through the spring afternoon.

A wild hoot of laughter greeted him.

'Where're your Cabinet colleagues? Have they left you to carry the can?'

'*What about the mining rights? The bush belongs to us.*'

'I'll be happy to meet a group of you inside Parliament Buildings to discuss any concerns you have. There should be no more than four in the group.' His words frayed.

'*Bull*shit, *bull*shit, bull*shit*.' The farmers took up voice against him.

'*What about New Zealand? New Zealand belongs to us. What have you done to New Zealand? Sold it out to foreigners. Well you can't have bloody Weyville so easily.*' Henare Muru's voice carried above the megaphone. One of the protesters started banging a kettle drum and the lone representative of the Weyville Pipe Band screeched into life, playing a dirge.

'Ladies and gentlemen,' Kit tried to shout above the racket, 'the decisions are not mine, I can only represent your concerns.'

'Yes, but are you going to?' Nick called back through cupped hands. Rose grabbed the handle of the pushchair.

Kit looked straight at Nick, and at her. He lowered the megaphone, handing it to Harry with a muttered aside, and turned abruptly on his heel.

Harry raised the megaphone. 'Ladies and gentlemen.' His voice trembled and he was greeted with jeers. 'Mr Kendall... Kit says he's got nothing to say to you until you're prepared to talk sense to him.'

'I didn't mean to get into the march, Kit. It was just happening.' Rose was drinking tea in his office and trying to feed Sharna a bottle at the same time. She thought that the child should be doing more for herself.

'I suppose Nick Newbone didn't either.'

'We were coming to see you.'

'Bullshit, as your chums out there would say.'

'All right. So I wanted to hear what you were going to say to them. As it happens you said nothing.'

'There's nothing to say yet.'

'About what? Mining rights. Unemployment? There never is.'

'There's a whole raft of proposals in the melting pot. Things are on track.'

'Jargon, gobbledegook.'

'What do you want me to say?'

'The truth. In newspeak, it's a scam, it's all a bloody scam.'

'I've got to be in Gamble's office in five minutes.'

'I get the message, don't talk about anything nasty. Where's Matt?'

'Talking to Smart.'

'Oh boy, so much for the non-alignment pact. You lot don't know what time of day it is, do you?'

'What did you want to see me about?' He raised his hand. 'Sorry, I shouldn't have asked. No, I still don't want to talk about the delicate state of our marriage, thanks very much.'

'I wanted to tell you that I think I know who's been bugging me all this time. Nick's been helping me.'

His curiosity flickered to life. 'Who?'

'Teddy O'Meara.'

'Not the cop you talked to?'

'One of them.'

He slumped. 'Are you sure?'

'Almost.'

'Jesus, Rose, you've got to be sure before you say things like that.'

'I am, I know. It's a long story for now, but I just know I'm right.'

He swivelled in his chair. The window looked out on to a concrete wall. 'It makes sense,' he said eventually. 'A pity we'll have to sit on it.'

'What do you mean? I'm going to blow it right open.'

He turned back to her, put his elbows on the desk, and leaned on his cupped hands. 'Don't you see anything? I stand for law and order. We can't go round knocking the cops. The Opposition would have a field day.' He shifted before her uncomprehending gaze. 'Think of what Banks and Meurant would do to us,' he added.

'You and I know about the cops.'

'There's some good ones around these days. Things have changed.'

'Maybe, but you can't guarantee there's no bad ones. Kit, Teddy O'Meara makes perfect sense, because he knew I'd never suspect him. Even after '81, we're the kind of people who still go on trusting the police.'

'So what do you propose to do?'

'I have to think about it. Maybe actually go to the police. Jeffrey Campbell might be all I've got.'

'Do you think he knows?'

'Oh God, I don't know. Surely not.' But she really didn't know.

'Drop it, Rose. The whole thing is most politically unsound.'

'What do you want me to do? Live with it? It's gone too far for that.'

He was silent.

Finally, she said, 'I think you're still suffering from jet lag.'

He glanced at his watch and then at Sharna. 'I've got a babysitter organised for her. For Gamble's party.' It was the first time he had acknowledged Sharna's presence. Then, as he passed her, he spoke with unexpected gentleness: 'I know you loved Larissa, Rose. I know.'

She could have sworn there were tears in his eyes, but her own were so close to the surface again that she couldn't see him well enough to be certain.

'The bitch came and took her away.' Larissa's face was screwed up with fury. 'That's what people like that do to you. I always said she was rotten.' She'd been drinking for hours.

'Then why d'you go running after her? If you'd listened to me. You never listen to nobody.'

Gary's shaven head gleamed in the caravan's light. He had had a skull and crossbones tattooed on it while Larissa was away. A slight inflammation flared around the fresh needlework. 'Ought to give you a fuckin' good hiding, taking off like that.'

'Just you try it. I can do anything. I can drive cars. Tell you, this geezer let me drive all the way across the desert. Amazing. I'm going for my licence.'

'The fuck you are.'

'Anyway, I'm gunna get that kid back. She can't go round pinching kids like that.'

Gary spat, laughed. 'They'd get her off you in five minutes.'

'Told you,' Jason said, pushing his eyelids into shape with his finger and thumb, 'told you what the cop said I was to tell you, Larissa.'

'What cop? You been talking behind my back, eh?' Gary bunched his knuckles.

'Told you, Campbell came round, with a message for Larissa. I told you, didden I, she's bringing the kid back here tomorrow. Your auntie rang. That's what Campbell said.'

'See,' said Gary, 'I told you, you're nothing but friggin' trouble. Friggin' trouble, Larissa. I told you not to get the cops on my back. Miss Goody Two-Shoes, eh. Ought to smack you in, really should.' He drank some more beer and wiped his mouth with the back of his sleeve.

'Shut your mouth, Gary.' Jason leaned his head between his knees, and then threw it back in a desperate effort to clear it. Through the awning he could see the weight of the stars on the world. He had been reading about wormholes in the galaxies and how superior beings could tunnel through them to get to other universes. The stump of his leg ached and he hated with renewed passion the artificial limb which kept him bound to this caravan site, to the interminable days which followed one after the other.

Aloud, he said, 'We're oppressed.'

'Pass a tube, mate,' said Gary. 'You piking?'

Jason didn't answer. On reflection, he couldn't think of anything he particularly wanted to do, had never known any alternative but singing tyres beneath him, which were now denied him. He might have liked to be a farmer, perhaps. He chuckled softly to himself. A gentleman farmer with a crutch. If he and Larissa could break free, maybe there was something they could do together. If she would love him. It came to him that Larissa might go away sometime soon, that her trip to Wellington and the crazy dude in the car had shown her a route out of Weyville. The thought swept him, changing his mood to one of desolation while at the same time he exulted for her, if it were to come true.

'We got too much time on our hands here,' he said.

'Yeah, and whose fault is that?' Gary was getting ready to have another go at Larissa. 'We had a sweet little number going and she led that bastard straight to us.'

'Campbell was following O'Meara,' Jason said.

'No fucking way. He was following her.'

'Anyway, we got out in time. Unless you got something going I don't know about, Gary.'

Gary ignored this last comment. 'He makes me uneasy, very uneasy, does Campbell,' he ruminated instead.

'He can watch Verschoelt. Hear he's growing a bit of stuff in his packing sheds.'

'Horticulture, yeah. Ol' Larry's spending up, I hear.'

'What's O'Meara got going with you anyway?' Larissa had relaxed her guard. 'D'you give him a rake-off?'

'Told you not to ask questions like that Larissa.'

'But I want to know. Protection, why? Why you?'

'The ultimate shit,' said Jason dreamily, lapsing into space again.

'What?'

'You watch it.' The edge of danger in Gary's voice hardened.

'Some things,' Jason said, 'some things O'Meara would do to your aunt, and some things he couldn't quite bring himself to do. Like crap in her sitting room.'

'Bastard.' But it was Larissa whose arm Gary twisted up behind her back.

'Why? Tell me.' Larissa's voice rose, shrill with pain, but unable to stop asking.

'And the biggest crap, just taking the mickey. What a laugh, her own family, near as nothing, sitting there growing dope in her backyard. And Gary, our bro, feeding out all the story on Auntie Rose as it happened. Well, that's what O'Meara thought. Pity you fell out with her, Larissa.'

Larissa looked from one to another.

'Besides, Gary doesn't trust women. You'd have thought O'Meara would have worked that one out.'

He ducked, seeing Gary's fist flying at his face and his boot hitting Larissa all at the same time. The next time Gary hit him he tried to fight back, but he was never much good, with or without his leg.

'Friggin' puffball.' Gary stood over him and kicked his ribs. Jason's consciousness faded and then swelled briefly, long enough for him to hear Larissa whimpering, before it faded again.

The holiday brochures mocked Campbell. The twinkling blue seas shone with an unnatural glitter, the white sand winked at him.

'Why did you invite Gabby and Denise to come with us?' He had asked his wife three times now.

Each time she had looked at him with puzzled eyes, as if he was coming down with the first symptoms of Alzheimer's, he thought.

'They're company,' Lola explained patiently. 'We need a few people.'

'I hardly know them.'

'But you'll like them. Denise has got style.'

The renegade solution of just calling the whole thing off tempted him. But at what cost? A vision of them going on and on like this with no let-up, and her silences, appalled him. She would get over it in time, but the need for change, rest, respite would go unsatisfied.

She would be shamed, too, and he knew he couldn't bear that. Different they might be, but she deserved better than to be made foolish in the town where she lived.

Maybe she had read his thoughts, for when he looked up again, resigned, ready to capitulate, her irritation with him had been replaced by a look of pleading.

'It's all right,' he said. 'It'll be fun.'

Her smile was as instant as a camera click. 'I nearly forgot,' she said. 'There was a message. It came while you were on your way home. Some chap called Daniels, ringing from Wellington. Said he'd remembered something.' She handed him a slip of paper with a car registration number jotted down. 'He reckoned you'd know what it was.'

Studying it, he thought, another piece, and checked it out in his notebook. It was almost all together now. The Studebaker had been the following car that forced Daniels off the road, and in the oncoming car was another person who did not want Daniels in town. That was Teddy O'Meara. One more piece of evidence and he would be ready to move. It was where to find it that eluded him. He felt totally alone and longed to confide in someone. His wife had begun to buff her fingernails with a little chamois pad. In his mind's eye, he saw the circle of laughing young men at the station, Teddy's friends. There was not one whom he could be certain was not a confidant or mate. He should have told the bosses long before it came to this, but he had kept on hoping he was wrong, that it was he who had made the mistake. The men stuck together. Us and them. Not Teddy, please, not any of them behaving like this. Teddy might be an abrasive young bastard, and he was already under a certain amount of suspicion, but let him not have got into this. There was a difference between those who succumbed to temptation and the deliverance of evil.

Well, he could see it was past that. But there was one more thing that he wanted before he blew the whistle. Early in the day Rose had told him by phone that the mysterious caller was at work again.

The link he needed was Rose Kendall.

13

Somehow everyone finished up going to Rex Gamble's party. Or at least all that remained of the old party faithful from Weyville.

Nick had ended up going with Matt and Harry though he hadn't meant to. Just as they were saying awkward goodnights to Kit at Parliament, Gamble had appeared as if from nowhere, magnanimous and smiling.

'Of course you're all coming,' he said, 'we're going to have a good time. Let me tell you how to get to my house, okay? Go up to the top of Kelburn Parade, take a sharp turn right into Glasgow Street, there's a parking bay on the left-hand side: to the right there's a new green garage with a bubble roof. At the bottom of that you'll find the numbers. Go to the top, on the left you'll see a white house, then a green house with a barrel roof, the house behind that's got a trampoline in front of that. Keep going till you see a bramble hedge, very nicely cut I might add, and no I didn't do it myself, with lights on either side of the gate, and there're ten steps up to my front door. Can't miss it. All right, what's y'names, Harry? Nick?'

They repeated the address back to him like dutiful schoolboys, in the process committing themselves to the invitation.

Rose returned to the House, after putting Sharna to bed back at the flat. An efficient young woman had arrived, laden with an armful of books. 'I can stay the night if you like,' she said.

'I'm sure I'll be back soon,' Rose said, promising herself early release from the party.

The group from Weyville squeezed into the lift, clanking down to the chequered floor of the lobby. Rose crossed it as if in a dream, looking for something but she couldn't think what it was. As she pushed through the revolving door, she remembered that it was a marble table top.

They spilled out into the night, Parliament looming behind them. Light fell across the shadowy trees in the grounds. At the top of the long flight of steps that led to the courtyard, Rose paused. She had stood here so often, breathing power. She had forgotten, in the long months of distrust and dismay and the terror that had overtaken her, how it had all been, back at the beginning. There had been many nights like this, the country on fire, electric with promise. When the House rose, Government supporters had raced, joyous, out of the debating chamber, laughing and planning, set to deliver the promise of accord.

The phrases were tired. People talked about pragmatism and the real world these days.

Yet she'd never get over the place, its suggestion of freedom and a touch of grandeur. It had been so easy to believe in it.

Gamble's ministerial residence was a recent acquisition, which he had had a hand in choosing. It was a small architectural masterpiece, built like a tower on a narrow section, rising floor by floor to odd pointed ceilings; each room was painted stark white, the dull red brick floors were inset with turquoise mosaics on every level. The paintings which adorned his Beehive walls paled beside those which hung here.

Rose and Kit arrived shortly behind Gamble, but already twenty or so people packed the second level near the entrance. Most of them had been to another function; they were nearly all smashed. Rose found herself looking anxiously over her shoulder for the others. Nick was to drive Harry and Matt up from Parliament. Rose and Kit had just squeezed into a park in the line-up of Alfa Romeos and Porsches. Probably it would take them awhile to park and find their way to the tortuous address. She realised that she had no idea what the party was for. Perhaps Gamble was one of those people who simply gave parties.

An osteopath who had been treating Gamble for a back injury was mixing Pimms at the bar, adding greenery and elaborate twists of lemon. 'Pimms, my God, we drank that when we were kids.'

'Ssh, it's back in fashion,' Kit muttered.

A young woman with blue eyes and a hyper-tan stood close to Gamble, staring into his eyes. He caressed her bare back and her bottom with one hand, while with the other he held a glass and sipped from it. She was Gamble's fourth woman friend since his last wife left him and the third this year. The rumour going the rounds was that the woman's parents had been on campus at Kent State when the shootings happened there in '68, and emigrated; she had been back-packed out of the line of fire and lived in seclusion with them 'down the West Coast' for twenty years. That was the story, but nobody had been tactless enough to ask if it was true.

She didn't look like a flower child, Rose decided.

At the door, Matt, Harry and Nick hesitated. Gamble released his girlfriend and gave an amiable wave, welcoming them in. They clustered uneasily near Rose and Kit.

Across the room a woman with brown eyes and heavy make-up stared fixedly at Kit. He glanced, and started. Rose knew it must be Violet.

'Bit of a bastard, your mate,' Rose said to Kit, raising her voice slightly, meaning Gamble to hear her, only he had disappeared. The noise throughout the house was rising. Dancing had broken out on one of the lower levels.

'Keep your voice down. I didn't know she'd be here.'

'Who?'

Kit looked miserable, seeing the trap she had laid for him.

'I think I'll go.'

'Do what you like,' he said.

'Rose.' Gamble emerged from the kitchen with a distracted air, clutching bowls stacked with packets of potato crisps and nuts. He put them on a table and began tearing the bags open. 'You're just the person who can save this party.'

'It seems a great success already.'

'I've got a problem.'

'And you want me to do the dance of the seven veils? I'd say you had plenty of takers for that.'

'Now now. Rose, don't be like that, baby.'

'Don't call me baby, I'm one of the grown-ups,' she snapped, in a voice she hardly recognised.

He raised his hand, a conciliatory gesture. 'Could you cook something?'

'Me? You're not serious.'

'You can cook, can't you?'

'No, Kit and the children ate grass.'

'Balls. Look, I promised food and the caterers have let me down. I haven't got a cracker ready.' He contemplated the chips with distaste.

'So you want me to butter crackers?'

'Could you be an angel and throw some pasta together or something? There's plenty of everything in the kitchen. I'm hopeless.'

Behind him, Kit was mouthing something that looked like 'sorry'. She couldn't decide whether it was on account of Gamble, or if he was still on about Violet.

'What about your friend?'

'I loused it up, I've got a friend who cooks but I didn't invite her. Anyway, tell her what to do, she'll help. Her name's Stella.' He gestured towards the girl from Kent State in the backless black dress. 'Please,' he implored. 'Everyone else is too plastered to do a thing.'

Over the rail, on the lower level, Rose saw thin women in expensive dresses dancing like grasshoppers.

'Designer beanpoles,' she observed.

His gaze followed hers. 'Pity they're nearly all growing moustaches. Must be what dieting does to women. Nice clothes, though. Would you like some addresses in the ragtrade?'

'I can find them if I need them. Thank you. Anyway, I'm broke.' She knew straight away she shouldn't have said that.

'You'll make us some pasta then?'

'What've you got?' She followed him into the kitchen.

'Fettucine.'

'There's not enough there.' She was examining his cupboards with him.

'Lasagne.'

'I thought you wanted to eat tonight.'

'Spaghetti. San Remo.'

'It'll do.'

'Fresh herbs.'

'You've got a herb garden?'

'My last wife's, bless her, though the maintenance is killing me. She had some homely touches.' He opened a door which led on to a patio poised above a precipice. The smell of boronia and herbs and the sweet sour burden of early honeysuckle greeted her on the night air.

'Nice. Isn't it nice?'

'The sage has gone to wood.'

'You don't give much away, do you, Rose?'

'I want to go home.'

'You're lost on Kit.'

'D'you want me to make you some food or not?' It must be easy for seduction to happen, whatever your perspective. The men and women in there were being seduced in some form or another by this party, and all the parties that had gone before. She hesitated; it was so much easier to be on the inside. A vision flitted before her, of Gamble crouched on the floor of his ministerial car, giggling at her.

The young woman from Kent State was trying to slice French bread and making a mess of it.

'Didn't anybody teach you to slice bread?'

'My mother *made* bread.' Stella gave a pouty smile.

Of course, Rose thought, she would. 'Perhaps she'll teach you one day.'

'My mother had a very traumatic life.'

'So did my daughter's. Long strokes on the diagonal, Stella.'

'Rex is so lucky to have friends like you.' Stella had decided to be affable after all. 'You could teach me things when we get married.'

'Who feeds him when there aren't tame women around?'

'Oh, I don't know. I think he has a housekeeper now and then.'

'Politicians don't know what life's all about. Or they forget. You'll spend all your life in a supermarket queue if you're not careful.' She considered adding, if it lasts that long, but it didn't seem like her province. Her sauce was thickening, pungent and rich. The smell of onions and garlic clung to her hands. It made her oddly comfortable, performing the familiar routines of cooking, although she could see how she debased herself. Or how Gamble was doing it for her. She supposed it was premeditated.

The smell had infiltrated the room beyond. The dancing had stopped and the dancers were wafting expectantly round the long dining table. When Rose went out to set up a cloth and some cutlery, only Harry was performing a distracted awkward dance with someone who looked like an older version of Belinda.

Nick was deep in conversation with a woman with light brown hair and an air of competence. Rose could have sworn she had seen her before. She racked her brain trying to think who it was, sure she should know. The woman was drinking orange juice.

Alan Smart had just arrived, having waited quite properly for the House to rise. Remarkably, he was with his own wife. Mary had had a crisp new tint put through her hair. She wore a business suit, as if she hadn't had time to change. Somebody said she'd just been appointed to run an international company.

'Is this a delegation from Auckland?' he asked, looking around and seeing some unfamiliar faces. Smart's electorate was in the South Island, Gamble was from the north.

'No. Weyville in the raw,' said Matt, who had been drinking rather quickly for him. Rose thought, too late, that she should have asked him to help with the cooking, but he didn't look particularly friendly anyway.

It surprised Rose that Smart was there. From what she had heard, she would have thought that Smart and Gamble were so diametrically opposed that they were unlikely to attend each other's parties.

She supposed that in a world where policies were the game plan and the point was power, it probably didn't make much difference.

Harry hiccuped. 'Home base for the Gucci revolutionaries.' His voice was thick.

Kit turned a pained expression on him. *And there's no way you can get rid of him,* Rose thought, with what, she had to admit, was satisfaction.

As she set plates out nobody noticed her much. Most of the people in the room had forgotten she was a guest. Nick tried to catch her eye but she avoided it; the woman he had been talking to was still sitting close to him and she was still sober.

'Don't go putting words in my mouth, just put your tongue in.' The osteopath was administering free manipulation to the base of one of the expensive women's spine.

'Is the Minister of Finance coming?' Matt was getting bold. Someone had said on the way up that there would be senior Ministers at the party.

Gamble's teeth gleamed. 'Probably. Probably. I expect so.'

'What about Lange, is he coming?' Smart's voice was irritable. He poured himself a Scotch.

'Probably. Probably not. I'd say on the evidence, it's unlikely. I've got a can of beans put aside for him if he does.'

'I thought you said he was coming.' Rose guessed that this was why Smart had come. But now he was here, it appeared unlikely that he was going to hurry away. He had turned back to the bar to get ice, but not a lot.

'I think it's positively peculiar that his wife doesn't live with him.' The osteopath had taken his jacket off; his forearms were like those of a rugby player.

There was a chattering like crickets in the room:

'She'd be peculiar if she did, wouldn't she?'

'Is it true that he's got a girlfriend?'

'And I said to her, how do you like your eggs in the morning? And she said, unfertilised. Cute.'

'Is the Minister definitely coming?'

'Which one?'

'Finance, you said Finance.'

'Nothing's definite in this world. Justice might come.' Gamble laughed. 'After all, you've got me. Kit, there's another consultative committee coming up. Are you interested?'

'Does that mean the Government's got another decision it wants to put off for a year?' Harry said. He was trying to get Violet to dance and she was resisting, but he had grasped her firmly by both hands and pulled them backwards and forwards as if he was in a woodsawing competition, twitching his body in time to the music. Any moment, Rose decided, Kit would throw him out bodily. Could be sport, she might join in, take Violet with her.

'And he said to me, Julie, he said, why do you try all that feminist shit on me? I mean, Julie, I just look at you, and I just about cream in my pants. It takes all sorts, I said to him, we're all feminists at heart, we women. I mean, would you like me to stop shaving my armpits or something, I said to him.'

'The Report on Social Policy, my dear, was five thousand pages thick, and so wet it was printed on bark. Read it? Of course I haven't.'

'Darling you must see Ellie Smith, she's divine. What? I know you can see her on the Lotto ads but she's doing Judy Garland.'

'No, I don't have a system for Lotto but my brother has, you can cover the odds for eighteen grand. Why don't we form a syndicate?'

'I'm a Luddite, yes, all right that's what I am. Right, Matt? Eh, Nick? Never thought I'd say it, but yes, I want to go back to the old days.' Harry was looking increasingly morose. Nobody had offered him another drink for ten minutes, and he was not quite drunk enough to help himself with Smart's familiarity at the bar.

'The barbie, oh it was a wash-out. There was a bunch of Islanders playing their bloody boong music on the beach. Not that I'm racist or anything, but we asked them to tone it down, nicely of course, but they didn't. Well it was just that we couldn't hear a thing. I mean, truly, I do like Islanders, one of them did some work for me the other day. But noise. I mean noise is pain to me.'

Gamble passed, patting the speaker's bottom on the way. He said, 'Never, darling. Pain is a high brain function.'

The kitchen was hot. Stella had been drinking the cooking wine. 'It's too good to put in the sauce,' she said, holding the label out toward Rose.

'Never cook with wine you wouldn't drink. How's the bread?'

'Yummy, I've tried it. You *are* wise. You will be my friend, won't you, Rose?

'I'll bear it in mind. My friends don't have a lot of luck.'

'Did Rex say if the Finance Minister was coming?'

'He said somebody might.'

'Oh I do hope so. Though he could have gone gambling, I've

heard he does. Mind you, if he came here he'd be gambling, wouldn't he?' She clapped her hand to her mouth. 'That was rather good, don't you think.'

'Very good. Yes, that's very funny.'

'I'm glad you're nice to me. Not everybody is, you know. That Mrs Smart out there, she's not. She's really moral. I could tell her things about morals. My parents are really moral. They live in Blackball.'

'That's certainly moral. How's the spaghetti? Have you tried it?'

'Will you?'

'Al dente. We're ready to go.'

'Marvellous. Thank goodness you came.'

'I'll tell them you cooked it.'

'Will you? Oh gosh, really, that's nice of you. I can make blackberry wine, you know.'

A temporary quiet had descended. Everybody except Violet was eating. Harry looked almost sober.

'Shouldn't we have waited for the Minister?' asked the osteopath. He twirled spaghetti with a deft elegant hand, surprising at the end of his brawny arms.

'We're all waiting for the Minister,' said Harry. 'We're waiting for him to do something.'

'Just where do you people from Weyville stand?' said Gamble, leaning back and wiping his mouth on a napkin. Rose wondered if she should tell him that there was a strand of spaghetti in his beard. 'Or, more importantly, where does the member for Weyville stand?'

'Good point,' Alan Smart said. 'What I'd like to know too.'

Rose thought, *Amen to that*. The question had got repetitious, one way or another.

'Here, I'm not on trial,' Kit said. He helped himself to more spaghetti. Rose remembered how difficult it was to get him to eat pasta at home. He always said he didn't like it.

'Stella made it,' she said, though not necessarily to him. Nobody was listening.

'Actually,' Matt said, speaking to Kit, 'you probably are.'

'Some friend you turned out to be.' Kit was still making light of it.

'What say we convene a court? All those in favour say aye.' Gamble's face shone with excitement.

A chorus of ayes went up.

Nick half rose to his feet. Faintly, he said, 'No.' He looked across to Rose. She found herself shrugging, why not?

Kit had turned pale and stopped eating. She thought, this is my husband. We have two children whom we love. We've worked hard together and lived in an L-shaped Beazley house. (Well maybe we don't now, but we did, and we were happy.) We believe in the same things. We come from Weyville, where we will grow old together.

Only some of the argument fell apart. Looking round at the glittering gathering, the public relations consultants and newly respectable Treasury men, the assortment of instant names, the political commentators who would not dare to repeat exactly what happened in this room tonight, but who would find ways to make very good capital out of it all, she realised that each and every one of them saw themselves as true stars in their own right, entitled to spectacle. As she and Kit had once perceived themselves to be stars.

'No,' she whispered, but only to herself.

Kit had regained his composure. He picked up his fork and commenced eating spaghetti bolognese again.

'What's the charge?'

'Conspiring with the loony left,' said Gamble.

'Selling out to the right,' Harry and Matt said, more or less at once.

'Who are the witnesses?'

Violet picked up her handbag. 'You're all nuts,' she said and walked out.

'Fancy, and you never even got to read a charge,' Gamble said, addressing Rose. He was watching Violet's departure.

'Look at this,' said Harry. He picked up a bottle of wine and shoved it under Kit's nose. 'South African.'

Smart moved uncomfortably, looking sideways at the bottles accumulating around the room, but he was still drinking Scotch, even with his pasta.

'It won't do, Rex,' he said.

'I'm not on trial,' Gamble said. To Harry, he said, 'You've been drinking it too, mate.'

'You only brought it out when we began to eat, so we wouldn't notice. Kit, look at it, see what he's doing to us.'

When Kit didn't stop, Harry tipped the remains of the bottle he was holding over his head. A little sizzling sigh went round the room. Kit put out his tongue to catch the drops running down his nose.

'You don't give a damn about mining the reserve.' Harry was trembling, his eyes full of fervour.

'Perhaps Prebble might come,' the osteopath said.

'You've sold out to capitalism.' Matt's voice was aggrieved.

'Who d'you think's going to run the world?' Gamble asked him.

'Who do you?' Smart said.

'Well I tell you, it won't be your mate, the member for Weyville, but he's in with a chance if he sticks with me.'

The woman with brown hair was jotting something in a notebook.

'You've got to stand up for yourself,' Smart said to Kit, quite kindly. 'You get too upset when they heavy you in caucus.'

Gamble said, 'A bit of rough and tumble. He can take it, can't you?'

'He nearly cried when Finance heavied him a couple of months ago.'

'Bully-boy tactics. There you are.' Harry was triumphant.

'That was one of the girls,' said Kit, going on the defensive at last.

'That's it. Guilty of being a girl,' Gamble cried. 'I tell you lot, you're born losers. You think Lange's got a conscience. You think he might take charge again. I tell you it won't happen. We've got the country on the right path, thanks to the Minister. If he goes we'll all go down the booby hatch. You stick with Lange and you'll find yourselves in Siberia when he gets thrown out. It's one or the other, none of you can have it both ways much longer. I know where I stand. I know which side the proverbial bread is buttered on.' His voice had risen to a high and excited pitch.

'Are you the judge?' Nick asked, speaking at last.

'Yes, yes I am.' With that Gamble snatched Kit's half-empty plate and upended it on his head. Strands of spaghetti and sauce trickled down over his ears.

Applause broke out. Nearly all the audience was laughing so hard that tears streamed down their faces.

'Oh dear, and I was still hungry,' said Kit politely.

'There, get him some more Stella. If there is any. It's very good, angel.' He patted Stella's bottom as she made her way to the kitchen. In a minute she emerged with the pot.

'It's gotten cold.'

'You don't mind, d'you old chap? Here.' He handed it to Harry. 'Would you like to do the honours this time?'

'But I still don't know the verdict,' said Harry, puzzled.

'Ask him.'

'Your charge or mine? Ours?'

'I've given mine. This one's yours. Are you a hanging judge?'
'Kit, how do you plead?' Harry begged.
Smart said suddenly, 'Hasn't this all gone far enough?'
'There's a ministerial car along the road,' said the osteopath. He had been watching down the hill.
'Not guilty,' said Kit softly. He looked at Rose through the spaghetti strands. 'Not guilty, your honour. As of now.'
The osteopath said, 'There really is a ministerial car.'
Harry looked down at the pot. 'Then I guess this is just to keep you on the straight and narrow from now on.' He plonked the saucepan on Kit's head. The remains of the meal cascaded down over his shoulders and tie and into his lap. Kit sucked some strands in at the corners of his mouth.
'You're a fool, Kendall,' said Gamble, 'but I admire your spirit. Bravo.'
More clapping followed and one of the beanpoles switched on more music, Madonna belted out with ear-splitting splendour.
Stella was crying. 'I want to sit on a rock-hard dick and come twenty-five times,' she said between sobs.
Matt and the woman with brown hair fetched towels as the door opened. A messenger had arrived with regrets from the Minister, but in the bedlam nobody caught which one it was that couldn't make it.
'Shall we go?' Nick was standing at Rose's elbow.
For a moment she thought of staying to help Kit clean up, but it was too late for that.
'Great movie,' he said, as they found their way down the path.
'That's what I thought. Pity we forgot the jaffas.'
'Where to now?' They were in his car. He looked up the stairs as if expecting to be followed but there was nobody in sight.
'Now?' She was blank for a moment. 'Back to Sharna.'

It was nearly midnight. Fog had descended on Hataitai. Haloes of light flickered in the trees, the perfect V-shapes of the roofs and the innumerable spindly balconies outlined in the gloom. In the laundrette Nick and Rose folded napkins as they came out of the drier. Welfare had bought Sharna a set of new ones which gleamed in an icy pile under the harsh light. They had sent the sitter home. 'The child has no clean napkins,' the sitter said in an aggrieved way, as if Sharna was neglected. Rose had forgotten that babies got wet so often. She insisted that they walk to the village; she would die without fresh air she told him, and more or less meant it. They wheeled Sharna, still sleeping in her collapsible pushchair, down the hill together. Sharna, always sleeping.

'I thought people bought disposables nowadays.'

'So they do. I never thought of it. Anyway, they're full of toxins. D'you want her to be sterile?'

'What are you going to do about her?' He loaded another washing machine. She had told him of her decision to return to Weyville in the morning.

Rose sat down in one of the ugly little plastic bucket seats where people waited for their washing. She put her face in the warm fabric of the napkin she was holding. 'Take her back to Minna, I suppose.'

'I thought you loved the kid.' His tone was slightly accusing.

'I do.' She jiggled the pushchair up and down as though to soothe the child, although she looked perfectly relaxed. It was an old reflex. 'Oh yes, I love her all right.' She leaned over and cupped Sharna's face in her hand. 'I can't keep the kid while O'Meara's on the loose.'

'We'll get him.'

'He might get me first. That wouldn't do her much good.'

'What do you want, Rose?'

'You sound like Toni.' She leaned her head on the handle of the pushchair. 'I'm just working through the things I don't want.'

'Like Sharna?'

'Don't.' She hesitated. 'Everything that Katrina had.'

'You can't be serious.'

'Oh, but I am. Not the men,' she added hurriedly. 'Well, not those particular men. But something. Something she had.'

'She hasn't got much now.'

'There's some things you can't take away from Katrina. So I keep taking her kids. I wish you wouldn't wear those white shoes, Nick.'

'I probably won't any more,' he said. 'D'you want me to come to the cop shop with you tomorrow?'

'I want to catch him first. We could, you know.'

He looked at her. 'I guess.'

'Nick, when did you first start believing in me?'

'I always did.'

'Oh stop being stouthearted. Nobody did, except Toni. Did she really convince you?'

His look was shamefaced. He sat down beside her, stretching his legs. 'When I knew you were being followed.'

'Was I? You didn't tell me that. Who followed me? How did you find out?'

'Remember when you and Toni were supposed to meet me at the

Oaks that evening and you stood me up?' She nodded. 'There was a woman there who was expecting you. She kind of picked me up, started talking about you. Very casually. But she was waiting for you.'

'But how could she? Nobody knew we were supposed to go there. She'd have had to have heard our telephone conversation... Oh my God, she did?'

'She must have.'

'I told Toni I was being spooked. They must think I'm weird.'

'You made odd complaints, I guess.'

'That they didn't believe.'

'Perhaps they were worried you could have opened Kit up to blackmail.'

'Stuff Kit. What about me?' He didn't answer. 'Did you ever see her again?'

'I often see her. She was there tonight.'

'What?'

'The woman I was talking to. Amiable chitchat.'

'The one with mousy brown hair who looks kind of busy? I'm always bumping into that woman, she's everywhere I go.'

'No,' said Nick gently, 'you haven't been bumping into her. I wouldn't express it like that.'

Rose considered this. Presently she said, 'Whose side is she on then?'

'I don't know. Nobody's, I imagine. She's probably just doing her job.'

'Who'd want a job like that?'

'I like watching you.'

'D'you think she's watching us now?'

'I think we gave her the slip. She wasn't expecting us to leave when we did.'

He put his arm around her and kissed the side of her face. 'I'm sure she's not.' Rose pushed the pram backwards and forwards. He seized her hand, stroking it, winding a finger around her ring.

'It's a fake,' she said, holding the topaz to the light. 'It's a fake, Nick.'

14

'Supposing I won't take her?' Minna said when Rose turned up with Sharna. She had been watching *Days of Our Lives*. 'Aren't Don and Marlena getting old?'

'I don't know which ones they are.'

'They're the ones that used to be married. They change them around so nobody stays married to anyone for too long. Otherwise it'd get boring. It's like politics.'

While she was talking she pretended to ignore Sharna. But the child had opened her arms at the sight of Minna and begun to laugh, as if, at fifteen months, she could not believe what good fortune had been delivered to her.

'She's not pass the parcel, you know,' Minna said. 'I expect you'll be back to get her when it suits you.'

'Not if you want to keep her.'

'You think you're God Almighty, don't you? Anyway, you don't know for sure whether she can stay. They'll probably take her away.'

'They might. I can say a word, if it'll help. If that's what you want.' She was determined not to look back as she went out the door.

The Blake Block looked a little more appealing in the spring than when she had last been there, though not much. At least a big bright yellow forsythia bush bloomed on the front lawn and a blackbird warbled away on a telephone line stretched above a collection of old cars and a stack of worn tyres. She told herself it would be all right.

But Minna followed her down the path, holding Sharna in her arms. She said, 'Ellis Hannen says he'll marry me, if it'll help. So we can foster her.'

Rose turned back, unable to hide her amazement. 'Marry *you*. Ellie?'

'People have been known to marry me.'

'I'm sure... I didn't mean that. But why should he do that for Sharna?'

'He's out of a job, he might as well.'

'Then wouldn't he be better to marry Katrina?'

Minna gazed back, looking at her oddly. 'She's not exactly available, is she?' Then she added, in her strange inflectionless voice, 'It doesn't really matter which one of us he marries.'

★

Jane Marment gave a sigh of satisfaction. Her house was immaculate, the blinds pulled to exactly the right level. The state of the royal marriages was looking better than it had done for some time. She often worried about the Heir Apparent. The papers said such terrible things. It must worry the Queen. This morning she had polished the glass on her picture. The Queen's dress shone like a blue flame in the dusky light of the room.

It was time for her to sit down and take things easy for an hour or two before she began Teddy's meal. She planned to give him a good steak tonight. He deserved it; he had been so thoughtful to her lately. 'Meat and three vegies, Mrs M, you can't beat them,' he often said, giving her a fond smile. If her ankles weren't troubling her too much she would make an apple turnover. When he rang in to check what supplies she needed, she would tell him cream. 'I've got a little surprise for you tonight,' she planned to say. He nearly always knew it would be apple turnover, though sometimes, just to trick him, she did steamed pud and custard sauce. He liked it just about as well.

She arranged herself comfortably in her chair, back straight, both arms lying along the sides of her La-Zi-Boy recliner, a nice sense of balance all over. She pressed the lever so that her feet shot up on the foot rest.

When the doorbell rang, her look was grim. At first she decided to ignore it, but it went on and on. Besides, one needed to know who was lurking around the house. Putting her eye to the spyhole in the door, she saw the woman outside. For a moment she panicked, wondering if she should ring the station and get hold of Teddy.

She knew about this woman, *pure evil*, Teddy had told her, and she believed him. One of the loonies. One of the spoilers. She drew herself upright and opened the door. It was only yesterday she had seen her hanging around next door.

'I told you not to bother coming here,' she said to Rose.

'I want to see Teddy O'Meara,' Rose said.

'Who?'

'You know who I mean.'

'You're trespassing. I'll call the police if you don't leave.'

'He lives here, doesn't he?'

'Nobody lives here except me.'

'A man with very important work. You told my friend.'
'Her. She got what she deserved.'
'You remember, then?'
'He's gone.'
'Who's gone, Mrs Marment?'
'Go away.'
'His socks were on the line yesterday morning.'
'You're a spy. Everybody knows you're a communist.'
'I'm coming inside, Mrs Marment. I'll wait here till he comes.'
'No.' Mrs Marment lunged across the doorway. Then she stood back. 'Oh come in, if you wish.' Her eyes glittered.
Rose hesitated, saw the trap. 'I'll wait outside.'
'You'll still be trespassing.'
'We'll have to see about that.'
'I won't have it, not on my doorstep,' cried Mrs Marment, provoked into shouting. 'Teddy'll take you away, you'll see.'
Suddenly her face lit up at the sight of something behind Rose.
'Time to go, Mrs Kendall,' Teddy O'Meara said, advancing towards her. His eyes were very cold.
She opened her mouth to say something.
'I'm going,' she said. He followed her, his face inches from her own, his feet tripping at her ankles when she turned to run.
'No, don't touch me.'
'You're in trouble, ' he said.
She stopped, looked back to him. 'I know things,' she said. Her fingers were bunched to her mouth like a child's.
'So do I.' He caught her wrist. 'Why don't you come inside then?' He looked at his landlady and grinned. 'What do you reckon, Mrs M?'
'We can fix her,' she called. Her face was alight with pleasure.
'You're crazy,' Rose gasped, pulling with all her strength.
Then Nick was alongside the house, honking as they had arranged.
She ran the rest of the way down the path, choking on her breath, her arm stinging where he had held it, and threw herself into Nick's car.
'Go.'
'He won't follow us.' Nick's pale skin was flushed and his eyes gleamed with excitement and fear.
'He might.'
Teddy was, indeed, following. A few moments later, his Laser nudged up behind them as they rounded the corner of Power Street,

just before the telephone box. Nick swerved, mounted the footpath, and narrowly avoided the phone box, pulling away as Teddy followed suit, crashing to a halt inches away from it and reversing.

'Caught by his own phone box,' said Nick, elated.

'It's not funny, Nick.'

But it had given Nick a burst of courage and he roared down the road intersecting Blake Pass and on to the main road leading into town.

'Where are we going?' Glancing behind her, she saw Teddy's car coming up behind them again.

'To the cops,' said Nick. He had stopped laughing.

★

'Why did you do it?' Jeffrey Campbell's voice shook with anger.

'I had to do something.'

He folded his arms across his chest. 'You've wrecked it. We were almost ready to move.'

'You mean you knew?' She stared at him.

'It's just been reported.'

'By whom? Who to?' As she sat watching him, understanding before he answered, she felt a deep sickness, all the bitterness and anger of the past year welling up inside her. Her eyes filled with tears; she felt her face go crimson with a rage that more than matched his.

'You've been very helpful, Mr Newbone,' said Campbell.

Nick stood awkwardly, seeing himself dismissed.

'Mrs Kendall will have to talk to CIB. It's out of my hands now. Thank you, Mr Newbone.'

When Nick was gone, Campbell sighed.

Close up, Rose could see the puffy pouches under the sallow skin, a permanent chapped look around the corners of his eyes as if he lay in bed at nights rubbing them. Large freckles stood out on the backs of his hands. He must be fifty-three or fifty-four, she supposed.

'Investigations within the police force aren't easy, Mrs Kendall. An independent officer from outside the station is to be called in to assess what evidence we have.'

'What is the evidence?'

'I can't tell you it all at the moment.'

'Why not? It's my case.'

'That's not the point.'

'Then what is? I've told you everything I know.' She and Nick had spent an hour laying out all the information that they had accumulated, ending with O'Meara chasing them through the streets.

'I'm trying to explain. Since I last saw you some other information has also come to me. It may be enough to convict O'Meara of minor offences and put him out of the force.' He raised his hand, seeing the look on her face. 'He's thought all of this through and taken measures to protect himself. Your friend, Mr Newbone, was correct when he said that O'Meara has been perfectly placed to harass you without detection. Piece by piece, one shred of evidence sifted out from another, there is almost nothing to go on, unless he gets too confident. Or he's pushed, which is what I would like to do if I knew how and where to apply the pressure. But now... Petty criminal acts, perhaps, but nothing that would really put him out of circulation. I nearly had him when your friends and relatives took up trade at the bottom of your garden, but he got away on me.'

'You think they're the second strings, then?'

'They have to be.'

'And my niece?'

He shrugged. 'Who knows?'

'And you've got no proof?'

'Not enough. Not a fingerprint. My word against his. Sure, we could go and turn your niece's and her boyfriend's caravan over, or their mate Jason's, and sure as God made little apples I'd find a bit of dope there, perhaps some stolen property, probably some weapons —but what does that prove about O'Meara? Tell me?'

He sat back. 'In order to put him away I have to have a bigger hook than phone calls.'

'What about my dog?'

'Who did it? Him? Gary? You don't know.'

'It couldn't have been Gary.'

'That time.'

'My car?'

'Sure, nobody'd notice him throwing a bit of paint stripper out of a police car. Perfect alibi, a police car. Policemen in police cars are always going about legitimate business—or so we'd tell you, and that's what the people, them, out there, that's what they think, unless they see us doing otherwise. Oh sometimes they'll tell you they saw one speeding, or there'll be a nasty accident and everyone will say how badly the police drive and how they didn't have their flashing lights on, or their siren going, all of that. But to most people, police cars and their occupants go around preventing crimes not committing them. You prove to me that there was a tin of paint stripper in a police car one night six or seven months back. Eh? Where's your evidence?'

'I don't think there's much point in this conversation. This is all stacked against me.'

'There's real crime in this town, Mrs Kendall. Murders, muggings, rapes.'

'Oh yes, attempted murder too. My sister. Well, you've got her.'

'Right.'

'I'll tell you what, I'm sorry she missed Mungo Lord.'

Shocked at herself, she glared at Campbell, gathering up her handbag and half rising before he spoke again.

'Wait, Mrs Kendall. Please.'

Reluctantly she sat, still clutching her purse, leaning forward on the edge of her chair.

'I am totally frustrated, Mrs Kendall. I don't want him here any more than you do. Who can fight crime, deflect its course, undermine its intent, when the corruption lies within? It's not an original dilemma, I assure you, but it is new to me. And I don't even know why he's doing it Mrs Kendall. Do you?'

As she turned her gaze on him, he thought to himself that she was not a pretty woman, only moderately attractive, although she might become handsome in time as some ageing women do; nor was she always sensible, or even very clever. But she wore an air of determined courage, and she was a thoughtful person, who did well enough, especially when her head had charge of her heart; she was kindly and stood up for what she believed in, even if it took her time to formulate just what those beliefs were. He would describe her, and this came as something of a surprise to him, as unswerving.

'It is coming clearer,' she said. 'I have an idea.'

He gave the slightest nod. 'I thought you might.'

'What do you want me to do?'

He rubbed an imaginary piece of fluff between his fingers. 'I want you to talk to CIB. I think they'll ask you to go to the house and just wait.'

'Wait? I can't do that.'

'Somebody will be with you.'

'You?'

'No.'

'How will I know I can trust them?'

He flinched. 'We'll do the best we can.'

'What am I waiting for?'

‘I don’t know.’ Seeing her look, he added, ‘It might have been a phone call to begin with. But that won’t happen now.’

‘I’m sorry, I can see I’ve frightened him off.’ Absurd as it seemed; it was what she had wanted so much.

He relented. ‘About the information I have.’

‘Yes?’

‘Your Mr Daniels was very helpful.’ He smiled, the first time that afternoon.

When she had gone to talk to his colleagues, Campbell sat and looked at his desk for a long time, mentally packing it up, for good and all. Not much longer. He anticipated the long night of questions that lay ahead, with O’Meara in the hot seat. It saddened him that the officers at the station would be so divided by what was about to happen.

The worst, and most likely outcome that he could foresee, was that it would all be to no avail. O’Meara’s story was sure to hold.

Jason walked quietly and steadily in the morning light, only the ungainly beat of his crippled leg setting him apart. Over and over in his head, like a poem, he had rehearsed what he would say to Rose Kendall.

‘I took your message at the camp last night,’ he would say, but this time I didn’t pass it on to Larissa.

‘Why you motherfucker’—she wouldn’t say, but would certainly think—‘why, fancy, how come you got a message that was meant for Larissa and didn’t give it to her?’

‘Because she would tell Gary or he would find out somehow from her that you were in town because she can’t hide anything from him, that girl, he reads into her soul because he is a devil and has taken it over, I know because I have seen, and because my mother who is all-knowing has told me and there is little hope that she will be saved, I am giving up. But I have come to save you, for, and on account of one kind word from you, and because you too would like to save Larissa if it is not too late, I think she would like to be saved but she cannot be, she is in thrall to the devil, to the beast in him.’

‘This is strong stuff, Jason,’ she would say. ‘Are you sure that you know what you are talking about?’

‘There is little time,’ he would say. ‘It is best that you know that Gary and O’Meara are out to get you some way or another because O’Meara is a devil too and he is obsessed, and there is no way that obsession like his can be stamped out, only it is him that must be stamped out. I know these things, and I will tell you them because I do not wish you harm, Mrs Kendall.'

He knocked on the door, and as he waited he felt a quivering in the air, as if the trees down Cedarwood Grove were watching him.

'Who are you?' asked the man who answered his knock.

'I've come to see Mrs Kendall.'

'You'll have to give me your name.'

'Jason. Tell her, please, it's Jason from the camp.'

He saw her in the stairwell then, smaller than he remembered, although her bottom bulged a little in her jeans, like most women's, and her Indian cotton shirt was tied in too tight to her waist. Her face was stripped of make-up, and shiny, as if she had just washed. He knew he had been right to come.

At the same moment, at the other end of the driveway up which he had just walked, he saw O'Meara. Straight away he knew it was a trap, and he recognised the man at the door, one of the new young police constables that had come to town, a man called Tippet.

He turned. O'Meara stood impassive at the gate.

'What is it, Jason?' called Rose Kendall, advancing towards him.

'I've got something to tell you.' He shouted it as loud as he could, as if that would somehow convey all that was in his head.

'Come inside then. Constable, it's all right, Jason can come in.'

'I can't. I can't tell you now.' O'Meara walked towards him. 'You're being followed by devils.'

And then he was off, racing across the paving stones, his artificial leg making a queer pounding against them, and down through the bushes. He knew this territory better than O'Meara, and he doubted that he would pursue him at this moment, with the woman watching.

He took the back way out of Cedarwood Grove, doubled back, and emerged near the end without actually having traversed it. At the end of the road he looked back over his shoulder and saw the police car nudging out of the Kendalls' driveway. He was almost out of places to run: too late, he realised he should have laid low out the back of the greenhouse where he and Gary had done business.

There were fences that an able-bodied man might scale, but he could not. Just when it seemed that O'Meara must surely catch up with him, the grey snout of the Studebaker appeared round the corner.

'Get in, fuckwit.' Gary held the door open, slowing down to a crawl, so that Jason had to throw himself across the passenger seat. Gary picked up speed and they hurtled away towards the camp, the door swinging wildly.

'Where are we going?'

'Where do you think?' Gary turned the car into the camp. Herbert's face appeared at the toll-gate, incensed at their speed.

'Slow down,' screamed Jason, 'we're here now.'

'We're not staying.'

Gary had switched the motor off and was already running towards the caravan. 'We gotta get armed.'

'I'm not going anywhere with you and a gun.'

'Then I'll blow your fucking brains out now.'

Gary flicked his leg sideways, tripping Jason, and while he struggled to his feet again, Gary vanished inside and reappeared with the shotgun. Behind him stood Larissa.

'Get in the car.' Gary motioned to Jason.

'We haven't done anything.'

'We done plenty.'

'You gotta tell me.'

'I'll tell you in the car.'

'Larissa.'

Gary grabbed her arm as she moved forward, twisting it behind her back. 'You stay put. You caused us enough trouble. You're in for it when I get back.'

'I won't be here.' She raised her voice defiantly as Gary, pointing the gun at Jason, moved back towards the car.

Jason saw that her hair was blue again today, and so were her fingernails. Her face was pointed and pale. He tried to say, I love you, but nothing would come out.

Herbert stood guard at the entrance to the camp.

'Get in.' Gary prodded Jason with the barrel.

Jason found his voice. 'Go, Larissa,' he called. 'Be sure to go.'

Gary aimed the car at Herbert who fell sideways in a heap as the Studebaker ripped past within inches of him.

'Promise, Larissa,' Jason screamed out the window, praying she could hear him. Behind her, his mother pottered through the line of caravans planting another plastic bottle of water by a picket fence. Poppy's parrots tossed brightly backwards and forwards on their perches, felt wings glowing; then the camp was behind them and they were gunning down the road.

'O'Meara's after us.' Gary's voice was edgy with hysteria.

'You're nuts, we've done nothing.'

'Campbell's got evidence on all of us. They told O'Meara.'
'They're having him on.' It didn't matter whether it was true or not, he wanted to live.
'He's scared shitless we'll give evidence against him.'
'That's dumb. He should just keep his mouth shut.'
'Yeah? That's what we were gunna do, arsehole. What were you doing grassing round Mother Kendall?
'How d'they know about him? Slow down for Chrissake.'
The car slewed on two wheels, righted itself, and careered on up through Blake Pass.
'It doesn't matter, I tell you, they've got *evidence*.'
'Tell him we'll take the rap.'
'Oh yeah?' The gun lay across Gary's knees, steadied as they tore round more corners by the flat of his hand curved down from the steering wheel. 'So you'll do time and take me with you?'
'I don't wanna be dead.' Life suddenly appeared amazingly sweet to Jason.
'Nah, you won't die, not if you stick with me.'
'They'll bring guns after us. Herbert saw you take that thing.'
'Shit man, O'Meara's already out with a gun.'
'They wouldn't give him one.'
'Not theirs. His.'
They had passed the Blake Block and hills lay before them, and the bush reserve. 'Just let me out,' Jason pleaded. It felt like his last chance.
Gary looked at the bush and the shining trees that stretched before them. 'I need you, bro. I need someone to show me the way.'

★

Lola stood in the kitchen, as if drying her hands on a tea-towel, but by her stillness Campbell knew she was listening.
He walked out to the car where Max Tippet waited with the engine idling.
'All of us?' Campbell asked him stupidly. It was so long since he had done it. The morning rippled before him and bellied out. He could smell his own fear. When he was younger and it had happened, he had thought how much alike hunter and hunted must feel.
Lola had followed him to the car, untying her new flowered apron as she walked unsteadily towards her husband.
'Is it an arms call-out?'
'Go back inside. Go and get ready for work, dear.'
'Tell me. Jeff, please. Don't go.'

'It's nothing, it'll be over soon.'

'Sweet soul of Jesus,' she said and walked back inside.

When he had gone she wanted to cry out in a great long holler like she had seen people do in the movies. Only it felt for real. She opened her mouth and tried it, but only a little squeak came out and she felt silly and closed it again.

Outside there was a commotion. It was the Kendall woman running up to the house, calling out all the way for Jeff.

'He's gone,' she said, opening the door to Rose. 'Jeffrey's gone.'

'I know. They told me he was going. I've got to catch them. Jason wanted to tell me something.'

'Looks like they know all about that.'

'But he didn't get a chance. He might speak to me, you see. Which way did they go?'

'He didn't tell me.'

'You don't understand. Larissa might be with them. I have to go.'

'I don't know anything about it.'

'You know everything.' Rose flung the words at her.

Lola looked at her, caught. Even in this moment of her own distress, she knew when she was cornered. God knows what harmless little bit of gossip this woman had had passed on to her that might be turned against her. She remembered with embarrassment how freely she had talked to Rose Kendall's friend, Toni. Not that that made much difference now. But one never knew.

'They were going up Blake Pass,' she said.

As Rose got back into Nick's car, prised from him just minutes before, Lola called after her, 'Look what you've done to us. See what you've made of it. He's due to retire soon.'

The terrain was causing Jason difficulty. He breathed in short, laboured gasps. Gary urged him on. Jason knew this territory. He had boasted how he used to trail ride in the firebreaks when he was a kid. The one thing that was good and beautiful, he had told them one night under the stars. Hurling himself across cliff faces on those little machines that had led on to the big bikes. You got to know where every ridge and dip was, because if you didn't you were a gonner. Those hills, he had often said, looking at them with longing. And Larissa had got round to looking at them too, he'd noticed. Now he and Gary were at large amongst them, and Jason could not keep up.

'We ought to split, man,' he said.

'No way, you're staying with me.'

They paused for breath below a ridge. 'I won't grass, I'll tell them it was me that done it all, Gary.'

'Too late, mate. They know you got things on your chest.'

'We weren't that bad. We wouldn't do much time.'

'Armed robbery, breaking and entry. You gotta be joking.'

'All right, I'll tell 'em I did the lot.'

'I should shoot you, you know. Like a bloody dog. That's what you're worth.'

Jason stiffened. 'Look.'

Gary's eyes followed his down the ridge to an almost imperceptible movement in the trees.

'O'Meara,' said Jason. 'Him, too.'

'Let's go.'

'My leg's hurting.'

'Move.'

Then they were on the run again, only now the native bush merged into low scrub, where fires had passed. At the top of the ridge, Jason flipped himself on his side, plunged at the firebreak and began rolling down it, protecting the skin on his face with his arms, but his hands getting mangled by the harsh earth and the protruding stumps as he went. A moment later Gary followed him, sliding on his backside so that he could hold the gun upright. He emitted high yelping screams as he hit stones and thorns. Further down the hill Jason rolled away off the break.

'Where are we heading?' Gary demanded.

They rested a moment while Jason got his breath back. They were almost unrecognisable to each other, covered with dirt and blood.

'The tip.'

'The fucking tip. There's hundreds of bloody people there.'

'That's right. We can pick up another car there, nobody takes their keys out while they dump rubbish.'

Gary flashed him a look of respect. 'It's a chance.'

'It's the best we've got.'

Behind, O'Meara beat steadily towards them, even as they headed towards the gully where the tip lay.

'The cops might think of it, too.'

'You think of something better.'

'If it wasn't for him we could stay holed up here for a week.' Gary's eyes glazed as the undergrowth moved near them. 'You're on, let's move it.'

★

She had followed the police cars as they headed in a steady high-pitched volume of noise towards the tip, blue lights flashing. Nobody noticed the speed at which she was travelling, not even a traffic officer clearing the intersections for them to go through. As she had hoped, she was seen as part of the convoy.

At the entrance to the tip she panicked momentarily. A man wearing a yellow mud-splattered coat operated the barrier at the entrance. He was examining passes and raising and lowering the bar to allow authorised people through. She scrabbled frantically in Nick's glove pocket with one hand, found a computer print-out card and waved it at the attendant. The bar lifted. But now she was hard on the heels of the convoy and she could see Campbell two cars ahead. Any moment now, in the close confines of the road to the tip, leading between the hills, he would spot her in his rear vision.

The hills crouched in bands of scrubby bush and grey rock around them. At the far end of the tip the line of police cars stopped. She pulled up behind them. The smell appalled her, as it always did, but here in the hills today a high wind was blowing and strengthening all the time, its wild and violent motion in the gully sending papers flying in the air and casting the stench far beyond the tip's epicentre. People moved there, figures lost amongst the bright hard light, the chaos and the whirling debris. Nothing grew in the razed earth, but close by some people had taken up residence in a packing case, and a child dressed in rags stared grimy-eyed across the wasteland. Smoke billowed from a fire, adding to the confusion.

Through a loudhailer Constable Tippett was addressing clusters of people who had been dumping rubbish, advising them to vacate the tip with all possible speed. The graders which shovelled the banks of rubbish forward into the pits slowed down, halted.

Campbell walked back along the line towards Rose, his face like cold slate.

'What are you doing here, Mrs Kendall?'

'Is Larissa in there?'

'No. Now get out.'

'Jason'll speak to me, I know he will.'

'O'Meara is in there with a weapon. I'm ordering you out. You're under arrest if you don't leave.'

But it was too late.

Two figures emerged from the bush in the far distance. It was difficult to see them properly, but one of them walked in evident agony; even through the haze it was clear that his trouser leg was covered with blood.

'Drop your weapon. Drop your weapon, we have you covered,' Campbell called over his loudhailer. Gary hesitated, the bravado melting as Jason had prayed, if that were the right word, that it might, and flung the gun in front of his feet.

'Put your hands on your head, and keep walking towards us.'

But Gary stood immobilised, looking across his shoulder at the figure emerging from the bush near where they had walked out.

For O'Meara it was foreign country. He was nearly as scratched and bruised as Jason and Gary but his toughness, the physical perfection of his body, had kept him in touch with the men ahead.

Now he saw it all, himself against the world. Gary, Jason, standing mad and still in the infernal landscape. Advancing towards him walked the line of men who had been his friends, and behind them the woman. The world was full of evil. He had tried to stop it. He had tried to tell them all.

A cold day gleaming with a distant rim of sunlight behind dense grey cumulus. Twenty-two of them, men and women, sat across the roadway into Weyville.

O'Meara had been looking forward to the game. He hoped to be on duty inside the grounds. He was good at rugby; he made the All Black trials once. If he had been selected it would have been great, but even the trials were wonderful. There had been an all-night party up home in the King Country. The cars had parked in the paddocks until four in the morning; pretty well everyone in the neighbourhood there, waiting for him to arrive back home. When he turned up they had all stood on their horns for him. The sound ricocheted around his dreams, the moment never to be forgotten, the kid who made it (or near enough, nobody seemed to care that he didn't make the team), that's what their siren sound told him.

So he had waited, that day when the Springboks would play in Weyville looming closer and closer. At the after-match function he would talk to them. 'Nearly made it into the team myself once.' He could hear himself drop it into the conversation, modestly, of course. 'Made the trials, well you know there's a lot of competition for a spot in this country. Like yours, you know what it's like.' He expected they would win. Indeed, he could not bear to think of their defeat at the hands of a provincial team, it would be unworthy of the local team to beat the 'Boks. 'Great game,' he would say. 'See you warming up a few moves there, you won't be so lucky when you hit the tests, the All Blacks'll chew you up.' A bit of chaffing.

Only when it came to it, he wasn't inside the grounds. As the day drew closer, he could see it wasn't going to happen. He was outside, and a bunch of creeps and weirdos were blocking the roadway, and him and his mates had to deal with them.

'Give 'em enough rope and they'll hang themselves,' were the orders.

He stuck to the rules, like everyone else in the squad. The supporters went down the road after the protesters.

Amandla, Amandla, Amandla Ngawhetu.

The cry chilled his heart. What goddam spook language was this? Even at this last moment, before he withdrew the final vestiges of sympathy he might have for what would befall these people, he wondered, why couldn't they just be New Zealanders like everyone else? Like him?

The crowd behind him shouted:

We want rugby, we want rugby, give us rugby, go home commies give us a four what do we want rugby rugby rugby tour.

The squad entered a property by a back entrance and crouched beside a fence.

There was a thwack of bottles in the distance, and then silence. Someone peering through the cracks, said that senior officers had gone and quietened things down. Campbell, he supposed, talking to the protesters and the spectators, negotiating. Pleading, he thought with disgust. Stupid dopey old Campbell, playing nursemaid. He was an old woman. He couldn't stand Campbell.

O'Meara felt his pulse fluttering. He knew, with great clarity, that he did not want things to quieten down. It was time to take a stand. Under his hand was a beautiful baton, fifty-five centimetres long, with a thirteen centimetre handle at right angles to the shaft. A beautiful smooth, shining, never-before-used-in-New-Zealand, American PR24.

Suddenly he was glad to be out here, dressed in his riot gear, and not inside the grounds. He was about to keep his country beautiful, worth living in, and living for. As long as there was action.

The command came. As one body, the squad rose from behind the fence, moving down the road towards the protesters with a rhythmical, even tread.

'Move, Move, Move,' they chanted, and it was like the high chords of church music, a song he had known from his childhood.

He could still see their faces, their silly cowering afraid faces. There was one in particular that he remembered, a woman with frizzy hair and largeish hips, a real do-gooder, her and her bloke, one of those greenies; a couple who were always looking for something to make a fuss about, and get away with it. This time they weren't going to. He took the man first. The PR24 sang through the air and connected with just the right solid note; then there was blood.

The woman tried to protect him. He was a little kinder, going for the side of her arm so that her body was hurled away. Afterwards he was sorry that he hadn't given her the full treatment too. Women, out there, making trouble in a world of men. He thought of his mother, she wouldn't do that.

The next woman was easier.

The second woman had got her comeuppance in the end; she was dead now. But the first one kept coming back to haunt him. It had been war from the beginning, from that first moment. She never learned her place.

And now, here she was, walking towards him with the line of policemen, his mates who had gone soft on him.

The police were calling something, he didn't know whether it was to him, or to Gary and Jason who had been his prey because they had let him down just like everyone else. He couldn't hear, as his breath rasped in his chest from the chase, and the wind roared and the spiral of papers in the sky swelled above him.

The raw stump of Jason's leg was causing him intolerable agony. He knew he should be walking towards the police, but it was impossible for him to take another step. He stooped, releasing the strap which held the leg, hopping on one foot, and reached for Gary's shoulder in an impossible attempt to hold his balance. But Gary had begun to move at last, waving the gun around as if uncertain whom he should point it at. With the other men, Campbell raised his weapon.

'We're matter,' said Jason, quite reasonably. 'Just matter in the universe.' He hopped, about face, holding his leg aloft.

In that moment O'Meara took his eyes from the oncoming police and the woman, startled by Jason's sudden movement. He saw something pointed in the sky; a weapon, he thought. In the blinding and uncertain light he raised his own gun and fired.

Someone else fired too, but he was not sure who it was. The shots resounded round the walls of the gully, as if to frighten the huddled bulldozers. Gary screamed in pain, rolling on the ground and clutching his foot. O'Meara laid down his gun and walked towards Jason's body, waiting for the others to come.

15

Nick sent Rose a Virago postcard from London. He had gone there to order new equipment for Lyle Warner's business which he had bought out at a rock-bottom price. The card was edged with a dull burgundy stripe and inscribed with a long quote from *Maurice Guest*, a novel by Henry Handel Richardson whom Rose had not heard of before, and at first thought was a man. Part of the quote read: 'He heaped on her all the spiritual perfections that answered to her appearance. And he did not, for a time, observe anything to make him waiver in his faith that she was whiter, stiller, and more unapproachable—of a different clay, in short, from other women.'

She wondered if the title was a low blow, but then she remembered that Nick had held her hand, and his clumsy kiss. It was not true, this message that he had sent her. Once it might have been, but that was before the last wound, the sound of gunfire. Consumed by the presence of violent death, she would never be entirely still again.

★

There was plenty of money in her bank account, Morris Applebloom told her.

She realised the shares Kit had put in her name. It surprised Rose that he had bought ones which had survived the crash so well. She wondered if he might have forgotten he still owned them, and insisted that half the proceeds go to him. 'We're civilised,' she told Morris as she drew out all the money that was left and closed the account. It was during her absolutely last visit to Weyville.

Which was more than she felt could be said of Morris and the beautiful and inexplicable Sarah. They had bought a restored Bentley and drove around Weyville in it together. They had never looked happier.

'What are you going to do with the money?' Morris asked Rose when she collected her cheque.

'I'm helping to finance a co-operative of women film makers,' she said.

'You're crazy,' Morris offered, and she knew if he could have stopped her from taking the money he would. Probably he believed she was as mad as her sister.

★

Hortense said, 'Morris'll never take Kit's seat now. This electorate doesn't wear philanderers very well.'

'You used to think Morris was a bit of a devil,' Rose observed. 'Some people might still like him.'

Hortense looked serious and reminded her that women comprised fifty-one per cent of the electorate and explained, as if to a child, that tastes had changed, and that where once women might have admired Morris, they now perceived him as a rat. 'The fact is, we're stuck with your ex,' she said.

'Does it make much difference?' Rose asked.

'I suppose not. Six of one and half a dozen of the other. When Nick comes home we'll just have to get stuck into Party work again and hope for the best.'

'Is that what Nick wants?'

Hortense stared at her, suddenly convulsed, as if an impossibly funny idea had just occurred to her. She shook her head, dismissing whatever it was. 'He will,' she announced.

'Good luck,' Rose said.

'What about you?'

'I've left the Party.'

Hortense looked blank. 'Shit.'

★

'You're saner than me, Sis,' Rose whispered when she saw Katrina. She had managed to have her brought south.

'Ah bullshit.' Katrina seemed quite genuinely not to care. She smiled, as she had smiled throughout her short court appearance. 'I'm nuts, stop trying to comfort yourself.' She stared around the psychiatric ward with apparent nonchalance and allowed Rose to hold her hand. 'Have you heard from Larissa?'

'No, but Minna says she's gone. There were some housetrucks going over to the East Coast. They stopped in Weyville and had a bonfire by the lake one night. The next day they'd gone, and so had Larissa. Ellis's mates are watching out for her.'

'Sorry, old kid,' said Katrina gruffly. 'She was as much yours as mine.'

Rose shook her head. 'Gone to gypsies. Maybe it'll suit her. She might be happy.'

'Yeah? What's happy?'

'Where did we come from, Sis? What did we ever really know about our parents?'

'You know,' said Katrina, 'I used to wonder. But I see Elsie Diamond and I become nothing. I don't wonder any more. Not since I lost Basil. I used to wonder what made him so weird, and I used to blame his father, bad blood and all that stuff. Yet all that time the kid was sick. It didn't make any difference. Anyway, if we're a bit queer, there's always Jim. You can't get much straighter than Jim. I'm glad he didn't come to court, it would've been too much of a shock for his system. Is he back from dreamland yet?'

'Yes, they toured all over. Fay got enough Elvis souvenirs from Memphis to fill a whole wall of their living room.

'You see then, we're all right, aren't we, we've got Jim and Fay.'

'We should have kept dancing,' Rose said, 'All of us should.'

'You just never found the right stage,' said Katrina with an amused tolerance.

'I'm on the lookout,' said Rose, and could have laughed.

Before she left, she offered Katrina the topaz ring.

'Thanks,' said Katrina, as if she had been expecting it. She put it on her finger, turning it this way and that to the light. 'It's a pity it's not real, isn't it?'

Rose caught the unit back into Wellington. Later she would meet Olivia. It was a meeting she anticipated with mixed feelings. Olivia was angry that her parents had separated; she blamed Rose. Her letters were full of barely concealed accusations that it was Rose's fault. She was appalled, too, by the scandal which had surrounded her parents for months. Rose wrote to say that she understood, but it didn't change anything. She suggested they meet in Wellington when Olivia was on her way north to spend Christmas with friends in Auckland. In response, and to Rose's surprise, Olivia had agreed. *Of course, I'm grown up now* she had announced in her reply. All in all, Rose thought it could be a tricky meeting.

The Beehive loomed above her as she walked uptown from the station. She wondered what Kit was doing up there on the hill. There were only nine days till Christmas, and the House was still in session. Political crises rocked the country almost every day as Lange made his bid to re-establish his power base, eroded by the attacks on his leadership. Events like this fascinated but no longer touched her. She had not been in contact with Kit since the sale of the house in Weyville was finalised.

Hardly any cars moved up and down Lambton Quay. The city was unearthly in its quietness. Power cuts had affected different parts of the country all day. The national grid had been shut down as electricity supply workers went on strike. She had not realised how strange and dead the city would be. All the large department stores were closed. A handful of smaller shops were open, lit by candles, staff hovering near the doors to prevent shoplifters absconding in the gloom.

Rose sat down in a bus shelter to wait for the airport bus that would take her to meet Olivia from the plane. Glancing up again at the Beehive, she saw that the lights had gone out there, too. This, then, was Christmas under the Government of their dreams. All that work, all this loss.

Beside her a woman sat apparently transfixed, with one of the familiar transistors to her ear.

'Lange's got rid of Douglas,' she said out loud.

'Are you sure? Has he sacked him?'

'It's very confused. Listen.'

Together they heard the newsreader elaborate on the shock resignation.

'The lights are out, and Douglas has gone. Surely things can only get better,' the woman said, putting down the radio. She was dowdy and clutched a bag of groceries.

'Who can tell?' Rose was thinking of Kit, that maybe he had jumped the right way after all. Perhaps things would get better, for him, for the country.

But she was not sure, and she could not see how anybody could know for certain at this stage. Maybe all the people had gone too far down some dreadful path, away from their best intentions and ideals, to turn back.

She reminded herself that she was a film maker now, of sorts anyway. Perhaps the group could make a documentary. One of her partners looked like Katrina.

She glanced up towards the towering buildings. The window panes hovered in the dark air. Random light slanted down between two walls, a sudden illumination of the street.

'Tell you the truth, I could kill them,' said the woman. 'These politicians.'

'Anarchy rules, okay?' Thinking of Hortense.

The woman didn't notice any irony. 'You've got it. What are you going to do?'

Rose didn't answer straight away, partly because she had been asked this question, or a version of it, so often of late. She thought of saying: 'Shooting for the stars', only it made her think of O'Meara.

Anyway, she was still working out the stars.

Remembering all of them. Toni. Wiki. A small space for Hortense, in spite of herself. Katrina of course. Larissa. Minna. Sharna (she'd grow). The cast was huge. It filled her life.

There were bit parts for the chaps.

She could see the exact point where they would commence the opening sequence, in the empty park, alongside the Henry Moore sculpture. While she was squinting to establish angles the airport bus rattled past, leaving her behind. She considered a taxi rather than leave Olivia standing on her own. Then she thought that that was what grown-ups did. She decided to wait for the next bus.

She hoped Olivia would thank her.

She turned to answer. She was going to say, 'I'm working on it,' but the woman had gone. Rose felt comfortable in the silence.

★

OTHER NEW ZEALAND TITLES AVAILABLE IN VINTAGE EDITIONS

Holy Terrors and Other Stories by Amelia Batistich
Man with Two Arms and Other Stories by Norman Bilbrough
Strangers in Paradise by Jonathan Eisen and Katherine Joyce Smith
To the Is-land by Janet Frame*
An Angel at My Table by Janet Frame*
The Envoy From Mirror City by Janet Frame*
Owls Do Cry by Janet Frame*
The Carpathians by Janet Frame*
A Population of One by Alice Glenday
Strained Relations by Gaelyn Gordon
Wakeful Nights by Fiona Kidman
Finding Out by Elspeth Sandys**
The Peace Monster by John Smythe
Always the Islands of Memory by Noel Virtue*

*Available only in New Zealand
**Available only in Australia and New Zealand